M000309829

FOUR LETTER WORD

A NOVEL

GRETCHEN MCNEIL

HYPERION
Los Angeles   New York

Copyright © 2024 by Gretchen McNeil

All rights reserved. Published by Hyperion, an imprint of Buena Vista Books, Inc. No part of this book may be reproduced or transmitted in any form or by any means, electronic or mechanical, including photocopying, recording, or by any information storage and retrieval system, without written permission from the publisher. For information address Hyperion, 77 West 66th Street, New York, New York 10023.

First Edition, March 2024
10 9 8 7 6 5 4 3 2 1
FAC-004510-23355
Printed in the United States of America

This book is set in AGaramond, Melior/Monotype; Badhouse Light/House Industries
Designed by Marci Senders

Library of Congress Cataloging-in-Publication Data

Names: McNeil, Gretchen, author.
Title: Four letter word / Gretchen McNeil.
Description: First edition. • Los Angeles ; New York : Hyperion, 2024. • Audience: Ages 14–18. • Audience: Grades 10–12. • Summary: Izzy and her family welcome foreign exchange student Alberto into their home, but after a series of mishaps and coincidences, and with a serial killer on the loose, Izzy begins to suspect Alberto is not who he seems.
Identifiers: LCCN 2023010967 • ISBN 9781368097437 (hardcover)
Subjects: LCSH: Serial murderers—Juvenile fiction. • Student exchange programs—Juvenile fiction. • High school students—Juvenile fiction. • Mothers and daughters—Juvenile fiction. • Identity (Psychology)—Juvenile fiction. • Eureka (Calif.)—Juvenile fiction. • Detective and mystery stories. • CYAC: Mystery and detective stories. • Serial murderers—Fiction. • Student exchange programs—Fiction. • Mothers and daughters—Fiction. • Identity—Fiction. • Eureka (Calif.)—Fiction. • LCGFT: Detective and mystery fiction. • Novels.
Classification: LCC PZ7.M4787952 Fo 2024 • DDC 813.6 [Fic]—dc23/eng/20230703
LC record available at https://lccn.loc.gov/2023010967

ISBN 978-1-368-09743-7
Reinforced binding

Visit www.HyperionTeens.com

SUSTAINABLE FORESTRY INITIATIVE   Certified Sourcing

www.forests.org
SFI-01681

Logo Applies to Text Stock Only

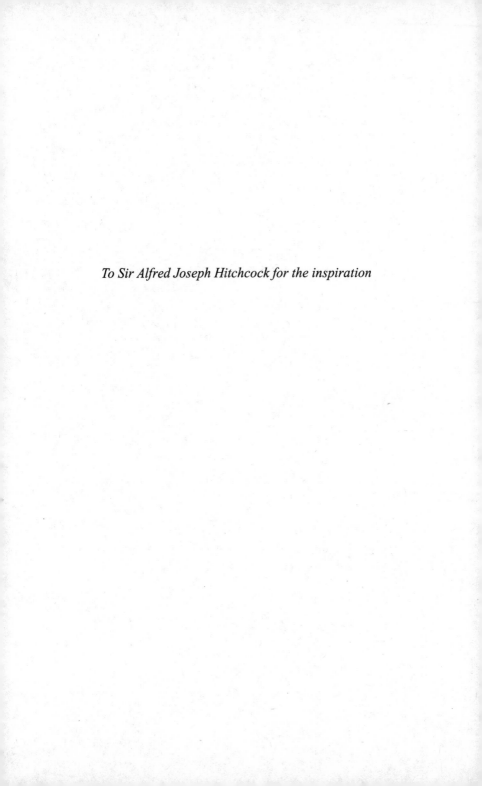

To Sir Alfred Joseph Hitchcock for the inspiration

"It is fate. But call it Italy if it pleases you, Vicar."

—George Emerson, *A Room with a View*

ONE

IZZY BALANCED HER LAPTOP ON CROSSED LEGS AS SHE LIS-
tened intently through her earbuds.

"*Il libro di italiano è sul tavolo.*"

Something about a table and a book, right? Maybe? *You can do this.*

"Eel leebro dee ee-ta-lee-a-no eh sool tavolo," she repeated out loud,
cringing at her atrocious pronunciation in comparison to the lilting
female voice on the language app. "The Italian book is on the table."

"The Italian book is on the table," the instructor said.

Izzy exhaled in relief at getting the answer right. One down,
ninety-nine to go.

"*Mi presti la penna per favore.*"

"Mee prestee lah penna pear favoreh?" She recognized the phrase for "please," and *"penna"* might have been pen. Or pencil? Something else altogether?

Her fear of making the wrong choice overwhelmed her executive functioning while the Italian lesson barreled on without her.

"Lend me the pen, please." The recorded instructor paused as if in judgment. *"È una bella giornata per una passeggiata sulla spiaggia."*

Izzy's shoulders sagged. She wasn't even going to attempt that one. The vowels and consonants all bled together, making it difficult to know where one word ended and the next began. No matter how hard she tried, she couldn't make her mouth create those sounds, and parsing out the meaning? For-freaking-get it.

Her thumb hovered over the podcast app on her phone. A new episode of *Murder Will Speak*, her favorite true crime docuseries, had dropped that morning and she'd been itching to hear updates on the Casanova Killer, California's newest and grossest serial killer. Maybe she'd just leave the Italian for later. . . .

As if sensing her drifting attention, the instructor's voice resumed her questions and answers.

"It's a nice day for a walk on the beach." Wow. That's what it meant? *"Il treno per Milano parte alle sette e mezzo."*

Before Izzy could officially bail on her failing Italian lesson, a nasally voice pierced the silence of her attic bedroom.

"Mangia, mangia!" Her brother Riley's perfectly coiffed brown pompadour bobbed up the staircase, coming into view a full two seconds before the rest of his head. *"Pappardelle in la luna. Mamma mia, ciao!"*

Izzy paused the language app as Riley ascended the stairs just high enough to rest his elbows on either side of the opening in her floor. His honeyed smile and narrow amber eyes lent a smarmy quality to what was otherwise a handsome pale face, and his teasing struck even harder than usual because, though the words were nonsense, his accent was significantly better than Izzy's.

"Your comedy would have slayed in 1933," she said with a tight smile.

Riley ignored the barb. "Gonna be ready to converse with this exchange student in his native tongue when he arrives?"

"Fluently," she lied.

"You can talk dirty to each other across the dinner table." Riley pumped his eyebrows. "Mom and Dad'll be clueless."

"First of all, ew." At nineteen, sex was basically all Riley thought about. She vaguely remembered her two other older brothers being this sex-focused, but Riley's approach was particularly gross because, as an extrovert, he shared every porny thought that popped into his brain. "Second of all, Mom speaks Italian, dipshit." *Much better than I do.*

"Wouldn't stop me."

"Once again, with feeling, *ew!*"

Riley rolled his head to the side and stared up at the ceiling as if in deep contemplation. "Can't believe Mom is letting some hot Italian sausage in the house with her precious little girl, and she freaks out because I'm seeing Kylie again."

"He's coming here to study English for a semester, not date an American high school student."

"Says you." Riley smirked. "Besides, you can't tell me you haven't fantasized about some sexy Italian dude sweeping you off your feet. Like in that boring Brit movie Mom loves."

Izzy jutted out her chin, feeling oddly protective of her mom's favorite movie. "*A Room with a View* is *not* boring."

"Uh-huh."

"And it's also fiction, so no, I'm not expecting Alberto to show up here and suddenly make Eureka not suck balls."

"Alberto? His name's Alberto?" Riley laughed, sharp and barking. A harbor seal begging for fish. "Oh, Alberto, you're so hot!" he cooed in falsetto.

She hated the smug look on his face. Especially because he was right. The moment Alberto Bianchi had been assigned to the Bell household as a foreign exchange student for his first semester of college, Izzy had looked him up. He didn't have much of a social media presence so there weren't many photos to go by, mostly group shots from before he graduated from secondary school, but he wasn't bad looking. Plus he wore his sandy blond hair a bit long and floppy on top, which reminded Izzy of Julian Sands in *A Room with a View*.

And *that* was hot.

A Room with a View was her mom's comfort movie, the one Izzy would put on whenever she sensed her mom was feeling depressed, or slipping into one of her "blue moods," as she called them. Alone with her mom while her brothers were off at college and her dad was working late night after night, Izzy had watched that movie so many times, she knew every line by heart. At first, she'd pretended to care about the plot because it made her mom happy, but over time, George and Lucy's romance had grown on her.

Their connection was fate, their love enduring. Izzy had nothing in her life but her family and her best friend, Peyton, so yeah, of course she'd imagined Alberto striding toward her through the golden haze of a Tuscan field at sunset, enveloping her in his arms while some operatic soprano belted out "Chi il bel sogno" in the background. How could she not?

But she wasn't going to let anyone know that. Especially not Riley.

"What do you want?" she asked, her words clipped in irritation.

"Mom says you have dibs on the car this afternoon."

"So?"

"So I need it."

"Why?"

Riley ran a hand gingerly over his hair. "Hot date with Kylie."

"On a Tuesday afternoon."

"Five days before I leave, so I gotta squeeze it in when I can." He pursed his lips. "Literally and figuratively."

How the youngest—and douchiest—of her three older brothers had become the heartthrob of Eureka, California, during the summer between his freshman and sophomore years at San Diego State was a bigger unsolved mystery than the existence of Bigfoot. And his on-again, off-again relationship with Kylie Fernández, a bartender down at the marina, was an even bigger mystery. Kylie had been the cool, tattooed girl in her brother Parker's class, the one who oozed confidence and didn't give a fuck what anyone thought of her. Half the school had wanted to date her, the other half wanted to be her, and somehow, she'd gotten involved with Riley, who was three years younger and three million times less interesting. Baffling.

"I thought you broke up."

"We did." Riley shrugged. "But then I saw her reading an article about the serial killer in Los Angeles who has sex with his victims *after* he kills them. I told her I was focusing my thesis on the psychology of sexual deviancy and boom, back in."

Riley only knew about the LA serial killer, dubbed the Casanova Killer, because of Izzy, and the idea that he was using her true crime podcast obsession to con a woman into having sex was almost as disturbing as the serial killer himself. "Aren't theses for doctoral candidates?"

Riley waved her off. "Kylie doesn't know that."

"Yeah, you're disgusting."

"So how much for your car privileges?"

Izzy picked up her phone with a sigh of resignation and texted Peyton.

> Riley needs the car. Can you drive?

The silence in the attic was stifling as she waited for a response. Riley drummed his fingers against the floorboards, slowly articulating each knuckle, eyebrows arched in annoyance as the seconds ticked by on the massive old grandfather clock beside the stairs. She should have just told him to fuck off, but she didn't. She never did. Probably never would.

Anxiety was the great silencer.

Not that anyone in her family noticed Izzy's reticence to speak up for herself. As the youngest child and only girl in the family, Izzy had spent her entire life overshadowed by the Bell Boys, as they were collectively known. Taylor, former high school baseball star and now an urban search-and-rescue specialist with Humboldt Bay Fire. Parker, the valedictorian who was heading back to Pasadena to start his PhD in aeronautics after graduating summa cum laude from CalTech. Riley, aspiring politician, who charmed everyone and everything in his path. Izzy was pretty sure most people in town didn't even realize that Harry and Elizabeth Bell *had* a daughter.

Her phone vibrated as Peyton's response popped up on her screen, all caps like whenever she was excited or agitated.

> BE THERE IN 10 BUT TELL RI HE'S GROSS

"Twenty bucks," Izzy said, tossing the phone onto her bedspread.

"Deal." He pulled a crisp new bill from his wallet and tucked it into a seam between floorboards. "I'd have gone as high as sixty. Don't be afraid to aim up, little sis."

Fear. Her weak spot.

With a self-congratulating laugh, Riley turned and descended the stairs. The door at the bottom slammed shut, sending a gust of air up into the attic. The twenty-dollar bill shuddered like a palm tree in a hurricane, then flew out of its crevice and fluttered across the room, landing prosaically in Izzy's trash bin.

"That's about right."

She contemplated returning to her Italian, but sadomasochism wasn't one of her interests. She swung her legs over the side of her bed and strode across the room to scoop Riley's twenty out of the garbage. The aged floorboards creaked in symphonic harmony with each step, and she realized with a cringe that Alberto, who would be sleeping in Riley's room for the next three months, would be directly below her. If he heard her moving around at night, would he assume that she was going to the bathroom? Which would probably be true. Or think she was an insomniac? Which could also probably be true. Or some crazy old cat lady tucked away in the attic who puttered around aimlessly at all hours of the night and day due to a free-floating lifelong anxiety she couldn't quite shake? Which was not true yet but probably would be someday if she didn't get the hell out of Eureka.

She shoved the twenty into her messenger bag, then paused in front of her windows, three narrow dormers behind her bed that faced the harbor. The skies were gray, though it was August, technically the warmest month for the extreme northern end of California. But "warm" on the coast meant seventy degrees, and only if the sun was strong enough to burn off the ever-present layer of moist, heavy fog that blanketed them 365 mornings per year.

Blessedly, the fog had crept back out beyond Woodley Island, but the weather was anything but glorious. A thin marine layer blurred the sun and cast the whole area in a purplish-gray light, muting the colors of summer and hinting that Izzy would have to wear a jacket to the airport tonight when they picked up Alberto. She knew that Florence, Italy, was significantly hotter and sunnier than Eureka, and she hoped the relative lack of cheerful summer weather wouldn't send Alberto running home early.

You're being ridiculous. It didn't really matter if Alberto stayed the full semester or not. He wasn't the romantic lead in the rom-com of Izzy's life. He was a stranger whose main purpose in her house was to help with her Italian so she could pass the second-year equivalency exam her first semester at college and immediately petition to study abroad. Basically her entire life plan.

Is that really what you want?

Izzy pushed the question aside. It didn't matter what she wanted. The plan was to attend Middlebury College, like her parents had done; study art history in Florence, like her mom had *planned* to do her senior year of college; get an internship at the Uffizi, like her mom had always hoped for herself; and then maybe fall in love with a hot Italian guy and live in a villa in the country and literally never come home.

Izzy's future, all mapped out by her mom, looked a lot like how Elizabeth Bell had always envisioned her own life. A vision that was interrupted when she got pregnant with Taylor.

Despite her dreams, Izzy's mom had never been to Italy. She never studied art history in Florence, nor did she ever view Caravaggio's *Medusa* in person at the Uffizi. And she certainly didn't live in an Italian villa.

It didn't matter that this plan, this whole insane road map for the rest of Izzy's life, wasn't actually *her* dream at all. It mattered that planning for Izzy's future made Elizabeth Bell happy again.

For that, Izzy would have endured anything. Even the sound of her own voice butchering the Italian language.

Besides, Italy offered her an option, an escape. There was literally nothing to tie her to this town.

She thought there had been something . . . someone. She'd made an unexpected connection earlier that year, a deep friendship that bordered on more, with a person who made life in Eureka seem not so horrible. But just a few weeks ago, he'd completely ghosted her, and once again, Izzy was left with nothing.

Her eyes trailed back to the window where she could see fishing boats beginning to return to the harbor, the same in-and-out flow she'd witnessed every day of her life from her attic room. If Italy was the solution to *this*, so be it.

TWO

"IZZY?"

Her mom's voice drifted up two floors through the old vents in their 1907 home. It had been a fun feature when Izzy was little. Curled up on the floor in front of the wrought iron register like it was an analog radio circa World War II, she'd opened the damper all the way and eavesdrop on the goings-on of her brothers and parents from the anonymity of her attic bedroom. She'd listened to her parents huddled around the kitchen island discussing how to pay for Taylor's shoulder surgery, heard the strain in Parker's voice when he came out to his brothers, witnessed her mom crying alone in her bedroom when no one else was home. Every sound in the house drifted up to Izzy's attic.

Then her dad had figured it out one day while repaning a window in her room. Now the family used the ventilation system as a low-tech intercom to summon Izzy when needed, and the vents had lost their charm.

"Izzy, can you come down?"

She sighed, looping her cross-body bag over one arm. Izzy wasn't sure she could fake enthusiasm as her mom went over the day's checklist one more time. She'd been single-mindedly planning for Alberto's arrival since they'd gotten the email assigning him to their home, mapping out every mundane detail from how many face towels he might need to which of her nine thousand casserole recipes might make the best welcome dinner. Izzy was pretty sure her mom hadn't spent this much time preparing for anything since Taylor's birth.

Izzy descended the stairs to the second floor, where the rest of the bedrooms were located, and slid her palm over the smooth, worn railing at the top of the staircase before she gripped the mahogany newel post, topped by a finial carved to look like a giant artichoke. She jumped and swung around it like Gene Kelly on a lamppost in *Singin' in the Rain*, landing on the second step of the main staircase. She'd been doing the same airborne move since she was tall enough to reach the artichoke finial, and the wood was eroding after countless trips down the stairs. Her dad, who had installed the newel post after rescuing it from a restoration project, didn't mind Izzy's habit, but her mom hated it.

She saw danger everywhere.

The Bell house was relatively quiet as Izzy trotted down the rest of the stairs, which was less of a rarity now that Taylor had his own place and Riley and Parker had both gone off to college. Still, Izzy had reacclimated to the increased volume with the younger Bell Boys home for a few weeks during summer break, and the current silence felt oppressive, pierced only by the slightly off-rhythm tick-tocks of the half-dozen mantel clocks that dotted the living room.

Over the years, her dad had picked up all six timepieces, as well as five more on the upper floors of the house plus two grandfather clocks, at local salvage yards and estate sales, restoring them to pristine condition in his workshop. They had all been gifts for Izzy's mom, who had once made the mistake of admiring a Victorian mantel clock at a restaurant, after which her husband had, in true Harry Bell fashion, gone completely overboard. She'd gotten a clock for every birthday since.

And she hated all of them.

"I'm not just going to take your word for it, Riley." Her mom's voice cut through the ticking. "You lost that privilege when you almost drove Dad's pickup into the river because you were making out with that waitress."

"Kylie's a bartender, not a waitress," Riley said, sounding quite pleased with himself. "And that was ages ago, Mother. I was a *child*."

"It was spring break!"

"Are you sure?" Riley asked slyly. "Maybe you don't remember."

"I'm not senile, Riley. And you can't gaslight me into thinking I am."

"Shit, Mom."

From the dining room, Izzy tensed. If there was one thing her mom hated, it was curse words.

"Riley Anderson Bell, you watch your mouth."

He instantly sulked. "Sorry, Mom."

"No four-letter words while our guest is here, do you understand me?"

"Yes, Mom."

"And *NO CAR*."

"Izzy!" This time it was Riley bellowing her name. "We need you!"

"Here." Izzy slunk through the formal dining room, where every inch of exposed wood from the legs on the threadbare Victorian chairs to the hanging ceiling beams glistened with Old English, and found her mom and Riley in a kitchen standoff.

Elizabeth Bell leaned back against the farmhouse sink, delicate arms crossed over her chest, while she glared up at her youngest son. She was a mite of a woman, as Izzy's dad liked to joke, five foot nothing and wiry like a cross country runner. Izzy, at five foot six with a size nine shoe, was burly in comparison.

Her mom's long, chocolate brown hair was swept up into a high pony-tail on the top of her head, a stark contrast to her milky white complexion, and with her outfit of cropped leggings and a sleeveless button-down blouse, she looked like a 1950s bobby soxer. The retro style mixed with her petiteness made Izzy's mom look younger than her actual age. No stranger would have guessed that she had four strapping children, three of whom were legal adults. But tiny of stature didn't mean small of spirit, and Izzy's mom was not someone you wanted to cross.

Her head whipped around the moment Izzy stepped into the kitchen, ponytail bouncing around her delicate, pale face. "Did you tell Riley he could use the car this afternoon?"

"Yep."

Her mom clicked her tongue, disappointed. "But you're supposed to pick up bagels by three thirty, remember?"

"Peyton's on her way over."

Her mom's combativeness ebbed the instant she heard Peyton's name. Izzy's best friend always had that effect. Her mom probably would have let her daughter drop out of school and join a free-love commune as long as Peyton was going with her. "Well, fine. But be back by six for dinner. I don't want us to be late to the airport. Flight number—"

"Thirty-seven sixty-five," Riley and Izzy recited in unison. "Nine twenty arrival."

They sounded like captured soldiers repeating their name, rank, and serial number under interrogation.

Izzy's mom snatched a frilly half apron from a hook. Her transformation into a '50s housewife was complete. "I just hope Alberto doesn't hate it up here after a week in San Francisco," she grumbled, attacking a Yukon gold potato with a peeler.

"He won't, Mom," Izzy said, while Riley pressed a finger to his smiling lips and tiptoed out the side door. "The house looks beautiful, and you've worked so hard to make him feel welcome."

"Thank you." She smiled, thanking Izzy with her soft brown eyes, then paused her potato peeling. "Did you practice your Italian today?"

Izzy experienced a full body clench at the question. "Yep."

"E come va?" she asked in perfect Italian.

Shit. Izzy attempted to translate her mom's question, which she was pretty sure meant "How's it going?" but she didn't dare answer in Italian. She didn't want her mom's vicarious dreams to fall apart just hours before Alberto was set to arrive.

"It's going well," she said with a shrug, opening the fridge to hide her embarrassment. She wasn't hungry but pulled out a slice of cheese anyway.

"Bene." Her mom's smile returned as she reached for another potato, then her eyes drifted over Izzy's head to the oversize bay window that faced the water. "I hope the goddamn fog doesn't roll in tonight."

"It won't." *Of course it will.*

"And your father'd better not be a jerk." Her next swipe at the potato seemed angrier than the last.

"He won't." Though Izzy certainly wouldn't have bet on it. Her dad wasn't really a jerk so much as a white guy of a certain age who thought all his jokes were funny and all his opinions deserved to be shared, and who didn't believe in hiding his true feelings behind social niceties. He wasn't on board with the Italian exchange student plan—or the "Italian Scheme," as he'd dubbed it—and though he wasn't a mean-natured man, his sardonic sense of humor frequently came across that way. Thankfully, he spent most of his time on jobsites or tucked away in the garage workshop and would probably only see Alberto at meals.

Izzy's mom dropped the peeler and reached her hand toward her daughter. "I just want this to be a good experience for you."

"I know," Izzy said, gripping her mom's fingers with her own.

"A chance to improve your Italian, get into that exchange program . . ." Her eyes hadn't left the window. Izzy knew her mom wasn't seeing gray skies and fishing boats, but the sun-drenched fields of a Tuscany she'd never experienced in person.

"It will be, but—"

"Don't get stuck here, Izzy." Her mom's face hardened as she reached for Izzy's forearm. "It's fine for your brothers, but not for my Elizabeth."

Izzy choked back the knot in her throat. Elizabeth, her given name. She was her mother's namesake, which meant she carried the weight of her mother's broken dreams.

"Promise me." Her mom's fingernails pierced Izzy's skin. *"Promise."*

"I promise," Izzy managed to whisper, her throat constricting along with her mom's icy grip.

"Fate is also a four-letter word," her mom said, her tone suddenly more bitter than plaintive. "And yours isn't here. I . . ." Her mom's voice cracked, misery overcoming the flash of anger, and just as she thought her mom was about to break down sobbing, Izzy's phone vibrated in her pocket.

"Answer it," her mom said when Izzy made no move toward her phone.

"Peyton," she said, without even looking. No one else would have texted her.

Not anymore.

Izzy's mom released her daughter's arm, turned slowly back to the sink, and picked up the peeler and the potato gingerly, judging their weight in her hands as if she weren't entirely sure what they were. "You should go."

"Back by six!" Izzy said enthusiastically, hoping to circumvent her mom's darkening mood, but her mom didn't respond, and as Izzy slipped out the side door, she noticed that her mom's eyes had found the window again.

THREE

"DID YOU TELL RI HE'S DISGUSTING?" PEYTON ASKED AS IZZY climbed into the passenger seat.

"Twice."

"Good." Peyton grinned wickedly. Even though she was practically engaged to her boyfriend, Hunter, her flirtation with Izzy's least likable brother had been in full swing since they were tweens. Not that anything would have happened between them—dating your little sister's best friend had to be some kind of social no-no—but Peyton was definitely hot in that shoulders-back, outgoing, overtly sexual kind of way that guys usually found attractive, and Izzy had always been afraid she'd walk in on the two of them making out in her living room.

"What are we doing today?" Izzy asked, changing the subject.

"Existentially or literally?"

Izzy snorted. "I can't handle existential musings right now."

"Fair. Well, if we're not going to contemplate the very nature of our existence all afternoon, then I thought we'd just chill."

"Chill?"

Izzy eyed her friend. Peyton wore a skintight, bright yellow halter that accentuated the spray tan on her usually pale skin, and she'd dabbed a peachy convertible color on both her lips and her cheekbones. She wouldn't have bothered with either if she was planning to "just chill" with Izzy all afternoon. Hunter would definitely be part of the day's agenda, and Izzy steeled herself for another afternoon of playing third wheel.

"I promise I won't bail on you with Hunter," Peyton said with a smirk, as if reading Izzy's mind.

"Just make sure I have a snack before you disappear into his room," she said. "And a fresh bowl of water."

Peyton usually would have responded with a witty retort, but she unexpectedly changed the subject instead. "Hey, have you talked to your dad recently?"

"Well, we live in the same house and I see him every day, so . . ."

Peyton pulled away from the curb. "But not, like, about anything specific?"

What was she fishing for? "Not that I can remember." Her dad wasn't exactly the "serious talk" kind of parent.

"Oh."

Peyton fell quiet as she chewed at the inside of her cheek, brows knitted together. Something was bothering her.

"You okay?" Izzy asked.

Her friend nodded, then shook her head rapidly, casting off her darkening mood. "So where am I going?"

"I need to pick up bagels at Frankie's before they close, so let's do that first," Izzy said, content to let things go for now. She'd ask Peyton about it again later, just to make sure there wasn't something wrong.

"Check. Then we can meet the boys."

"Boys?" *With an s?*

"Did I forget to tell you? Jake's home."

Izzy had to fight to keep her face passive as a hot wave of shame washed over her. *He didn't even tell me he was back.*

Peyton had no idea how close Izzy had gotten with Jake, her boyfriend's best friend, since last spring, had not been privy to what Izzy had thought were strengthening feelings between them. Izzy had kept her connection with Jake a secret, even from Peyton. And though he'd stopped communicating with her a few weeks ago, Izzy had held on to the hope that once Jake returned from his summer internship, things between them would go back to the way they had been.

But he couldn't even be bothered to give Izzy a heads-up that he was home. The rejection was complete, and Izzy was hurt and embarrassed that she'd ever thought she meant anything to Jake Vargas.

"Is that okay?" Peyton asked, eyeing Izzy closely as she zipped across town to the only New York deli within a hundred miles.

"Why wouldn't it be?"

Peyton shrugged. "I dunno. You just looked weird all of a sudden. Pale."

"I'm always pale."

"Like you'd seen a ghost."

"Ghost" was an interesting word choice.

It had all started in the spring when Jake accepted the summer internship at the Monterey Bay Aquarium. His girlfriend, Lori, had freaked out because Jake would be missing her older sister's wedding and demanded he turn the internship down. They'd gotten into a huge fight.

A few days later, while Jake and Izzy were watching the end of a horror movie after Hunter and Peyton had disappeared into the other room, he'd opened up to her about it. Izzy wasn't exactly sure why Jake had chosen her as a confidante—maybe because they were thrown together so much after their respective best friends started dating—but he did. Jake had shared his changed feelings for Lori, his love of oceanography and how desperately he wanted this internship, his dad's expectations that Jake would follow in his footsteps with a military career. Izzy had learned more about Jake that night than in the previous three years they'd known each other.

The conversation had been interrupted by the reemergence of Hunter and Peyton with ruffled hair and wrinkled clothes, but it hadn't ended there. Jake had texted Izzy later that night. And again the next morning.

Again and again.

Buried on Izzy's phone were months of heartfelt, in-depth messages between the two of them. In a short amount of time, Jake had become a very important part of Izzy's life, the only person other than Peyton in whom she'd confided her fears about studying abroad. And the only one, Peyton included, who knew just how tough Izzy's mom's mental health situation had gotten over the last year. She'd even confided in Jake about her mom's official diagnosis—Bipolar II—and her struggles to find medication that worked. Jake, more than anyone, understood why Izzy was going along with this Italian Scheme.

In an odd twist, Elizabeth Bell's mental health had been a source of bonding between Jake and Izzy. Jake's dad, a former Marine Corps sergeant, suffered from PTSD, a diagnosis Master Sgt. Alejandro Vargas, USMC, Retired, kept hidden from everyone outside his family.

Jake and Izzy had commiserated over parental expectations, and the importance of that connection had surprised Izzy. Delighted her. Their secret correspondence had continued through Jake's breakup with Lori and his temporary move down to Monterey for the summer. Jake was everything Izzy didn't know she was missing—a levelheaded sounding board with a smart sense of humor and an unexpected streak of empathy—and she'd looked forward to their daily texts.

Then a few weeks ago, Jake had gone silent. It had been a particularly rough period for Izzy as her mom had cycled rapidly through manic and depressive moods. Though Parker and Riley were both technically home, they made sure they were out of the house a lot. And her dad was always working, which left Izzy to manage her mom. Alone.

There was only so much *A Room with a View* could counterbalance, and her mom was spiraling as she obsessed over Alberto's arrival.

Izzy had texted Jake one night, voicing deep fears about both her mom's mental health and Alberto. She was getting more and more excited for his arrival. Something to look forward to. Something for *her mom* to look forward to. She was nervous that Alberto wouldn't like the house or her or would be offended by her wretched Italian.

Izzy had shared her fears with Jake and confided that she really wanted Alberto to like her.

Jake, who usually responded with encouragement and positivity, had merely typed a short, "Oh, I see." Then gone silent.

For weeks.

The suddenness of Jake's ghosting was devastating. Izzy had followed up, asked if he was okay, and gotten a few brush-offs like "Busy" and "Out on the boat all day" before she finally stopped trying. She felt foolish, ashamed that she'd imbued their friendship with more meaning than he had, embarrassed that she missed him, depressed that she had no one to talk to about it, and now angry that she was going to have to hang out with him again and pretend like nothing had happened.

"I was thinking," Peyton began slowly. "Now that Jake's back and, like, totally single, maybe . . ." She let her voice trail off as if Izzy was supposed to fill in the blanks. Which she wasn't about to do.

"Maybe what?" she asked sharply, her anger at Jake spilling over.

"Sorry." Peyton paused, eyeing her friend. "You guys seemed to get along pretty well last spring, and I just thought—"

"I'm not interested in Jake Vargas," Izzy snapped. Her anger covered the lie.

"Okay, that's totally fair." Peyton chewed at the inside of her cheek as the old SUV rattled to a stop at a red light. When she spoke again, her words felt carefully chosen. "I'd never push you into something you didn't want to do, Izz. I promise."

Something she didn't want to do . . .

So *that* was it. Peyton had been skeptical of the Italian Scheme from the beginning, worried—rightly—that Izzy was just going along with her mom's latest whim. In her charming but pushy kind of way, Peyton was trying to help Izzy find something else in life she wanted, something other than keeping her mom happy.

She didn't realize how close to home she'd hit.

"I just thought it would be cool to spend some time with Jake," Peyton continued, her eyes flitting toward Izzy in quick movements, like a hummingbird scanning for predators. "And it might take your mind off things."

Izzy arched an eyebrow. "Things?"

Peyton took a deep breath. "Like how your mom is trying to live vicariously through you by forcing you into something you don't really want. Like how some stranger is about to show up at your house to teach you a language you don't want to learn." She pulled into a parking spot at the deli. "Things."

Peyton didn't mean to, but she was exponentially increasing Izzy's stress level. "Alberto arrives in, like, eight hours," she said, trying to stay calm. "I think it's too late to cancel."

"But it's not too late to talk to your mom."

"And say what, exactly?"

"Tell her the truth!" Peyton shook her head. "She's your mom. She'll understand."

Peyton and her mom, Jeanine, had a very different relationship than Izzy and Elizabeth. It had been just the two of them since Peyton's dad passed away ten years ago. They'd bonded in their grief, and half the time acted more like sisters than mother and daughter, staging sleepovers in the living room and sharing secrets about crushes and sex and God only knows what else. Izzy and her mom were close, but the idea of that level of mother-daughter bonding was about as foreign to her as Italian.

"It's just . . ." Peyton gripped Izzy's hand. "You're not happy."

What else is new?

"And I know I can't, like, magically fix that or anything."

No one can.

"But I also know that me and Hunter, well . . ." She squeezed Izzy's hand, almost as fiercely as Izzy's mom had done in the kitchen. "I'm here for you, Izzy. Even though I'm with Hunter, I'm still here."

Izzy felt her chest muscles contract as her eyes welled up with hot tears. She *had* felt so alone since Peyton and Hunter got serious, more so than she realized. Which was why her connection with Jake had been so important. Would she still be considering Italy if Jake had reciprocated her feelings? That was a depressing thought.

"I know how much you want your mom to be happy," Peyton said softly.

Izzy stared out the window as the tears spilled down her cheeks.

"I know your dad's not . . . not around much."

That was an understatement.

"And your mom's . . . moods . . . are rough."

"Moods" was a simplistic way to describe it. A mood was something you could control. Mental illness was something bigger and darker and more elusive, triggered by things that were difficult to predict and even more difficult to avoid. Medication had helped a little, but the right combination had proved elusive, and her mom's emotional state had deteriorated since three of her four kids had moved out of the house. Izzy tried her best to keep her mom happy; she felt as if she was failing every day.

"Can we not talk about this anymore?" Izzy begged as she wiped her face with the backs of her hands. She hated how pathetic she sounded. And afraid. Always afraid.

"I just don't want to lose you."

Izzy glanced at her friend sidelong. "You make it sound like I'm joining a convent."

"I hear there are a ton of them in Italy," Peyton said, teasing. She always knew when to lighten the mood. One of the reasons she and Izzy were still friends. "Is 'meet a hot priest' on your agenda?"

"Ew."

"Cuz if that's what you want, I can probably dig one up in town."

"Double ew."

Peyton laughed. "See? No reason to leave Eureka!"

Izzy knew Peyton didn't get it. She saw her entire life contained within the confines of Humboldt County. She'd been born and raised here, like her parents. And her grandparents. And her *great*-grandparents. They'd never left, finding happiness in the town where they were born and raised and died, and Peyton had every expectation of doing the same. Even though they were about to be high school seniors, Peyton had already found her future husband in Hunter, who had a career lined up running his dad's fishing boat after graduation. Peyton would go to Humboldt State, just up the road from the house where she was born and raised, and then get some sensible white-collar job with health-care benefits and a retirement plan that would allow her to go part-time once she started making babies.

It was a good fit for her best friend, the dream future Peyton had mapped out since she was ten, but it wasn't what Izzy wanted.

The problem, of course, was that she didn't know what she did want— it was difficult to look out for your own interests when you spent all of your time thinking about everyone else—which made advocating for herself practically impossible.

"Pey, I know you don't want me to leave—"

"It's not that I don't want you to leave," Peyton said with a dramatic eye roll. "Okay, not *just* that. Lots of people leave for college. But they come back. If you go all the way to Italy . . ."

"I might not return," Izzy said, finishing her friend's thought.

"Yeah."

That was the plan, whether Izzy went to school in California, or Vermont, or Florence. She was leaving Eureka and never coming back.

"I'll always come visit you," Izzy lied. "You're the only thing in this town I give two shits about."

"Not ideal," Peyton said, feigning irritation. "But I'll take it." She reached over the center console and hugged Izzy tightly. As they sat in the idling car, hanging on as if it was the last time they'd ever see each other, Izzy was reminded of what a tight bond they had, and how important that bond had been to her for so many years.

It was almost enough to get her to stay.

Almost.

FOUR

BAGELS TUCKED SAFELY AWAY IN THE BACKSEAT, PEYTON headed toward the harbor. She seemed content not to renew their recent conversation.

They drove through Old Town, passing within two blocks of Izzy's house, through an area filled with Victorian homes. These painted ladies—mostly bed-and-breakfasts for the bustling tourism industry—made up most of Izzy's dad's clientèle. He specialized in restoring furniture and woodwork in old houses, and as they passed each vibrantly hued facade, Izzy could recall the refinished wardrobe that her dad had delivered to one, the wainscoting he'd installed in another. A replica corbel to match the one cracked during an earthquake. Restored porch swing that he'd found at a scrap yard when he was seventeen and kept at Grandma and

Grandpa's house "just in case" he ever needed it. The period replacement stained-glass doors he'd gone all the way to Santa Rosa to source. Each structure had some piece of Harry Bell's handiwork, either inside or out. Her dad's skill was on display all over his hometown. No wonder he loved it here.

Her eyes drifted down to the water, an incredibly beautiful view she'd taken for granted her entire life. Despite its location in the northern wilds of California, Humboldt Bay was oddly serene. Buffered by breaker islands, the natural harbor had been stumbled upon by Europeans before the signing of the Declaration of Independence, though its hidden entrance between rocky, inhospitable cliffs and the rolling monotony of sand dunes within had been discovered and forgotten more times than anyone could recall. Which seemed about right to Izzy. These days, Eureka was the kind of place she wanted to forget.

The boats continued to filter into the bay: fishing charters, mostly, like the one Hunter's dad ran. It was the same boat that *his* father had operated back in the seventies, when commercial fishing was still somewhat profitable. Now, Hunter and his dad ferried tourists and hobbyists out to fish deep-water halibut, rockfish, albacore, and crab, depending on the season, in a forty-three-foot Delta sportfisher named *Bodega's Bane*, a boat Izzy had seen coming and going from her bedroom window for as long as she could remember.

Everything and everyone in Humboldt County was connected to each other in that annoying and sometimes insidious way that visitors liked to call "quaint" in tones that denoted their regard for such small-town trappings, so long as they were only experiencing them from the outside. It was the kind of place where people didn't lock their doors when they left the house, where every single one of Izzy's teachers from kindergarten through high school had taught all three of her brothers before her, where you married someone you grew up with and stayed forever.

Don't get stuck here, Izzy. Promise me.

Peyton pulled into the parking lot near the entrance to Halvorsen Park, which was directly across the water from the *Bodega's Bane*'s slip, and leaped out of the SUV as soon as she cut the engine. Her eyes were fixed to the west, where three boats were slowly cutting through tranquil water. The first two—a shiny new sportfisher and a smaller skiff that probably fished the Klamath and Eel rivers—led the parade, and bringing up the rear was the much broader *Bodega's Bane*. As soon as the blue-and-white boat was in sight, Izzy spotted a figure on the bow, waving an orange-sleeved arm high above his head.

Peyton jumped up and down excitedly, blowing kisses to Hunter like he was coming home from war instead of a day at sea. They were close enough in the narrow channel of the inner reach to actually have a ship-to-shore conversation, and as the boat approached, Peyton called out to her boyfriend.

"Catch a big one, honey?"

Hunter cupped his hand to his mouth. "That's what she said."

"Kill me," Izzy grumbled. She wasn't jealous of their relationship, per se. Izzy had never been the kind of person who felt as if she needed a romantic partner to find fulfillment, but though she rolled her eyes at the copious public displays of affection and gross little sex jokes, the simple intimacy of her best friend's relationship looked kinda nice. Something she might want to find.

Something I thought I had.

But that felt impossible now. Izzy wasn't the type of girl that people remembered. She blended into the background, with lank, ashy blond hair that couldn't hold a curl to save its life; a pale, almost wan complexion; colorless cheeks. She had an utterly unremarkable face, with utterly unremarkable features, which were so utterly unremarkable that even the baristas at her favorite coffeehouse had to ask her name every single time she ordered, even though she'd been going there for years. Izzy wanted someone in her life that actually saw her. Made her feel special.

Jake had done that.

But unremarkable girls like Izzy didn't attract guys like Jake Vargas. And he'd made that abundantly clear through his silence.

As the boat cruised by, another figure climbed out beside Hunter. Izzy stiffened. Even with a woolen cap on, Izzy instantly recognized the burly stature of Jake Vargas.

He stood a good two inches taller than Hunter, but his build was thicker and sturdier than that of his lithe friend. Dark brown curls peeked out from beneath his cap, hinting that Jake's hair had grown out from the close-cropped buzz cut his retired military dad preferred, and Izzy felt a flutter deep in her stomach as she realized that she'd see him up close and personal in just a few minutes. Not the usual flutter of fear, though. This time, it was excitement.

Izzy pulled her eyes away from the deck of the boat. Excitement? Had she lost her mind? Jake wanted nothing to do with her. Most likely, he wouldn't even hang out with the three of them after the boat docked. This was as close to Jake as she was going to get.

Bodega's Bane turned into a row of slips on the barrier island across from the inner reach. Jake and Hunter hurried around the deck tossing orange buoys over the side. Izzy knew from experience that it would take at least half an hour before Hunter finished mooring the ship, unloaded the tourists and their catch, and drove over the bridge to the park. Peyton spent that time touching up her makeup and inspecting her outfit while

Izzy pulled out her phone, desperate to divert her thoughts from Jake. Thankfully, her mom was really good at monopolizing Izzy's mental space.

Six texts from her, all regarding Alberto.

What kind of coffee does he like?

Milk or cream? Real sugar or fake?

Should I get out extra blankets in case he's too cold in the house?

Did Dad add weather stripping to the front door like I asked?

Will Alberto need a plug outlet converter or should I get him an American voltage cell phone charger?

What kind of phone does he have?

Izzy didn't have answers. She and Alberto had exchanged a few messages over social media, but the Wi-Fi coverage in Alberto's town outside Florence was spotty, so they hadn't been able to do a face-to-face online chat. Their conversations had so far consisted of polite niceties and expressions of excitement, and Izzy had gotten the impression that Alberto's English was limited. Like he might have been running his sentences through Google Translate. It made sense that he was coming to the United States to study English, both at college and with Izzy's mom, though how he was going to function for an entire semester at Humboldt State was a mystery.

"Finally!" Peyton squealed as Hunter's white F150 pulled into the lot. She leaned back against the door of the Explorer seductively, hands on her hips. Hunter practically launched himself out of the driver's seat the instant the truck stopped moving.

"Heeeey, babe," Hunter said, slipping his arms around Peyton's back and pulling her close. Their kiss was deep and intimate, the kind of prolonged making out Izzy imagined might happen before sex, except instead of the privacy of Hunter's bedroom, they were standing in a parking lot while cyclists pedaled by on the coastal path and off-leash dogs chased squirrels up sycamore trees.

After watching for a few seconds longer than she should have, Izzy peeled her eyes away and found Jake standing beside her.

Izzy fought to keep her emotions in check, tamping down her nervous excitement. Which was difficult, because he looked really, *really* good. *Dammit.*

"Hey," Jake said.

Izzy's excitement dissolved into anger in a heartbeat. After weeks of avoiding her, he offers a nebulous "hey"? Like nothing had happened? That didn't even deserve an answer.

"How are you?" he pressed.

Lonely. Wounded. Pissed off. Izzy didn't think she could speak without screaming in rage, so again, she kept her mouth shut, merely offering a shrug in response.

Which seemed to confuse Jake. He whipped the woolen cap from his head, freeing the fledgling curls, and his brown eyes scanned Izzy's face. Was he looking for forgiveness or explanation?

After a few seconds of awkward silence marred only by the occasional slurping sounds from their mutual best friends, Jake opened his mouth to speak, but before he could formulate any words, someone hooted from behind them.

Another ship was passing through the inner reach, and two fishermen stood on the bow, applauding the make-out session. Peyton giggled and broke the embrace, though her hand still caressed the back of Hunter's neck.

Hunter gave the fishermen a thumbs-up, then swung Peyton around to face Jake and Izzy. "Dudes, should we go to my place?"

Sitting alone with Jake in Hunter's shabby-chic living room while he and Peyton hooked up was *not* part of the afternoon plan. Thankfully, Peyton was on the same page.

"Why don't we get some lunch," she said, then winked at Hunter. Izzy wondered if that was a promise of a later hookup.

"I'm starved," Jake said quickly, slapping Hunter on the back. "Aren't you?"

Everyone seemed really intent on getting lunch.

"Right," Hunter said with an audible huff. "Lunch."

Peyton grabbed his hand and spun him away from the water. "Let's walk. It's a beautiful day!"

Izzy glanced at the gray, damp sky and wondered if love made you believe that even the grossest days were gorgeous.

FIVE

PEYTON AND HUNTER LED THE WAY, HIS ARM STILL POSSES-
sively draped over her shoulders, and Jake and Izzy fell into step behind
them. L Street was relatively quiet in the late afternoon as tourists
geared up for dinner in Old Town, and the lack of other people accentuated the tense silence between them, thickening like cornstarch in
boiling water.

Finally, at the second intersection, Jake cleared his throat. "So how've
you been?" he asked.

One word. That was all he'd get from her. "Fine."

"Good fine? Bad fine?"

She stopped abruptly, her anger spilling over. "Well, you'd know that
if you hadn't ghosted me."

Izzy practically choked on her own words. She was so used to placating the people in her life, de-escalating tensions and trying to keep everyone happy, that speaking her true feelings felt like she was spewing poison.

"That's fair," Jake said softly. "I deserve that, and I'm sorry." He offered no explanation, just stared straight up L Street, hands shoved deep in the pockets of his Dickies work pants. Izzy wasn't sure if she was irritated or relieved by his response.

Yep, no. Irritated. She'd shared so much with him: her fears about what was happening in her life, her worries about her mom and about her future, her sense that her dad had completely checked out of the family. Jake's disappearance felt like a betrayal. An abandonment. And she needed to know why.

"That's it? I'm sorry?"

She watched Jake closely, catching his flinch. Guilt wrinkled his lips, and he couldn't look at her. "It's just . . . I mean . . ." Jake sighed, and his eyes shifted back to her face. "I had an amazing time in Monterey."

"Um, great." What did that have to do with her?

Jake began to walk again, slowly, with purpose. "It was nice to be around people who were interested in the same things I love. It showed me a future, you know? A path."

Izzy had no idea what that was like.

"And that path . . ." His voice trailed off, and he ventured a glance at Izzy walking beside him. He smiled at her shyly, then his eyes darted away. "You know, one of the other interns is going to be a junior at Humboldt State this year," Jake said, totally changing the subject. "They've got a top-five program for oceanography, and Tamara's double majoring with marine biology."

"Oh-kay . . ."

"She's got a job at their marine lab up in Trinidad that could turn into a full-time position once she graduates, and she said I can come any time and check out the facility."

So that was it. Jake had met a girl over the summer.

"That's *so* nice of her," Izzy said, bitterness creeping into her tone. She couldn't help it.

"Maybe I could take you?" Jake pressed. "For a tour of the campus. You might—"

They'd reached the restaurant, and Izzy stopped on the corner as Hunter and Peyton ducked inside. "Yeah, no. I'm the third wheel around here enough already."

"Third wheel?" He cocked his head. "Izzy, that's not what I meant."

"Sure sounded like it." She yanked open the brightly painted front door of the taco restaurant and dashed inside.

The restaurant's interior was a mishmash of decor that always made Izzy wonder if she'd just entered a fast-food joint or someone's living room. Tables and chairs were a mix of street finds like an old Formica breakfast table with chrome legs and a long wooden dining room monstrosity with intricately carved pedestals that was surrounded by six wooden school chairs from the early part of the last century. Then there was the industrial fast-food garbage can with the words "Thank you" engraved on the swinging refuse door that Izzy was relatively sure had been picked up from the old Burger King when it went out of business several years ago and a granite counter mounted on plywood. But whatever. The tacos were amazing. And cheap.

The restaurant was empty other than Hunter and Peyton. He was paying for their order at the counter, and she had taken up residence at the chrome-legged table that reminded Izzy of something her grandmother would have owned.

"Hey!" Jake said, following close behind. "Can we talk?"

Izzy ignored him, perusing the menu instead. As if she didn't have it memorized. "Carnitas or al pastor," she mused, then smiled at the cashier, a fifty-something Latina with blue eyeshadow and deep burgundy lips. "I'll take three al pastor tacos."

"I can get this," Jake said as the cashier rang Izzy up.

Izzy arched an eyebrow. "Why?"

"Just, um—"

She didn't need his guilt money. "I can pay for my own lunch."

"But, I uh . . ." He swallowed whatever words were to follow. Good. She'd heard enough.

Izzy turned back to the cashier, who was smirking at her as if she had an amusing secret she wasn't about to share. Izzy slapped some bills on the counter, half convinced the thing would collapse on impact, grabbed her order number, and retreated to the table. As she went, she heard the cashier say something to Jake in Spanish. He laughed and replied, but Izzy's two years of Spanish classes hadn't helped her much and she had no clue what they were saying.

"You still going to the bonfire Friday?" Hunter asked the moment Izzy sat down. "Even with that Italian dude staying with you?"

"Of course she's going," Peyton said. "I wouldn't let my boo miss it. I don't care who's living at her house."

The traditional Eureka High School summer-ending beach bash was one of *the* parties of the year. Peyton dragged her along every year, though Izzy had to admit she always had fun.

"Cool, cool," Hunter said, smiling at Izzy as if she'd been the one to actually respond to his question. "How's the Italian going?"

"Good," she lied. "I'm on the intermediate course already."

"Dude, can you say something?" Hunter leaned forward on his elbows. "Like, ask me how my day went?"

Izzy's mouth went dry. "Um . . . I could. But I'm pretty sure I know how your day went."

"Come on," Peyton said, backing up her boyfriend. "If you can't speak it in front of us, how will you be able to practice with Alberto?"

Jake slid into the seat beside her, and Izzy did her best to ignore him.

"Say anything," Peyton pleaded, patting her hand on the tabletop in anticipation. "Please?"

"Dude, it's not like we'll even know what it means," Hunter added.

He had a point. Clearly there was no getting out of this, and it was true that in a few hours she was going to have to get over her reticence and actually converse in Italian with Alberto. Izzy took a breath, trying to quell the panic seizing her central nervous system. *"Com'è stata la tua giornata?"*

She wasn't sure exactly what she sounded like, since the pounding of blood in her ears drowned out all other sounds, but judging by her friends' faces, which had suddenly gone rigid, she was pretty sure even *they* knew she'd just mercilessly butchered a romance language.

"Good job," Jake said, breaking the silence. He probably meant to sound sincere, but all Izzy heard was sarcasm.

Peyton's reaction was less veiled. "Tell me again why you're going to Italy?"

Izzy bristled. Peyton knew damn well why she was going. "Because I want to."

Do you?

"I think," Jake said, jumping in, "Peyton's just worried."

"Yes!" Peyton cried, eyebrows knitted with concern. "What if something happens to you? You get hurt or kidnapped into one of those white slavery rings?"

"You need to lay off the Lifetime Original Movies," Izzy said, forcing a laugh.

"It's dangerous out there," Peyton continued. "Look at that serial killer in LA targeting single women. That could be you!"

Hunter leaned forward, interested. "The guy who has sex with the bodies afterward?"

Of course that was the salient detail Hunter took away from the manhunt for the Casanova Killer. "It's called necrophilism," Izzy said, quoting from the latest episode of *Murder Will Speak*, all about the perviest new psychopath on the block. "Usually an attempt by the killer to exert control over his victim, even in death."

Peyton's eyes grew wide. "That's disgusting."

"The Casanova Killer isn't a necrophiliac," Izzy said. She felt like she needed to clarify this point, even though it sounded as if she were defending a monster. "But his DNA has been found on the mouths and faces of his victims, as well as in their throats and lungs, implying that he was making out with them at the time of death."

"That's even more disgusting." Peyton covered her mouth with one hand, as if afraid she might be the next victim of the Southern California murderer.

"Why do they call him that?" Hunter asked.

"Eyewitnesses say he's good-looking and charming, and targets women sitting alone at bars," Jake said. His face was hard, no hint of Hunter's delight or Peyton's distaste.

Izzy would have been impressed if she weren't pissed off at him. "Not exactly a barfly over here, so I should be fine."

"That's not the point," Peyton snapped.

Izzy tilted her head. "What is the point?"

"That . . ." Peyton stumbled. She was losing the threads of her argument. "That it's a dangerous world out there."

"It's a dangerous world, period," Izzy said as the cashier dropped off their orders. Once again, Izzy caught the woman smirking at her.

"It's true," Jake nodded. "When I was waiting to fly home, the local news ran a story about a body that washed up in San Francisco Bay with its face completely removed. Hannibal Lecter style."

"Who?" Peyton asked.

He cast a furtive glance at Izzy. "You know, *Silence of the Lambs*?" One of the many movies they'd watched together at Hunter's house after he and Peyton had gone off to have sex. Jake scrunched up his face like a lizard. "'I ate his liver with some fava beans and a nice chianti.'" Then he made a weird *fuh-fuh-fuh* sound with his lips.

"Rad," Hunter said with an appreciative nod.

"I'm not going to be cannibalized in a study-abroad program, guys," Izzy said. She couldn't believe how off the rails this conversation had gotten. "Or be strangled by a serial killer or end up as some Russian oligarch's sex slave. I'm just going to study art with a bunch of other art nerds."

Jake turned to her. "You're an art nerd now?"

"I . . ." She felt her face redden.

"See?" Peyton said, hands wide. "Even Jake can see this is bullshit, and he hardly knows you."

Hardly knows me. Izzy felt her chest contract like she'd been punched in the solar plexus. She clenched her jaw, trying to keep the tears at bay. She was under attack, and there was no safe harbor at this table. Her eyes shifted from Peyton to Hunter, and finally to Jake. His was the only gaze that faltered, and suddenly she knew why they were here, why Peyton had suggested lunch instead of hooking up with Hunter, why everyone was so intent on talking about her Italian.

"Seriously?" Izzy stood up, hands clenched at her side, while her carefully controlled temper ignited. "You're staging an intervention?"

Peyton clasped her hands in front of her heart, which meant she was about to lie. "We're just worried about you."

Izzy backed away from the table. Hunter was just along for the ride, but she wasn't sure whose participation she was more disappointed in: Peyton's or Jake's. "I'm going to Italy. I'm going to fucking love it there. And I'm never coming back to this shithole, so just get over it!"

Then she spun around and marched out the door.

SIX

IZZY RACED UP THE STREET, HER VISION BLURRED BY SHAME. Did her friends really think an intervention was the best option? Like she was a drug addict or an obsessive gambler. Why was it so awful that she wanted to leave, to see the world, and to maybe figure her shit out along the way? Why did every single person in her universe have their entire lives mapped out by the time they were seventeen? Who even did that?

Peyton's motivation she understood, but what right did Jake have to act like he cared what she did with her life?

Especially since he, and only he, knew all of Izzy's secrets. Her fear of going to Italy, her fear of staying home, her fear of what might happen to her family if she left. And her mom . . . She hadn't even told Peyton about how the Italian Scheme had started in the first place. One night a few months ago, Izzy's dad had been working late, and she'd come home to find her mom alone in the living room, weeping. A full glass of red wine and two prescription pill bottles on the coffee table, her mom's favorite movie paused on the TV screen. *A Room with a View*, the scene at the Basilica of Santa Croce with the Giotto frescoes.

Izzy had seen and heard her mom cry countless times before, usually silent tears while she worked in the kitchen or more robust wails as she sat alone in her room and thought no one else could hear. This time was different. There was no hiding her anguish. Agonized sobs ripped from her mom's chest, while snot and tears flowed unheeded down her face.

But the thing that had scared Izzy the most was the desperate look in her mom's eyes as she silently pleaded with her daughter for help.

"I'm sorry," her mom had sobbed, head buried in the palms of her hands. "I'm so sorry."

Izzy had rubbed her mom's back in slow circles with one hand while she picked up the pill bottles in the other. One shake allayed some of her fears—neither was empty.

"It's okay, Mom." Izzy had known for a long time that nothing about her mom's emotional state was "okay," and that her struggles to find the right combination of medications had only exacerbated the problem in the short term, but that evening had neither been the time nor the place for that conversation. She just had to keep her mom calm, let her know that she was loved, and ease her through the night until they could contact her doctor in the morning.

"I just . . ." Her mom had stared at the television. "I love this movie so deeply."

Izzy hadn't been sure how to respond but went with the first thing that popped into her brain. "I do too."

Her mom had caught her breath, eyes wide, mouth agape. "Really?"

"Um, yeah." Izzy had squeezed her mom's hand. "Don't I watch it with you all the time?"

Her mom had paused, eyes still fixed on the screen. *"Firenze,"* she'd said in a hushed voice. Then, all of a sudden, her mom had been in motion, talking a mile a minute as she transitioned from the film to the city to her own love of Italian Renaissance art, and by breakfast the next morning, a plan had been formulated: Izzy would follow in her mom's abandoned footsteps and study art history abroad in Florence.

Her mom, Parker, and Riley had been for the plan, her dad against it, and her eldest brother, Taylor, was impartial as usual. Like the friends she'd just left, they all had an opinion about her future, but . . .

She froze in the middle of the street, heart thundering. But no one had even asked her what she wanted. Not once. They'd either told her what she *should* want or scolded her for not knowing, but no one had asked.

Izzy felt rather than heard the footsteps pounding down the pavement toward her. She didn't turn around, afraid she'd immediately burst into tears. If Peyton wanted to apologize, she'd have to do it to the back of her head.

"Izzy!" a voice called from behind. Only it wasn't Peyton. It was Jake. "Wait up."

She didn't move, though she wasn't sure why. Did she really want another standoff with him?

"I'm sorry, okay?" Jake dashed in front of her, panting. "I didn't know it would go like that. Honest."

Izzy blinked. That was the only response he deserved. Jake sighed, shoulders sagging. The self-confidence drained out of him.

"I'm just worried that you've latched onto this plan for all the wrong reasons."

"I'm not going through a midlife crisis, Jake." *I'm not my mother.*

He stepped toward her, dropping his voice. "No, but that night with your mom and the pills . . ."

After disappearing from her life without a word, Jake didn't deserve to fall back into their intimacy so easily. "Oh, please, person I 'barely know.'" She added air quotes on the last two words to emphasize their ridiculousness. "Please enlighten me."

Jake grimaced. "You never told Peyton about our chats." It felt like an accusation.

"Why do you care?"

Heavy brows pulled low over his dark brown eyes. When he spoke, his voice was soft and measured, but his jaw quivered as if it took all of his concentration to stay calm. "You may find this difficult to believe right now, but I do care."

THEN WHY DID YOU DISAPPEAR? She wanted to scream the words in his face but realized that the answer wasn't something she really wanted to hear. She'd been a temporary crutch, a friend of convenience to help him through his breakup with Lori, but once he met someone cooler, more together, and more interesting, he'd dropped Izzy like a hot brick.

"Look," she said, exhaling all of her anger in one giant deflation of her lungs. "I'm glad you had such a great summer. And . . . and I'm glad that you connected with Tamara and are staying here to go to school with her next year."

"Uh, I'm not going to school *with* Tamara."

Izzy was confused. "But she's at Humboldt with their top-five oceanography program." Why else would he have brought that up?

"I *am* applying to Humboldt for next year," Jake said, then shook his head. "But that's not what I meant."

They'd reached the front gate of Izzy's house and she turned, one hand on the latch, to face him. "Then what did you mean? Why is everyone trying to get me to stay?"

"I'm not everyone." He stepped closer. Izzy had to tilt her head to meet his eyes, and she caught her breath at the sadness she saw in them. "I know you're mad at me, but I just need you to know that I'd really like it if you weren't so far away next year."

He hovered, eyes locked on Izzy's, and teetered toward her as if a gust of wind had suddenly caused him to lose his balance. Then he seemed to right himself. He stepped back, swallowing hard before he turned and disappeared around the corner.

SEVEN

IZZY'S EYES LINGERED ON THE SPOT WHERE JAKE HAD DISAP-
peared around the side fence of Miss O'Sullivan's Victorian Bed-and-
Breakfast.

It had seemed, maybe, that he was about to kiss her.

But that was impossible. Izzy wasn't the kind of girl who inspired
romance. She was plain and boring and quiet. A third wheel. That's the
only way anyone in this town would ever see her.

Besides, Jake had literally spent the last month pretending she didn't
exist while he was hanging out with cool college girls named Tamara. Izzy
must have misinterpreted his body language.

She shook her head, dismissing the feelings that had bubbled up inside
her, and unlatched the gate that opened onto her front yard. The ancient

iron hinges creaked like a surly old tomcat mewling for his dinner, and Izzy could feel the grinding metal vibrate beneath her hand. While her dad was maintaining the fancy Victorians in town, the Bell house was falling apart.

The stick-style Queen Anne had been a grand house in its day, occupying a spacious corner lot not far from the iconic Carson Mansion, whose peaked roof and ornate tower dominated the Eureka waterfront. The Bell house was decidedly less stately, though the carved roof posts around the front porch and intricate gingerbread trim indicated that the original owners had money to spend. Every detail of the house had been meticulously planned, from the stained-glass windows on either side of the massive oak door to the multitiered gabled roofline to the tone-on-tone green paint with brick red trim that harkened back to the native Humboldt County redwoods; it must have been a sight to see in 1907.

Today, not so much. Her parents had bought the house as a fixer-upper after years of neglect, and though her dad had spent almost a decade restoring it to its original glory, his attention and resources had eventually been pulled away by his business, and the Bell house hadn't received any significant TLC since Izzy was a child. The paint was faded and peeling, the once sharply landscaped hedges were overgrown blobs choking the front yard, and a portion of trim over the front door had broken off in a storm. If it weren't for the always-on porch light, strangers might have mistaken the decrepit old house for abandoned, possibly haunted.

Even though her family routinely left the front door unlocked, no strangers were going to venture inside. It didn't look like the kind of place that would have anything of value to steal.

Izzy slunk toward the house, dragging feet weighed down by the world. At the base of the front stairs, she froze. She'd left the goddamn bagels in Peyton's car.

She didn't want to text Peyton because she just couldn't face a renewal of that intervention—or worse, an effusive apology from her friend—but she didn't want to face her mom either. The missing bagels might tip her anxiety into the red zone.

While she contemplated whether or not she could make it upstairs to her attic undetected, a circular saw buzzed to life in the garage workshop. Her dad was the brand of dreamy optimism she needed right now.

The latch on the side door to the garage had been broken for years, and when Izzy pushed it open, she found her dad hunched over a table saw, goggles securely fixed over his eyes as he expertly guided a piece of cedar through the rotating blade. Sawdust billowed outward, particles dancing in a shaft of light that had pierced the cloudy sky and beamed through an open window. They circled upward toward the garage door rails and disappeared into shadow.

Her dad lifted his foot from the pedal that controlled the circular saw, pushed his goggles to his forehead along with a thick, unkempt fringe of salt and pepper gray hair, then held the long piece of wood up to his nose to examine his handiwork.

"Cornice trim or wainscoting?" Izzy asked from the doorway. Her dad didn't flinch at the sound of her voice, even though he couldn't have heard her coming.

"Bargeboard," he said, running a hand over the flat surface. "Or at least it will be once I'm done with it."

"For the Pink Lady restoration?" Izzy asked. The owners of the Pink Lady, one of Eureka's crown jewel Victorian properties turned upscale bed-and-breakfast, had been promising to hire her dad to restore and replace some of the rotting exterior woodwork. It was a huge job, both for the prestige and the paycheck, but after a year of stringing him along, a contract had yet to materialize.

Her dad shook his head. "Nah, just the Dickerson place."

"Sorry."

He turned to face her, a hearty smile wrinkling his tanned face. "Why sorry? The Dickersons are good clients, and their Stick-Eastlake Victorian is a rare bird. I'm honored that they trust her to me."

A rare bird whose owners *rarely* paid their bills on time.

"What's wrong, Izzy?" her dad said, tossing the soon-to-be bargeboard back onto the workbench. "You nervous about that Italian kid?"

"A little." Tip of the iceberg.

He snorted. "You sound about as excited as a mourner at a funeral."

"Depends whose funeral."

"Good one." He laughed. "Well, your mom's excited enough for all of us. I haven't seen her like this since she moved to California."

Izzy cringed at her dad's cluelessness. He worked a lot, both in his workshop and at various sites that sometimes kept him away until late at night, absences that seemed to have increased over the last few months. She should have been surprised that he had no idea about the true state of his wife's mental health, but she wasn't.

She also wasn't surprised that her mom hadn't been excited about much of anything since she moved from New England to sleepy little Eureka. She had been a twenty-two-year-old college graduate with a new baby, and she'd just had to let go of her own dreams. Instead of crossing the Arno River over the Ponte Vecchio or strolling through the Boboli Gardens, she was breastfeeding an infant in her in-laws' guest room with a view of the fog, the fog, and some more fog. Sure, she'd grown up in a coastal town full of ships and fishing and sea air, but even Mystic,

Connecticut, was a far cry from Florence, and it was nothing short of a miracle that Elizabeth Bell had lasted twenty-four years in this town.

"Speaking of your mom, I have a surprise." Her dad's dark blue eyes sparkled as he beckoned Izzy over to a table in the corner of his workshop where a stained tarp covered a small object. From its shape and size, Izzy knew what it was without even seeing it.

"Another clock?" She couldn't hide her disappointment and was pretty sure her mom wouldn't be able to either.

Her dad's face fell. "How did you know?"

"Because it's always a clock!"

He puffed up his chest as if she'd insulted his manhood. "And what's wrong with that?"

Ugh. "I'm sure it's a lovely clock, but—"

"But it's not just *any* clock, Izzy." Grinning broadly, he whipped the tarp off the table with a dramatic flourish, revealing a foot-tall rectangular desk clock with a key sticking out of one side. The box looked as if it had been used as a scratching post, and the hands were frozen at two and ten. "Behold! A genuine T. Boxell of Brighton library clock, circa 1860. Mahogany case with flame veneers, original bun feet, and beveled glass on the top and side panels. All the parts are in excellent condition. Just needs a little love."

He paused, joy radiating from every pore as he gazed at his latest restoration project. "It's super rare to find one of these in the States."

"Is it worth anything?"

Her dad gasped, horrified. "I'm not selling it! It's for your mom's birthday."

Izzy pictured the living room, littered with clocks. Every tick added to her mom's despair in that house, and the idea of adding one more . . . Izzy could see her mom's face as she opened the gift, the taut smile held in place by muscles long accustomed to displaying happiness where there was none, flared nostrils the only indication of her annoyance. Would her mom see it as a gift of love or just another example of her husband's thoughtlessness? Izzy already knew the answer.

"Dad," she said, closing the garage door behind her. "Don't you think, maybe, it would be nice to get Mom something *other* than a clock for her birthday?"

Her dad pulled back his head, brows knitted in confusion. "Like what?"

Izzy shrugged. *Something she might actually enjoy.* "Maybe a nice piece of jewelry? Something to make her feel special."

Her dad spun the clock around and opened the back, exposing the mechanical guts inside. "See that decorated pendulum rod? They don't make 'em like that anymore. How could this not make her feel special?"

He so wasn't getting it. She walked up to the clock, running appreciative fingers over the smooth, mahogany case while assiduously avoiding his eyes. "I . . . guess."

"What is it, kiddo?" Her dad folded his arms over his chest and squared his hips, his most fatherly pose. "You know you can tell me anything."

Izzy sighed. She didn't want to hurt his feelings, but she also wanted her mom to find a new spark in life. *And stop trying to live vicariously through me.* "I think Mom's feeling a little underappreciated right now, and maybe an unexpected birthday gift from you might help."

He chewed at the inside of his cheek as if the soft, gummy skin were his daughter's words. "I guess I could save the clock for Christmas."

It wasn't perfect, but it was something. "Good idea."

"Parson's shop has pretty stuff." The estate sale store had lovely old jewelry—Peyton's mom shopped there a lot—though Izzy was surprised her dad knew about it. He probably hadn't bought a woman jewelry since her mom's wedding ring.

A gust of wind ripped through the garage, throwing the unlatched door wide as it traveled through the open window on the opposite wall. The door had been broken so long there was actually a divot in the wall from the handle, which violently smacked into the wood dozens of times a day.

"You should fix that," Izzy said, even though she knew he wouldn't.

"It's on my list." He slid the goggles back over his eyes. Izzy's cue to leave.

"Thanks, Dad." Izzy leaned forward and pecked her dad on the cheek. "A nice bracelet or something would make Mom so happy."

He laughed again, all trace of disappointment over the clock vanished. "*You're* going to make Mom so happy. You're living her dream!" He recovered the clock and returned to his bargeboard without noticing that his daughter had gone rigid at his words.

Izzy slipped out of the garage somehow feeling worse than when she'd entered. So much for a cheerful pep talk from dear old Dad. She'd ended up parenting him more than he parented her.

But what else was new?

EIGHT

THE ARCATA-EUREKA AIRPORT—ALSO KNOWN AS THE California Redwood Coast–Humboldt County Airport—was, either way, appropriately named. Originally built by the US Navy during World War II, a few miles north of both Eureka and the college town of Arcata in the even sleepier hamlet of McKinleyville, the airport hugged the coastline in a narrow swath of grassy lowlands between the Pacific Ocean and the redwood forested mountains. Izzy was pretty sure the only thing that kept the tiny airport from being shut down completely was the presence of a major university in neighboring Arcata. Other than tourists and the forestry service, college students were the only people who bothered with Humboldt County.

Alberto was arriving on the last flight of the day, a late shuttle from

San Francisco that was set to arrive just after nine o'clock. According to the itinerary furnished by the foreign exchange student agency, Alberto had gone to San Francisco for a few days to sightsee before heading up to Eureka. Which was smart. But San Francisco was a beautiful place, and she hoped Alberto wouldn't request a transfer back down there after a few days in the Bell house.

Or maybe she hoped he would? If he hated Eureka and asked to leave, she'd be off the hook in terms of exposing her hideous language skills. Maybe the entire Italian Scheme would unravel organically from there.

Izzy glanced over at her mom, who was tapping the steering wheel with her thumbs and singing along to one of her favorite tracks. Something grungy from the nineties. Her mom was smiling as she added her slightly atonal soprano to the gravelly voice coming through the speakers in the family minivan, and she leaned forward in the driver's seat as if in anticipation, her dark brown ponytail bobbing back and forth to the beat.

Izzy hadn't seen her mom this happy in weeks, and despite her own anxiety, she joined in with the final chorus of "Even Flow."

Izzy's mom glanced at her as she pulled off the highway, nodding her head in approval. "I didn't know you like Pearl Jam."

"Yep!" Izzy didn't really, but she'd been forced to listen to this album so many times in the car with her mom that she knew every single lyric.

"Aren't you full of surprises."

"Gotta keep you on your toes," Izzy said, smiling.

Her mom snorted. "I think Riley wins that prize."

They both laughed at the truth of her words, and then Izzy's mom reached over and squeezed her daughter's hand. Even though it trembled slightly, Izzy was comforted by the gesture. Her mom was in a good place tonight, and Izzy wanted to keep her there as long as possible.

The song ended, and her mom switched the input to Izzy's phone. "Do you want to listen to one of your murdery podcast things? I know how much you love them."

Izzy did, rather desperately, want to relisten to the latest Casanova Killer episode of *Murder Will Speak*, but she knew graphic descriptions of murder made her mom uncomfortable. "No, I'm good."

"You sure?"

"Yep. We're almost there anyway."

Her mom shifted nervously in her seat as they drove up a dark road from the highway, the only lights coming from an illuminated Holiday Express sign mounted over what appeared to be a 1950s motor lodge and the occasional muted streetlamp piercing the evening fog. "I hope his plane's not delayed."

Izzy checked the flight tracker app on her phone. "According to this, he should be on the ground in five minutes."

"Are you excited?"

"Yeah," Izzy lied, mustering up as much enthusiasm as she could.

"This is going to be *so* good for you. When I was preparing for my Italian exams, my language skills really improved after I started watching old *Un posto al sole* episodes online. I wish I'd started doing that earlier so I could have applied for study abroad as a junior instead. . . ."

Her voice trailed off, but Izzy knew how that sentence ended. *Instead of waiting for senior year.* Because Elizabeth and Harry, smart Gen Xers raised during the safest safe-sex era of the AIDS epidemic, had skipped a condom one night. She found out she was pregnant the same week her application for senior year study abroad was due. Not only did her mom never make it to Italy, she just barely graduated, navigating the last semester of college with a newborn.

Even though her face was shrouded in darkness, Izzy could sense that her mom's emotional state was souring by the second. Without thinking, Izzy laid her hand on her mom's arm. "Thanks, Mom."

"For . . . for what?" she asked, confused.

"For everything." Izzy squeezed her arm. "You're an amazing person, and I appreciate everything you do for me."

She felt her mom suppress a sob, shuddering in her chest as she fought to control her emotions. It wasn't that her mom regretted her life as a whole—she'd talked openly with all her kids about choices and sacrifices and having no regrets—but Izzy knew that regret *had* seeped in. That's why her mom hated the idea of fate: if she'd been destined to end up in Eureka, rather than arriving there through choices made of her own free will, then fate was something to be loathed, not lauded. *Fate is also a four-letter word.*

By the time Riley had graduated from high school and headed off to San Diego last year, Izzy's mom was in a noticeable funk. Well, noticeable to Izzy. Not so much to anyone else in the family. And now, as Izzy was about to start her last year at Eureka High School, her mom had heaped all her sadness, her regret, and her unfulfilled dreams onto her daughter's shoulders like she was some kind of emotional pack mule.

The pressure was overwhelming, and Izzy couldn't see any other way out except through. And "through" meant Alberto and Italian lessons and hopefully discovering a love for Renaissance art.

Her mom gripped the wheel tightly as she pulled into a mostly deserted parking lot. The main terminal looked more like a high school gym than the airports Izzy had seen in movies—no bustle, low security, just a large open space with domed two-story ceilings and a wicked echo effect. A few check-in desks at one end and a single baggage claim belt on the other, the airport looked particularly small and lonely at this hour, with just a couple of security staff and a janitorial crew on hand for the last flight of the day.

"I hope we'll recognize him," her mom said, striding quickly across the terminal to the security gate where deplaned passengers arrived.

Izzy glanced around, noting just six other people, all locals judging by the pale, sun-deprived skin and mix of practical outerwear. Their tanned Italian exchange student from Tuscany should stand out. "I don't think that will be a problem."

Still, her mom shifted her weight nervously between her feet, the bobbing ponytail in constant motion, while she wrung her hands in front of her.

They'd only been at the terminal for a few minutes before a handful of weary travelers meandered down the corridor. Most of them were dressed in long pants and hoodies in anticipation of cool weather. Locals. She even recognized one guy, a fisherman friend of Hunter's named Greg Loomis who had graduated from their high school three years ago. Tall and traditionally hot with dark brown hair, blue eyes, and square shoulders, he'd been Peyton's obsession before Hunter. He had a reputation as having a bad temper and some unsavory habits, and thankfully wasn't interested in a gawky freshman like Peyton. Now Greg, who couldn't have been older than twenty-one, looked like a forty-five-year-old with weathered skin and yellowing teeth. He lit up a cigarette the instant he set foot outside and slowly sauntered off into the night.

See what Eureka did to people? Emotionally *and* physically.

"Oh!" Izzy's mom said, gripping her daughter's arm. "I think that's him!"

Izzy turned back to the trickle of passengers. Even if he hadn't been wearing cargo shorts and a sleeveless jacket, even if he hadn't been a head taller than almost anyone else coming off that plane, Izzy would have known Alberto right away. The sun-bleached hair and tanned face were exactly what she remembered from the few Facebook photos she'd seen, and his bright, cheery smile stood out among his fellow travelers.

He locked his eyes with Izzy's almost immediately, light blue and so alive with excitement that they mirrored her mother's. Alberto hiked his backpack higher up on his shoulder and increased his pace, striding right up to her. Without breaking eye contact, he reached down for her hand, his thumb brushing gently across her skin as he lifted her fingers to his lips.

Izzy had never been kissed by a guy before: not on the lips, not on the cheek, and certainly not on her hand like she was a noblewoman being courted by a gallant knight. Before she realized what was happening, Alberto's lips were pressed to her fingers, a gesture so quick and simple Izzy wasn't sure whether she should be offended or turned on.

"You are Izz-*ee*, *sì*?" Alberto asked, placing emphasis on the last syllable of her name, which made it sound significantly more regal.

"Y-yes," she stumbled. "Um, *sì*."

Alberto took a step closer, his handsome smile deepening as his eyes bored into hers. "*Ciao*, Izz-*ee*," he said softly. "I am Alberto."

Deep inside, Izzy felt a seismic shift. *"Ciao."*

NINE

ALBERTO BEAMED DOWN AT IZZY WITH THE KIND OF MILLION-watt smile that only A-list actors and con men seemed to possess. His light blue eyes, almost translucent in their paleness, glistened as he flipped his hair out of his tan face, a few errant strands arched coyly over one brow. He looked boyishly rogue, the epitome of George Emerson in *A Room with a View*, and despite Izzy's usual reticence to look new people in the eyes for longer than a heartbeat, she felt unable to break from his gaze.

Izzy's mom, oblivious to the fireworks moment happening between her daughter and the new Italian exchange student, stepped between them and threw an arm around Alberto's neck, hauling his tall frame down to her level. When Alberto pulled his eyes away from Izzy, it felt like her soul went cold, deprived of his warmth.

"Buona serata, Alberto. Benvenuto!"

Bent under the weight of Elizabeth Bell's embrace, Alberto winced noticeably, as if he'd pulled a muscle in his back. He didn't respond to the greeting.

"Com'è stato il tuo volo?" Izzy's mom continued. Her accent was flawless, her voice strong and confident despite not speaking Italian for almost twenty-five years. Had she been practicing too?

"Bene, bene," Alberto said with an uncomfortable little laugh. *"E tu?"*

Izzy wasn't entirely sure, but she thought her mom had just asked Alberto about his flight, to which he'd replied, "Good, and you?"

Her Italian was worse than she thought.

"You must be tired," her mom said in English, releasing her hold on Alberto. He straightened up and turned his megawatt smile onto Izzy's mom.

"You are-a Izz-ee's sister, *sì?*"

Izzy snorted. "More like my mom." The words were barely out of her mouth when she felt her mom's icy, hard stare boring into the side of her head.

"We're not *that* far apart in age, Izzy," her mom said. "Though I suspect Alberto is just being kind." She shifted her eyes back to him, lids lowered.

He laughed, light and easy, as he gripped Izzy's mom's hand. "Signora Bell, you-a tease me."

The handshake lingered, and Izzy saw her mom shift her feet. She broke away suddenly, gesturing toward Alberto's small wheelie bag. "Is this all your luggage?"

"*Sì*, Signora."

"For three months?"

"We Italians, we-a travel light." Alberto ran a hand self-consciously through his floppy hair as his eyes darted back and forth around the emptying terminal. "Your house issa far from here? I am, as-a you say, tired."

Her mom smiled warmly. "Yes, of course." She gripped the handle of his bag and headed toward the parking lot. "This way!"

Izzy hurried to stay beside Alberto as they followed her mom out into the darkness. A car stenciled with a Holiday Inn emblem waited at the door, probably for the pilots and flight attendants, and though it was too dark to see, the close, damp air that smacked them in the face as they exited meant that the fog had thickened during their short time indoors.

Alberto shivered, hunching his shoulders toward his ears. "Always it is so cold?"

Yes. "Not usually this time of year," Izzy lied. She suddenly wanted him to like her hometown. "September and October are our nicest months."

He peeked at her through his hair. "I look-a forward to spending them with you, *sì?*"

Izzy felt her cheeks heat up and shifted her eyes to the asphalt to hide her confusion. It must have been a translation thing. He couldn't actually mean that he was looking forward to spending time with her specifically. They'd literally met ninety seconds ago, and though Izzy wasn't beyond a romantic fantasy, she knew better than to think that she was either beautiful or charming enough for this world-traveling Italian to instantly fall for her. That only happened in the movies.

Right?

"Alberto," Izzy's mom said, popping the rear door of the minivan with her key fob. The brake lights blinked red in the night, glinting off Alberto's teeth. "My daughter has been practicing her Italian all summer. Say something, Izzy."

They stopped behind the minivan, and all the warmth that had just radiated through Izzy's body instantly drained away, leaving a debilitating panic in its wake, as cold and damp as the sea air surrounding them. The idea that Izzy had been practicing her Italian for months in anticipation of this moment made what was about to happen all the more horrifying. Once Alberto heard her wide American vowels and stuttering, staccato syllables, that beautiful smile would turn into a derisive sneer.

Her mom raised her eyebrows expectantly as she hit the "close" button. The motor on the mechanical door was the only sound breaking the ominous silence.

"Uh . . ." Izzy began. All of her memorized phrases and vocabulary abandoned her. "I . . ."

"No, no," Alberto jumped in, waving his hands before him as if in surrender. "No *italiano* tonight, *sì*? We in America! I practice my English first, *sì*?"

Her mom shrugged. "It can wait until tomorrow!" She opened the front door of the van for him. "Shall we?"

Izzy let out a breath through pursed lips. A stay of execution. Though the firing squad would be back in the morning, locked and loaded, and there was literally zero chance she'd go from Italian hack to fluent speaker by then.

Alberto bounced lightly in his seat as he fastened his safety belt. "The American minivan!" He sounded genuinely excited by the aging car. "I am-a exciting."

Izzy's mom smiled at him. "I am excit*ed*," she said gently, correcting his tense.

"Ah! *Mi dispiace.*"

"Your English will be flawless by the time I'm done with you."

"Grazie tante, Signora."

She started the engine. "Please, call me Elizabeth."

"Ah, *sì*. Eleeza—"

He was in the middle of elongating the second syllable in her mom's name when the car stereo connected to Izzy's phone, picking up the episode of *Murder Will Speak* she'd started earlier that day. The two hostesses, Mags and Amelia, were bickering lightheartedly about the nickname of the West Coast's newest serial killer.

"I think it's a terrible name," Amelia said with a groan. "Like, what octogenarian came up with it?"

Mags snorted. "It's not that bad."

"Lies."

"It could be worse."

"You're bananas."

"Only at breakfast."

The lightning banter was one of Izzy's favorite aspects of the podcast, like two friends shooting the shit about famous murderers. Her mom didn't share her love.

"Izzy, can you switch it off?"

"Yeah." Izzy fumbled with her phone. "Sorry."

"I'm just saying," Mags continued, "you could do a lot worse than 'Casanova Killer.'"

Alberto jolted in the passenger seat.

"Izzy!" her mom snapped. She hit the brakes abruptly in the middle of the dark road and reached down to turn off the stereo before Izzy could get her app open. "You've upset our guest."

"I'm sorry?" she said, not sounding or feeling the least bit apologetic. Alberto wasn't a child, and the clip hadn't contained any of the salacious details that Izzy knew would be discussed later in the episode.

"No, no. No need to apologize. I have heard of this Casanova." He said the name in perfect Italian, and Izzy suddenly remembered that the original Casanova had been Venetian, a fact Izzy's mom seemed to realize at the same time.

"Alberto, I hope you're not offended by the name," her mom said quickly, car still idling in the middle of the road. "It has no bearing on how we Americans view Italy or Italians. I doubt most people even know who Casanova really was."

If his Italian pride had been wounded, Alberto didn't show it. "Please, Signora. I have no offense."

"I *take* no offense," she corrected.

"Ah, *grazie*." He flashed Izzy's mom his beguiling smile. "Shall we go to the house?"

Izzy's mom eased the car into drive. "While you're with us, consider it your home."

"*Grazie, grazie*," Alberto said. "I think I shall like-a that very much."

TEN

ALBERTO'S CHIPPER MOOD HAD FADED BY THE TIME THEY reached the Bell house that night, and it was clear that he couldn't keep his eyes open. After meeting Parker and Riley, he politely declined the shepherd's pie Izzy's mom had prepared and merely requested a glass of water before being shown to his room.

When Izzy descended to the bathroom early the next morning, the door to Riley's room was still closed. And again when she passed by on her way to grab breakfast half an hour later. Her mom had laid out a tray of bagels, cream cheese, fresh local lox, capers, and sliced red onion on the kitchen island, and Izzy wondered with a pang of guilt if Peyton had dropped the bagels off last night or if her mom had raced out this morning to pick up another box. Whichever the case, Izzy's mom didn't seem to care. She kept glancing at the doorway every few seconds, and it was clear from her worried expression that Alberto hadn't yet emerged from his room.

"Do you think he's okay?" she asked as Izzy slipped two halves of an everything bagel into the toaster oven.

"It's not even eight o'clock," her dad said, sipping heavily sugared black coffee from the window seat, his work boots kicked up on the bench. "He's probably jet-lagged. Let him sleep."

"He's been in San Francisco for almost a week," her mom said. "He should have acclimated by now." She stared up at the ceiling as if she could see through the hundred-year-old floorboards into Riley's room.

"College kid alone in San Fran?" Her dad laughed. "He hasn't slept in days."

Riley, who sat on a stool at the kitchen island with an empty coffee mug in front of him, looked up from his phone long enough to smile sympathetically at his mom. "Not all of us keep business hours."

Izzy rolled her eyes. "And what time did you get home last night?"

Parker poked his head in from the laundry room. He still wore leggings from his morning run. "One thirty."

"You had a *second* hookup last night?" Izzy asked, disgusted.

"Kylie. Again." Riley grinned from ear to ear like a satisfied cat after polishing off a bowl of cream.

Parker arched an eyebrow. "Does she know how young you are?"

"Nope!" Riley held out his fist for a bump from his older brother, who pointedly avoided it.

"I don't know where that thing's been."

"Gross," Izzy groaned, eyeing her mom. This was normally about the time she'd lay into Riley for dating Kylie. Riley even braced for impact, tightening his muscles as he waited for the onslaught of "bad reputation" and "dangerous ex-boyfriend" lectures, but the Italian student asleep upstairs seemed to occupy all her maternal anxieties.

"It's going to be such a nice day," Izzy's mom said, watching the fog retreat toward the ocean. "I hope Alberto doesn't miss it."

"Same weather forecast for tomorrow." Izzy's dad stood up. His voice was light, but the smile on his weather-lined face looked forced.

His wife wasn't listening. "I wonder if I should bring up some food."

"Oh, leave him alone, Beth." Her dad rounded the island, coffee cup in one hand. "He's a grown-ass man. He can ask for food when he wants it."

Izzy tensed as she saw a shift in her mom's face from concern to distaste as she slowly turned to her husband. "I'm so glad I have *you* as an expert on grown-ass men," she said, her voice steely. "Oh, wait."

He dropped his cup in the sink without rinsing it, ceramic clanging against porcelain. "What's that supposed to mean?"

"It means you're about as 'adult' as the JV football team."

Parker had disappeared from the laundry room, and Riley was focused on his phone as if engrossed by the most interesting article ever written. Her brothers had a knack for avoiding their parents' fights, a luxury not available to Izzy. Someone would have to pick up the pieces if the confrontation escalated, and that someone was always her. Meanwhile her dad, who should have known better by this point in his marriage, refused to back down, planting his hands on his hips like a pouting child.

"I don't see *you* paying the bills," he began, the familiar first blow in all their fights. Izzy wondered if he realized how sexist it was to call out his wife's lack of earning power after she raised their four children, though pointing that out would only prolong the argument. With Alberto sleeping upstairs, she needed to de-escalate this standoff quickly. She didn't want his first day in the house to be marred by domestic strife.

Before her mom could respond, Izzy jumped off her stool and pointed to the clock on the wall, a smiling starburst sun whose cheeky grin mocked the tension in the kitchen. "Eight already? Dad, don't you need to be at the Dickersons to install that bargeboard?"

"Bargeboard," he said slowly. "Right." Izzy wasn't sure if he knew she was trying to distract him and just looking for any excuse to avoid the fight he'd started, or if he was truly clueless about her machinations, but either way, he turned from his wife and patted Izzy on the head. A dutiful puppy. "Thanks, kiddo."

"No problem, Dad."

He loped toward the laundry room, his wife staring daggers at the back of his head. "Should be there most of the day. Home by dinner."

"Okay, Dad!" Izzy said, trying to sound cheerful.

No one else responded.

Even after her dad's exit, the kitchen was tense. Neither Riley nor her mom said a word: he was still fixated on his phone, while she fretted over the breakfast spread, swathing it liberally in Saran Wrap so it would be fresh whenever Alberto emerged from his bedroom. Before she could be asked her opinion on Alberto's breakfast needs, Izzy grabbed her coffee and bagel and slipped back upstairs to her attic room.

Alberto's door was still closed.

The screen on Izzy's phone was just dimming as she flopped down on her bed, and she picked it up to see a string of missed texts from Peyton.

So? What's he like?

Is he hotter than his photos?

Don't make me show up there to see for myself.

What does your mom think? Is she happy?

Did you get the bagels I left on the porch?

One mystery solved.

Izzy started to respond, then paused. She and Peyton hadn't spoken, even by text, since yesterday's botched intervention, and though her friend was trying to sound normal, it was difficult not to infuse each message with subtext.

So? What's he like? *Maybe if he's a douche you'll rethink the whole Italian Scheme.*

Is he hotter than his photos? *If he's hot, I might forgive you.*

Don't make me show up there to see for myself. *I know you're still mad at me, but I'm trying, okay?*

What does your mom think? Is she happy? *I know you desperately want her to be.*

Did you get the bagels I left on the porch? *I'm sorry.*

Izzy sighed. She felt trapped up in her attic. Downstairs, her mom fretted and her brothers bickered. She couldn't text Peyton for advice or comfort without the fear of reopening yesterday's arguments, but as she held her phone in her hand, her thumb lingered over her messaging app.

A few weeks ago, this is when she would have texted Jake for some witty banter laced with sage advice, and once again, the weight of his loss crashed down upon her. She would have told him everything, held nothing back, and he would have responded kindly, thoughtfully, but with humor that would have diffused her anxiety and lessened the burden of her worries. She had no idea why Jake was the one person in her life who held this power, but he did.

Was she in love with Jake? She'd thought maybe she was, but then again, the way her stomach dropped out of her body when Alberto kissed her hand . . . That was the George Emerson effect. Instant chemistry. Which is how it was supposed to work, right? Slow burn friends to lovers felt like she would be settling.

Like her parents.

Harry and Elizabeth had been friends since their freshman year at Middlebury College. He was there on a football scholarship, and she was there because everyone in her family for three generations had graduated from Middlebury. Legacy Middleburian, Izzy's grandfather had joked one of the two times she'd met him. But Harry and Elizabeth hadn't gotten romantic until junior year when all their friends had started pairing off and they were the only two single people left in their group. Hooking up had seemed inevitable.

Then her mom had gotten pregnant, and that was that.

Izzy sometimes wondered why her mom hadn't terminated the pregnancy and gone off to Italy, but it wasn't something her parents ever discussed, and Izzy couldn't exactly bring it up. And it wasn't like they didn't have three more kids after Taylor—there must have been some love between them. But she'd always wondered if her parents had simply settled for each other because they didn't want to start over with someone else.

That wasn't going to happen to Izzy. Love wouldn't be a gradual realization but a lightning bolt. She wouldn't fall into something easy with the guy next door, she'd wait for magic. She wouldn't wake up one day and realize Jake was the one simply because they were both still around and both single.

The grandfather clock in her room chimed softly, the bell muted by layers of cloth wrapped around the hammer to dull the noise. The clock, another restoration job turned birthday present for Izzy's mom, had been banished to the attic. Her dad had intended the clock for the dining room, but her mom had drawn the line: only one enormous cabinet clock on the ground floor of the house. Her dad and Taylor had then lugged the heavy piece up to the second-floor hallway, but it blocked the linen closet. Her mom wanted to get rid of the monstrosity, as she called it, her dad indignantly refused, so up it went to Izzy's bedroom, where it had remained out of sight, out of mind.

Well, out of mind for her parents. To Izzy, it was an hourly reminder of their unhappy marriage.

Izzy picked up her phone again. She needed to get out of her own head, and her virtual BFFs, Mags and Amelia, always delivered. She popped in her earbuds, flopped back onto her pillows, and resumed her *Murder Will Speak* episode from where it had left off the night before in the minivan.

"I wonder if he's an actor," Mags said. "Failed, of course."

Amelia snorted. Her signature reaction. "Not everyone in LA is an actor."

"I suppose."

"Besides, we don't know he started his spree in LA."

"True."

Mags cleared her throat. She was about to get serious. "According to my sources, the investigation has widened. The authorities are now looking at cold cases in Las Vegas and Tucson, as well as two new missing persons in the San Francisco Bay Area. Which means our Casanova Killer might be on the move."

"Sucks for Frisco. First the faceless guy in the Bay, and now this?"

"As I always say, Ames, the world is a dark place."

ELEVEN

IZZY WOKE WITH A START. LAUGHTER AND LOUD VOICES drifted through her attic room, and for a disorientated moment she wasn't sure where she was.

Patchwork comforter? Check. Whitewashed dresser and bureau? Double check. She was definitely in her room, but the boisterous sounds were utterly unfamiliar. Stretches of murmured voices punctuated by sharp outbursts of laughter. Coming up through the air vents.

Laughter? In *her* house?

She sat up, realizing with a start that it was significantly darker than it had been when she'd accidentally fallen asleep, and a glance at her phone told her it was almost five o'clock. Had she really slept through the day?

Izzy hurried downstairs, wondering if everyone was drunk or whether a dangerous gas leak—one of the potential dangers of an old house that Izzy's mom always worried about—had turned her family loopy. She swung around the artichoke at the top of the stairs and double-timed it to the ground floor, but instead of empty bottles of wine scattered around the dining room table or the funky scent of propane, she found her parents and her brothers gathered in the kitchen, where Alberto sat on a barstool, telling an animated story.

"The waitress stare at me, just-a so." He turned to Izzy's dad, who hadn't been home this early in weeks.

"Oh, dude," Riley said, shaking his head. "You're so screwed."

Alberto nodded, blue eyes so wide they might have popped out of his head if someone had slapped him on the back at that very moment. "*Sì*. And she, how-a you say . . ." He raised his eyebrows at Izzy's mom. "*Urlare?*"

"She screamed," her mom translated with a chuckle.

"*Sì, sì*. She scream and-a drop whole plate of your chicken wings. *Tragico*."

This snippet of the story didn't seem particularly funny to Izzy, but the rest of her family exploded with laughter as if Alberto had been practicing his stand-up routine in their kitchen. Even Parker, who was usually reserved and always serious, slapped the counter in enjoyment. Alberto had charmed everyone, and Izzy felt a surge of jealousy at being left out.

"Sounds like a tragedy for whoever made the chicken wings," she said from the doorway.

"Izz-*ee*!" Alberto cried, sliding off the barstool. He approached her with open arms as if they were old friends. His hair was still wet from a recent shower, and he'd changed into slightly more appropriate clothes—a pair of straight-leg jeans that hit at the ankle and a button-down pinstripe shirt that rose to expose his flat stomach when he raised his arms. Alberto must have gone through a recent growth spurt because his clothes clearly didn't fit. It would explain why he was so much taller than he looked in his photos.

He clasped Izzy by the shoulders and kissed her on both cheeks, European style, but his eyes didn't bore into hers the way they had the night before. The entire gesture was less intimate than the kiss he'd planted on her hand at the airport and felt almost theatrical. Over the top, like his exaggerated Italian accent. Izzy wondered if he'd realized how Plain Jane she truly was in the sober light of early evening.

"Alberto," her mom said, once again with perfect Italian inflection, "was just telling us about his first night in San Francisco."

"Some waitress thought he was Harry Styles and completely freaked out," Riley said, still spasming with laughter. The situation didn't sound inherently funny. Alberto must have been an expert storyteller.

"I'd freak out too if I thought I had Harry Styles in my section," Parker said with a wry grin. "He's hot."

"Not as hot as Miguel," Izzy's mom said with a little nod. "Right?"

Parker stiffened at his boyfriend's name, and the tendons in his jaw rippled beneath a tight clench. "Right," he said. But his voice was all wrong. Had he and Miguel broken up after graduation? Is that why her brother had come home for the summer instead of staying in Pasadena?

Alberto wiped his dry cheek as if he'd been tearing up with laughter. "But the waitress, she still ask for Alberto's number." Then he turned away, dropping his voice. "Slut."

"What?" Izzy said. His comment was like a record scratch, piercing the affable mood of the house. She seriously hoped his use of that word was a lost-in-translation issue, not an intentional slur.

Riley held up his hands in mock horror. "Another of mom's dreaded four-letter words."

"For a good reason, you turd," Izzy said. How was she even related to him?

"Turd!" Riley pointed an accusatory finger at Izzy. "Four-letter word! Four-letter word!"

Parker elbowed him in the ribs, which was a nicer version of what Izzy wanted to do.

Alberto turned to Izzy's mom, blue eyes wide with concern. "Did I-a say something-a wrong?"

"'Slut' is not an acceptable term for a woman," Izzy's mom said gently. *"Non usare la parole 'puttana' per le donne."*

"Ah, no!" Alberto said, horrified. Thankfully. *"Scusi, scusi."*

"What were you trying to say?"

Alberto scrunched up his mouth in thought. *"La bimba."*

Izzy's mom smiled. "I can see where you were confused. That actually translates to something more like 'child.'"

"Ah, thank you, Elisabetta." He met her smile for a moment before Izzy's mom turned abruptly toward the oven.

"Shall we eat?"

Izzy's mom removed a giant pan of chicken enchilada casserole from the warming rack of the old 1930s stove while everyone ambled into the dining room. She placed the tray on a trivet in the middle of the elongated table and immediately began directing traffic.

"I'm here by the kitchen," she explained to Alberto, gesturing to the end seat nearest the door. "You and Izzy can sit on either side. Parker, Riley, you're at the other end with your dad."

"Aye, sir!" Riley said with a salute.

Their mom scowled. "And none of your gross talk about bartenders and whatever today," she said. "I don't want to offend our guest."

"Um, I'm sorry," Riley said, pantomiming confusion. "But didn't our guest just tell a story about a sexy waitress who wanted to bone him because he looks like Harry Styles?"

"'Bone' is a four-letter word," Parker said. "And so is 'dick.' Which you are."

Riley was about to reply when the doorbell cut him off. Alberto started as if a gun had discharged in the dining room, pushing his chair away from the table with such force that he almost toppled backward. His chair hung in the balance on its back two legs while he grasped for the table to catch himself, his face twisted up in fear.

Izzy's mom was equally as perturbed by the interruption. "Who's coming around at this hour?" she asked, fidgeting with her shirt as she hurried toward the front door.

"Don't answer!" cried Alberto. The chair thunked back into place like an exclamation mark.

Izzy raised her eyebrows. Why was he so disturbed by the doorbell?

Alberto's eyes landed on her face, and in an instant, his affable smile was back. "It is the salesman, *si*? We just pretend-a no one home?"

Izzy's dad snorted. "There haven't been door-to-door salesmen around since I was a kid."

"But should we not—"

Alberto's protest was interrupted by Izzy's mom, who threw the door wide open. "Peyton!"

"Hi, Mrs. Bell!" From Izzy's seat at the table, she could see her friend's brown curls bounced up and down as she stepped into the entryway.

"We're just sitting down to dinner," Izzy's mom said without asking why her daughter's best friend had appeared unannounced for no apparent reason. "Can you stay?"

It wasn't unusual for Peyton to join the Bell family for dinner, but normally she was already hanging out in Izzy's room. Never in the history of their friendship had Peyton just shown up at their door at dinnertime.

"Sure!" Peyton responded with a shrug, as if that hadn't been the plan all along. Since Izzy hadn't responded to her texts, she must have decided to check in on her in person. "My mom's having a girls' night out, so it was kind of lonely at home."

"And you can meet our new addition!" Izzy's mom continued, leading Peyton into the dining room. "Alberto, this is Izzy's friend Peyton."

Izzy half expected her friend to march up to Alberto and announce that he wasn't stealing her best friend away to Italy, or something equally as embarrassing and dramatic, but instead, Peyton paused in the doorway, eyes examining Alberto from head to toe. She ran her fingers through her long brown curls, quickly arranging them over each shoulder so they framed her face. Then, lips parted and shoulders back, she practically pranced across the room to Alberto.

"Hi," she said in a huskier voice than normal. "I'm Peyton."

Riley slid his chair over to make room for her. "You got a cold, Pey?"

She shot him a withering glance. "Why don't you be a gentleman and get me a chair or something?"

Riley rolled his eyes but did as he was asked, placing a chair behind her. "Yes, your highness."

"Alberto is from just outside of Florence," Izzy's mom said. Then she snapped her fingers. "What did you say the name of the town was?"

Alberto dragged his attention away from Peyton. "Rufina, *Signora*."

"Call me Elizabeth." Izzy thought her mom sounded annoyed.

"Sì, sì." The megawatt smile was back. "Elisabetta."

"Firenze must be beautiful," her mom continued.

Riley shoveled a forkful of casserole into his mouth. "Isn't that where you were supposed to go after college?"

Izzy kicked him under the table as her mom's face hardened.

"What?" Riley sputtered, unaware that his comment might be triggering. All the men in her family were clueless.

"Nah," her dad said, shaking his head. His eyes were fixed on his plate, avoiding everyone else at the table. "It was Rome."

Izzy watched a shadow pass over her mom's face. For the second time that day, she looked as if she wanted to murder her husband.

"It. Was. Florence." Her mom's voice was too even, too calm.

Leave it to Harry Bell to thoughtlessly bumble his way into an argument. "Oh, right. Florence, not Firenzy."

"They're the same city."

"Um, my mom was going to study at the Uffizi," Izzy said, desperately trying to diffuse the tension. "She has a passion for Italian art."

Alberto nodded. *"Bene."*

"That was a long time ago," her mom said, her eyes still fixed on her husband. "No one's ever taken me to Florence."

The table fell silent. Parker, always the introvert, had retreated into himself, staring pointedly at the untouched nonvegetarian casserole on his plate as if it were the most appetizing thing on the planet. Peyton, who had straightened her bra while Alberto's attention had been drawn away, was casting flirty smiles at him as she pretended to help herself to some food. Izzy's dad and Riley ate lustily, as if nothing had happened. The only sounds in the dining room were the clinks of their cutlery against the Bells' best china.

Izzy didn't know what to do to break the spell of her mom's darkening mood and was trying to think of some topic that might snap her out of it when she caught Alberto watching her. His eyes were soft, sympathetic, and with an almost imperceptible nod of his head, he shifted his chair to directly face Izzy's mom.

"Elisabetta, *scusi.* A question."

She waved her hand, dismissing her memories, her husband, or both. "Yes?"

"Though I no see it from-a my room . . ." Alberto paused, sniffing the air. "Can I smell the sea?"

"The harbor's right down the hill," Peyton answered before Izzy's mom could chime in. "You can walk there."

"It is large?"

"Molto grosso," Izzy's mom replied.

Alberto's eyebrows shot up. "Many boats?"

"Many."

"The big ones, *sì*?"

Riley snorted. "That's what she said."

"My, er, friend owns one," Peyton said quickly. "A fishing boat."

"Your *friend*?" Izzy asked. Peyton had been in love with Hunter since they were fourteen, and suddenly Peyton was referring to him as a "friend" in front of an Italian guy she just met? If that was love, maybe Izzy was justified in not wanting any part of it.

Peyton ignored her. "I could give you a tour."

What the hell was she doing?

"I would like-a the tour," Alberto said, lowering his chin so he stared at her from beneath his dark brows.

"I don't think the boat is booked for tomorrow," Peyton said, fluttering her lashes. "I could pick you up. Take you over."

"Wonderful," Izzy's mom said. She stood up and began to clear dishes from the table. Even the unfinished ones. "You *and* Izzy can give Alberto a tour of the harbor tomorrow morning, after our first English lesson."

Great. Now Peyton had wiggled her way into Izzy's first day with Alberto, and as she watched the Italian ogle her friend, she already felt like a third wheel.

TWELVE

ALBERTO WAS PERCHED AT THE KITCHEN ISLAND WHEN IZZY
came downstairs the next morning. He looked even more relaxed than he
had the night before, leaning on the gleaming quartz counter, both hands
wrapped around a mug of frothy cappuccino goodness while he listened
intently to Izzy's mom.

"I'm so glad you mentioned del Sarto! Most people have forgotten about
him, his fame eclipsed by his contemporaries—Leonardo, Michelangelo,
Raphael. But he should be included in the same breath."

"*Sì?*"

Her mom nodded vigorously, and Izzy inwardly smiled. It was nice to
see a sparkle in her eyes.

"Though Vasari and Browning weren't particularly favorable to him," she continued, "and de Musset characterized him as a cuckolded if sympathetic husband, del Sarto's contribution to Italian mannerism coming out of the High Renaissance should not be overlooked."

She spoke quickly while she fussed with some scrambled eggs, moving them heatedly around the pan with a spatula.

"He is a favorite, *si*?"

"*Si.*" She smiled at the brightly tiled backsplash, blissfully happy. "I remember when I saw a traveling exhibition at the Museum of Fine Arts Boston when I was in high school. His *Portrait of a Young Lady with a Book* just absolutely blew my mind. The intimacy of the painting, the enigmatic smile. I stared at it until my parents made us leave." She paused, her cheeks flushed as if suddenly self-conscious. She looked over her shoulder at Alberto. "I suppose I knew then and there that I wanted to study art history."

Izzy'd never heard her mom speak so passionately about anything. It was mesmerizing. Enviable. The only thing that got Izzy this excited was discussing serial killers.

"And you did," Alberto said, toasting her with a raised mug.

Her mom sighed, her spirits momentarily dampened. "Yes, back in Vermont. But I never got to Italy."

"Life. It-a rarely goes the way-a we want," Alberto said, then abruptly turned his head toward the doorway. "*Ciao*, Izz-ee."

"*Ciao,*" Izzy said, though her accent sounded more like she was describing pet food than the delightful inflection Alberto used with the word. "How's the English lesson going?"

She'd meant it good-naturedly, but her mom's blush deepened as if she'd been reprimanded by her daughter. "I suppose we got a little sidetracked."

"It was-a my fault," Alberto said, hand pressed to his chest. "I ask-a the questions."

"Plenty of time for lessons," her mom said, regaining her composure. "What time is Peyton picking you up?"

Now it was Izzy's turn to sigh. Not that she didn't love her friend, but she'd been hoping to spend time alone with Alberto. Peyton had a way of hogging the spotlight, and Izzy never felt as if she could compete. "Noonish."

Her mom arched a brow. "I thought I said morning?"

"To Peyton, that *is* morning."

"Jeanine really shouldn't let her do that," she said, mentioning Peyton's mom. There had been an unspoken hostility between the two women for years, some kind of parental one-upmanship that Izzy had never understood.

"Only on the weekends," Izzy said, feeling the need to defend her friend.

"It's Thursday."

"If-a you please," Alberto said. "Can-a we walk there early? Perhaps-a now? I would love-a to see the boats."

"The slips are on the island," Izzy explained. "We need to drive over the bridge to get there."

Alberto's face fell, a sad puppy. "Ah."

"But you can walk down to the park and see the boats across the inner reach," Izzy's mom suggested. She was going all out to make sure Alberto felt no discomfort whatsoever.

And it worked. His smile was back, blossoming slowly across his tanned face. "I would like-a that."

Izzy shrugged. "Sure." There was nothing particularly interesting about Woodley Island Harbor or the boats in it, but she couldn't exactly deny him this request on his second day. Besides, the park that skirted the waterfront was pretty, and judging by the sunbeams attempting to burn off the marine layer outside, it might actually be a lovely day. "I'll tell Peyton to meet us."

"*Stupendo!*" Alberto exclaimed as Izzy's mom slid a plate of scrambled eggs, bacon, and sourdough toast in front of him. "To-a the both of you." Then he dove into his breakfast as if he hadn't eaten in days.

* * *

The sun had just succeeded in banishing the cloud cover as Izzy held the front gate open for Alberto. Yesterday, while he slept, the marine layer had only capitulated to the sun's warmth for a few hours midday, but now the sun was winning a decisive battle. It was as if Alberto himself had pierced through the thick clouds, his megawatt smile and upbeat personality spreading sunshine in a gray world as easily as he'd inspired her mom's bright mood. Which was poetic and silly, but as they walked down L Street, Izzy felt the warmth of a sunny day growing with every step.

"Your town issa very pretty," Alberto said as they passed Miss O'Sullivan's Victorian Bed-and-Breakfast around the corner from the Bell house. "Do you not think so?"

"Yeah." Sure.

"Remind-a me of *mi nonno*'s house. He live-a by the sea."

Maybe Alberto wouldn't hate Eureka if it reminded him of his grandpa's place? Izzy found herself hoping that would be the case. For her mom's sake, at the very least. He seemed to have a magical effect on her.

They crossed Second Street, with the ornate tower of the Carson Mansion looming at the end of the block. Alberto stopped to admire the iconic Queen Anne. "It is like your house," he said, articulating every word. When he slowed down his speech, Alberto's accent practically disappeared.

Similar to the Carson Mansion? Hardly. That estate had been built by the richest man in Eureka, a timber magnate who almost single-handedly founded the city, while her house had just been a regular old family home. Plus the mansion had been meticulously maintained over the last century. The Bell house was falling apart.

"They're both Victorians," she said, not wanting to explain how not rich her family was.

"But it issa very nice."

"Yeah, thanks. Good place to grow up."

"Many antiques."

"Antiques!" Izzy said, tilting her head in appreciation. "That's some advanced vocabulary."

Alberto laughed. "I like-a the American television shows."

"Which ones?"

He scrunched up his mouth in thought. *"Yellowstone."*

"Like my dad."

"The nerd show. *Big-a Bang?*"

"Big Bang Theory. My grandma's favorite."

"The *Law and Order.*"

"So does my grandpa. How old are you?"

Alberto winked at her. "How old-a do I look?"

She paused, hand on her chin, examining him as if he were one of her mom's prized Italian masterpieces. "Twenty on the outside," she said, an easy guess since she knew from his profile that he was nineteen. Then she smiled wickedly. "Fifty on the inside."

She'd meant it as a tease, but the truth of it struck as she watched him ponder her words. His face was youthful, maybe a little older than Izzy and her friends, but then, the deep tan probably aged him. But there was also something mature about his personality, a watchfulness in his eyes, as if he knew more about the world than he was letting on. Alberto Bianchi was an anachronism. A worldly attitude mixed with clothes that didn't fit. The heavy, almost comical Italian accent peppered with idiosyncratic English that belied his supposed struggles with the language. He was simultaneously exactly what she'd expected and a complete and total surprise, and she had no idea what to make of him.

Suddenly, Alberto leaned toward her, eyes soft at the corners. "You are very pretty, Signorina Bell. Like-a your name. *Che belissima!*"

Izzy stopped abruptly. "Oh." No one had ever called her pretty before. Not even her parents.

Alberto plunged his hands deep into his pockets. "Oh?"

"Er, I mean, um, thanks?"

He continued walking. "You are very welcome, *Izz-ee.*"

Izzy felt her cheeks flush. She especially didn't know what to make of this. No one was ever interested in Izzy Bell. Certainly not this charming stranger from one of the oldest, most cultured areas in Italy. Yet here he was, smiling at her shyly as they crossed the overgrown train tracks at the end of L Street into the same parking lot where Izzy and Peyton had watched *Bodega's Bane* return to harbor just a couple of days ago. Alberto marched through the mostly empty lot to the grassy strip of land at the water's edge and stared out at the slips on Woodley Island.

"Fishing boats," Alberto said, less of a question than a statement of fact. If he'd grown up visiting his grandfather near the sea, then he probably knew more about boats than Izzy did.

"Yep."

"They go to deep ocean?" He eyed the tiny ripples lapping the rocky embankment below the coastal path. Buffered by the channel islands and some natural sand dunes, the water of the inner reach seemed downright calm compared to the roiling North Pacific Ocean currently crashing into the western side of the peninsula beyond Tuluwat Island. Even from five miles away, Izzy could make out the faint roar of waves on Samoa Beach, nature's own white noise.

"Yeah, they're deep-sea fishing vessels."

Alberto rubbed his chin while he scanned the rows of slips across the water, half of which were empty. "Not very many." He sounded disappointed.

Izzy laughed. "Everyone's working."

"Ah, *sì*. Of course." He narrowed his eyes as if trying to make something out on the island. "It is always this, eh, deserted?"

He wasn't going to need many English lessons from her mom. Alberto's grasp of the language was much better than Izzy thought it would be. "Only during the day when the boats are out."

"They work all the days?"

"Pretty much."

"Even your-a famous American weekends?"

Izzy knew the Italian word for "weekend" was literally *"il weekend,"* which meant the concept of a five-day workweek had traveled back across the Atlantic to Europe, but she had no idea why Alberto was so interested in the comings and goings of sleepy little Woodley Island.

"Boats go out when the tourists are here," Izzy explained. "So there isn't really a weekend until the weather turns." She wondered how different the Italian harbors must be from dank and dark Eureka. She pictured yachts with supermodels tanning on deck, moored up in a sunny port surrounded by the glittering warm waters of the Ligurian Sea and the craggy shores of Corsica in the distance.

"And-a the weather, it is always so clear?"

Izzy snorted. "I wish. When the fog rolls in, or a big storm, visibility is almost nothing. You can't even see the island from here."

"Ah," Alberto said, then shivered. "Like a haunted story."

That sounded way more romantic than it felt in reality. "I guess so."

Alberto stared at the boats for a few more moments, then abruptly turned toward the park. "Shall-a we walk?"

With no word from Peyton, Izzy readily agreed, and the two of them headed north up the coastal path. She'd learned to ride her bike on this asphalt as a kid, wobbling along behind her mom's more confident pedaling cadence while her dad chased them both on foot, attempting to steady her without training wheels. It was one of her happier childhood memories with both of her parents, and she smiled.

"You are happy?" he asked. She never even saw him look at her.

"Yeah." For the first time in a while, it wasn't a lie.

"Why?"

Izzy opened her mouth to reply, then stopped. She wasn't entirely sure—yeah, it was nice to have a guy call her pretty, something that had literally never happened before in her entire life—but there was something else about Alberto that made her smile. Maybe the effect he had on her mom, who seemed happier than she'd been in months, despite the episodes with her dad yesterday. But also, when Alberto looked at Izzy with those dancing blue eyes, she felt as if he actually saw her. Not what she looked like, but who and what she was. Izzy felt important when Alberto spoke to her, and she'd only ever felt something like that once before.

With Jake.

Her heart ached at the thought of him, and for the first time since his return from Monterey, Izzy wanted to cry. Maybe her feelings *were* more than just friendship?

Shit.

Izzy hadn't realized she'd stopped walking until Alberto stood in front of her. "Izz-*ee*. You-a no happy now. What-a is wrong?"

"I don't know," she said truthfully. It was many things and nothing, all at the same time.

She felt his fingers slide across her palm, then up to her wrist. She shivered, despite the warm day. "Can I help?"

Before she could answer, a blaring horn ripped through the quiet morning. Izzy turned to see a blue Ford Explorer stopped on the road that paralleled the park. Peyton leaned out the window. "What the fuck, you guys?"

THIRTEEN

PEYTON GLARED OVER HER SHOULDER AT IZZY AS SHE CLIMBED into the backseat. "Don't you check your phone anymore?"

Izzy flinched at the venom in Peyton's tone. The two friends had radically different personalities: the extrovert and the introvert, the brash girl and the shy one, the hot chick and the wallflower. They frequently disagreed about everything from boys to books to where Izzy should go to college, but never in the history of their friendship had Peyton been overtly hostile.

Don't you get up before the crack of noon anymore? The words itched on Izzy's tongue. But she said nothing.

Alberto didn't seem to notice the friction. He slid into the passenger seat, eyes glued to the panels of city-sanctioned graffiti art that decorated the retaining wall along Waterfront Drive. "Issa so colorful. My heart, it-a leaps with the love of the art."

"Cool, right? It began with—" Izzy was about to explain how the city had started a program where they commissioned artists to decorate utility boxes all over town, which then became walls on the sides of buildings in Old Town and finally blossomed to this art installation along the waterfront, but Peyton interrupted.

"It's just like the Venice Art Walls," she said. "I've always wanted to go see them. Is Venice far from where you live?"

Since when did art count among Peyton's interests? Besides, she didn't even have the right Venice.

"The Venice Art Walls are in Venice, *California*," Izzy said, trying not to sound as deprecating as she felt.

Alberto laughed. "I am sure issa similar wall in Venezia."

Peyton beamed at him, and somehow, just sixty seconds into this car ride, Izzy was relegated to sidekick status.

They looped back around to R Street, then over the Samoa Bridge, which looked more like a freeway overpass than the majestic Golden Gate. To the north, Eureka Channel opened up to the expansive Arcata Bay, protected from the onslaught of the Pacific Ocean by a narrow strip of sand dunes stretching from Humboldt Beach all the way down to the North Jetty. Below them, the fishing boats still moored at the dock bobbed in water that seemed uncharacteristically choppy.

At the end of the bridge, Peyton rounded a corner too fast, swerving into the oncoming lane. She had to slam on her brakes as a pod of cyclists swarmed her SUV, each of them flipping her off as they passed.

"Bike dicks," she muttered as she continued, more slowly, behind the peloton. "Think they own the road."

"You-a no like the bikes?"

Peyton chewed at the inside of her cheek, a signal that she was contemplating her response. Probably trying to guess Alberto's stance on the matter. Was he pro-cyclists? Anti-cyclists? Izzy shook her head. Why would anyone want to tailor their opinions to what a guy thought?

"I like the bikes," Peyton finally said, tossing her hair over one shoulder as she turned left into the marina. "Just not the cyclists."

"Nota bene," Alberto replied.

He spoke Latin too?

Peyton parked in an empty spot near the marina restaurant and slid out of the driver's seat. It was the first time Izzy got a look at her outfit, a form-fitting sleeveless mini dress and strappy gladiator sandals that laced up her calves. She looked like she belonged in Venice, Italy, in the hottest part of summer, not Eureka on a warmish day where, despite the sun, the wind was beginning to whip in off the ocean.

"This is the marina," Peyton said, then sucked in a lungful of air. "I love the smell of the sea. It makes me feel so alive."

Izzy had literally never heard those words come out of Peyton's mouth. She wasn't sure how much of this she could stomach.

"And-a your friend's boat?" Alberto prompted.

Izzy turned toward Dock B, expecting to see *Bodega's Bane* moored at the very end, but the berth was empty.

Peyton gasped, her eyes fixed on the same spot. "She's not here!"

"I thought you said they weren't working today?" Izzy said.

Peyton clicked her tongue, hands on her hips in disappointment. "They must have booked a last-minute trip," she said with a pouty frown. Then she held up a finger as if she'd just had a brilliant idea. "Hey! Why don't we have lunch first? They should be back by two."

The pose, the pout, the delivery—Peyton had planned this. She knew

Hunter would be out on a fishing trip today; she just wanted to have lunch with Alberto. Without her boyfriend around.

Izzy loved her friend, but that was pretty fucked-up. Peyton was practically engaged to Hunter and had never expressed any concerns or problems with their relationship. But after spending an hour with Alberto last night, she was suddenly willing to throw away two-plus years of a relationship on a guy she just met? And who lived on the other side of the planet? She had no idea what had gotten into her friend, but she didn't like this side of Peyton.

"Lunch sounds-a lovely." Alberto offered her his arm, and they pranced toward the side entrance to Woodley's Bar.

Izzy had only been to Woodley's once when she was a kid, but the dark wood interior and nautically themed accoutrements were exactly as she remembered. The bar looked empty, and for a moment Izzy hoped they weren't open yet and Peyton's lunch plans would be scrapped. But movement at the darkened bar caught her eye. A guy in the corner, hunched over his drink. He wore the work pants and woolen sweater of a deckhand, the sole customer.

"Let's sit outside," Peyton said, pulling Alberto toward the patio that fronted the marina. She didn't even wait for a hostess to offer, marching straight through the double glass doors to a shaded table above the water. Alberto pulled a chair out, and Peyton beamed up at him as if he'd just proposed. Her face visibly fell when he did the same for Izzy.

A woman emerged from inside, a curvy Latina with heavily tattooed arms and a frizzy French braid in her light brown hair. She huffed, glaring over her shoulder toward the bar as she approached the table, but even with her face turned away, Izzy recognized Kylie—Riley's on-again, off-again—immediately.

They'd met once last spring, when Riley drove their dad's truck into the creek while he and Kylie were getting handsy in the cab, and Kylie might have recognized Izzy as her fuck buddy's little sister except, from the moment she arrived at their table, her eyes latched onto Alberto and refused to let go.

She smiled and sucked in her abs as she approached, the scowl from seconds ago completely vanished. "How can I help you?" It definitely was not a plural "you."

"Buona sera, Signorina," Alberto said, wishing her a "Good evening" despite it being the middle of the day.

Kylie's eyes grew wide. "You're French?"

"Italian," Peyton said, her tone impatient, as if she could have told the difference between the two languages offhand.

Kylie ignored her. "Sexy accent."

Peyton growled deep in her throat and leaned possessively on the arm of Alberto's chair. "Are you the waitress?"

"Bartender," she said, not even looking at Peyton. "But we're short-handed today so I'm here to, uh, take care of you."

"Can we get some menus?" Peyton snapped.

Kylie smiled at Alberto as if he'd made the request, unruffled by Peyton's snark or her territorial display. She simply pointed to a plastic frame with a QR code sitting in the middle of the table.

"Oh," Peyton said. Point to Kylie.

"Grazie," Alberto said.

A thud from inside the restaurant was the only thing that could wrest Kylie's gaze from the Italian. It was followed by a crash, as if someone had knocked over a heavy item and then launched it across the restaurant. Kylie glanced over her shoulder again, and when she turned back to the table, her face reflected a new emotion: fear.

"I'll give you some time to look it over," Kylie said, hurrying inside. Izzy thought of the man sitting at the bar and wondered if one of them should go with her. Before she could voice the idea, Peyton angled her chair so she was facing Alberto.

"Did you see those tats? So ratchet."

Alberto smiled, amused. "You no like-a the waitress?"

"Not particularly."

"You know her?" he pressed.

"Uh, no," Peyton faltered. "But the way she threw herself at you . . . No class."

The same way you're throwing yourself at him? Izzy wanted to ask. But she didn't.

Alberto seemed to intuit Izzy's thoughts. As he pulled his phone from his pocket to scan the menu, he glanced at her, a twinkle in his eyes, then winked.

Kylie quickly returned to take their order, and so began the worst, longest lunch of Izzy's life.

Not that the food was bad—kinda hard to mess up a turkey sandwich and potato chips—but the atmosphere on Woodley's patio was uncomfortably tense.

It was like watching two walruses battle for dominance on a beach: rearing, maneuvering, retreating, regrouping. Kylie made twice as many trips to the patio than were absolutely necessary for the ordering and delivery of food, lingering as if she didn't want to go back inside, and Peyton made sure she was touching Alberto whenever she saw the tattooed bartender approach the glass door.

The conversation between Kylie's visits was no less painful. Peyton peppered Alberto with questions about his life in Italy, his family, his friends, not-so-subtly fishing to see if he had a girlfriend. He answered happily as he ate his steamed chicken and vegetables, easily the least appealing item on the menu, and attempted to include Izzy in the conversation every chance he got.

It felt like hours before Kylie brought the check. The bartender smiled coyly as she slid the paper across the table to Alberto, and before he picked it up, Izzy caught an added scribble at the bottom: Kylie's name and phone number.

Poor Riley.

Kylie swiveled around to leave, hips moving hypnotically as she walked, and Izzy hoped that Peyton didn't catch the inscription at the bottom of the check. No such luck.

"Are you kidding me?" Peyton said, eyes wide. She didn't even wait until Kylie disappeared inside.

"Excuse me?" Kylie said over her shoulder from the door. "Is something wrong?"

Let it go, Pey. Izzy tried to will that sentiment into her friend's brain, but Peyton was already on her feet, ready to throw down. "Yeah," she said. "You."

Kylie narrowed her eyes. "Watch yourself, little girl."

"Come," Alberto said, whisking the receipt off the table. He shoved it in his wallet, then pulled out two fifty-dollar bills—easily twice as much as the meal actually cost—and tucked them under the QR code frame. "*Grazie*, Kylie."

He tried to guide Peyton toward the door, but she wasn't done. She looped an arm through his, leaning on him possessively. "What kind of a skank slips her number to a guy when he's out with two other women?"

The question was directed at Alberto, but Peyton said it so loudly, it was clear she wanted Kylie to hear. The bartender clenched her jaw, bearing down for a fight, but before she could respond with words or fists, another voice joined the argument.

"You gave him your fucking phone number?"

A man had just emerged from the restaurant. Izzy recognized the work pants and navy-blue sweater of the deckhand who had been sitting at the bar, but now that she could see his face, she recognized it as well: Greg Loomis.

"Shit," Kylie said under her breath. She didn't turn and look at him, but her entire body stiffened in fear, and when she spoke again, her voice quavered. "We're not dating anymore, asshole!"

"Who issa this?" Alberto asked, but before anyone could answer, Greg stormed across the patio, tossing a chair out of his way. It clattered against a nearby table, tipping it sideways so the salt and pepper shakers crashed to the floor.

"First that pansy-ass college kid and now this turd?"

Kylie's fear spread to Izzy as she realized that the "pansy-ass college kid" must be her brother Riley, and Greg was definitely one of Kylie's exes.

Greg sneered at the back of Kylie's head as he approached, his crimson face gleaming with sweat, and Izzy caught a whiff of alcohol when he opened his mouth again. "I asked you a question! Answer m—"

Three things seemed to happen simultaneously as Izzy stood rooted to the wooden planks of the patio deck. First, Greg cocked his right arm back, fist balled, locked and loaded. Second, Kylie began to turn toward Greg, arm raised to her face as if expecting the blow. And somehow, before Greg could even unload a punch, Alberto had disentangled himself from Peyton and wedged his body between Kylie and her assailant.

He moved with confidence, easily deflecting Greg's drunken punch with his arm before using the fisherman's own body weight and forward momentum to swing him around. Greg careened face-first into the glass-plated table, which toppled at impact. Greg sprawled across the deck, landing at Izzy's feet. She stumbled away from his flailing limbs, tripped over an upended chair, and lost her balance, landing hard on her left hip.

"Izzy!" Peyton cried. She sprinted around the table to Izzy's side. "Are you okay?"

This was the Peyton she knew and loved, not the boy-crazy mean girl from lunch. She smiled at her friend, more embarrassed than injured. "Yeah, just clumsy."

Peyton helped Izzy to her feet while, inches away, Greg clawed at the table and chairs as he tried to regain his footing.

Alberto didn't give him the chance. With a swift donkey kick, he slid a chair out from beneath Greg's arm, and the man slid back down onto his stomach. When he rolled over, Alberto loomed above. He placed a sneaker-clad foot on Greg's throat.

"You will-a leave the lady alone, *sì?*"

"Who the fuck are you?" Greg sputtered.

Instead of answering, Alberto pressed down against Greg's Adam's apple. "You will-a leave the lady alone," he repeated. *"Sì?"*

"That means 'yes,' asshole," Kylie added.

"You can't just—"

Alberto applied more pressure, and Greg gasped for air. *"Sì?"*

"Yes!" Greg choked, still trying to inhale. His crimson face had turned a deep shade of eggplant. "Yes!"

Alberto waited another moment before he removed his foot. Greg clasped his throat as he rolled onto his side, gulping for air.

"Now, you-a go." Alberto's voice was so calm it was unnerving. He was like some kind of Italian James Bond, ruthlessly efficient as he doled out justice, and Izzy had a difficult time reconciling this version of Alberto with the cheerful, smiling college student sleeping in the bedroom below hers.

Greg was dealing with no such dilemma. He only knew one side of Alberto—the one who had just kicked his ass—and he didn't need to be told twice to get the hell out of there. He clambered to his feet and staggered back toward the restaurant, spitting on the ground before he disappeared inside.

FOURTEEN

NO ONE SPOKE UNTIL THEY HEARD THE DISTANT SOUND OF A car door slam, followed by a screech of tires indicating that Greg had peeled out of the parking lot in a shame-fueled, drunken rage. Izzy let out a breath and felt her heart rate begin to normalize.

"Are-a you okay?" Alberto asked, a hand on Kylie's arm. She looked unsteady on her feet until she caught Alberto's eyes, then she smiled, leaning toward him.

"My hero."

Peyton tugged on his sleeve. "Uh, *my* hero."

And boy-crazy Peyton had returned. Bummer. Thankfully, before Kylie and Peyton threw down on the patio, Izzy spotted a familiar outline on the water. *Bodega's Bane* had returned.

"They're back!" she exclaimed in relief.

"Who?" Peyton asked.

Izzy turned to her, eyes narrow. She'd had enough. "Your *boyfriend*. And his daddy's boat."

Peyton sucked in a breath through her teeth as if she'd just burned herself on scalding hot tea.

"Boyfriend," Kylie said with a knowing smile. "Gotcha." She laughed and managed to sound condescending and triumphant at the same time before she touched Alberto lightly on the arm. "I'll see you later."

Peyton exhaled sharply, but before anyone could add another word, Alberto looped one arm around her, the other around Izzy, and maneuvered them both off the patio.

* * *

Bodega's Bane was pulling into its slip at the end of Dock B as they left the restaurant. Alberto eyed the towering vessel with admiration. "Issa this the boat?"

"Yes!" Peyton preened as if the fishing vessel were her firstborn child. The competition with Kylie was forgotten. "This is *Bodega's Bane*." She hurried down the concrete gangplank that connected the island down to the floating docks. "Come on!"

Alberto trotted behind. "She issa beautiful."

Izzy wasn't entirely sure he was talking about the boat.

She brought up the rear, as usual, carefully picking her way down the gangplank, conscious of the "Caution: Slippery" signs mounted everywhere. The floating metal structure bounced slightly beneath their weight, and Izzy reached for the railing to steady herself.

Hunter was just exiting the wheelhouse when Peyton reached the end of Dock B. She moved fluidly, like an eel skimming across the water, her hips and chest sinuously weaving from side to side with every step. Izzy had seen that walk from Peyton many times—it was her sexy walk, the one she used when she was feeling hot, on the prowl, or had one too many beers at a bonfire.

"I caught a big one today!" Hunter cried, a reference to one of their couple jokes. But Peyton didn't respond. Hunter looked momentarily confused as his eyes traveled from his girlfriend to the new guy and then to Izzy.

Izzy didn't have much time to feel sorry for him, as she was distracted by movement at the stern, where Jake was packing away gear. Like Hunter, he wore his usual work pants and knit cap, but he'd discarded his waterproof jacket in the warm sun to reveal a form-hugging T-shirt. She was used to the loose-fitting flannels that made up three-fourths of his wardrobe, and Izzy wasn't sure if she'd ever seen this much of Jake's upper body. If she had, she might have remembered his strong shoulders and back muscles.

"Hey, babe!" Hunter cried, trying again, as if Peyton just hadn't heard him the first time. "You look hot."

As soon as he spoke, Jake's head turned sharply in Izzy's direction. His eyes met hers and she faltered, heat rising in her cheeks.

Had Jake just caught her perving?

Shit, had she just been perving on Jake?

As she was floundering in her own embarrassment, Alberto whispered in her ear. "This issa the boyfriend?"

The heat in Izzy's face intensified. "I don't have a boyfriend."

Alberto chuckled. "*Her* boyfriend."

Right, duh. Of course. Izzy cleared her throat, attempting to regain her composure. "Hey, Hunter, this is Alberto." She gestured toward the Italian, who had already stepped onto the deck. "Thank you so much for giving him a tour of your dad's boat."

Hunter cocked his head to the side. "I'm giving him a tour of the boat?"

"Yes!" Peyton squeaked with a nervous laugh. "I told you last night."

She clearly hadn't.

"Oh, um, sure, dude."

Hunter's dad, Mike, an overly tanned white guy in his early fifties, poked his head out of the wheelhouse. "H-Man, you can mess around with your friends after work."

"Aye, Cap'n!" Hunter said, hopping to. Izzy had never heard him refer to his dad as "captain" before, and the change in his demeanor was instantaneous. He was no longer Peyton's adoring boyfriend but a seasoned deckhand with a job to do. He hustled Alberto off the boat. "Can you wait on the dock?"

Alberto looked disappointed but acquiesced, and Izzy hoped Hunter would be this take-charge when it came to Peyton flirting with the new guy.

The three of them waited silently on the dock while Mike bro-talked with the customers, a group of eight middle-aged white dudes in cargo shorts and boat shoes who looked as if they walked right out of a Tommy Bahama catalog. Hunter and Jake whizzed around them on deck, disappearing into the cabin occasionally as they stowed equipment. They were admirably efficient, their various tasks cemented by rote into a fluid choreography that hinted at years of practice. It took less than twenty minutes to secure the boat and offload both the customers and their catch.

As Hunter's dad disembarked, he vaulted over the gunwale. "Got your keys?"

Hunter patted a hip pocket in his cargo pants. "Aye, Cap'n."

"Then just lock up when you're done." Mike cast a friendly smile at

Peyton and Izzy as he walked by. It dimmed slightly as his eyes passed over Alberto. "You kids have fun."

"Thanks, Dad!" Hunter waved as his dad retreated down the dock, then reached a hand out to Peyton. "May I, milady?"

Normally, Peyton would have played up Hunter's chivalrous offer, batting her eyelashes while she indulged in the romanticism of being helped onto a midsize fishing boat, but today she looked more annoyed than flattered by Hunter's attention.

"I can do it," she snapped, swatting his hand away as she stepped on board.

Once again, Hunter's face registered his confusion, and for a split second his otherwise buoyant nature seemed weighed down. He shook if off, chuckling, and ushered her by with a sweep of his arm. "Of course you can. You can do anything!"

"You-a handle the boat well," Alberto said to Peyton as she pranced down the side deck.

"Oh yeah," Hunter bragged. "She's spent a ton of time on the old *BB*. Right, babe?"

Peyton cast her boyfriend a deprecating smile over her shoulder; then, as if the universe felt the need for retribution, the boat bobbed, and Peyton skidded on the slippery deck, the grip on her gladiator sandals impractical even on the grooved flooring. She stopped herself awkwardly at the railing, her pale skin flushed with embarrassment.

"Water's choppy today," Hunter said, riding out the dissipating rolls with practiced ease. "Jake says a storm's coming in."

"Storm?" Peyton snapped, taking her frustration out on her boyfriend. "In August?"

Alberto glanced at the clear blue sky above them and laughed. "I no see-a one cloud."

Jake climbed out of the cabin, eyes narrowed, face pinched. He pointed toward thin, wispy white streaks in the sky. They looked like spun cotton candy, stretching toward them from the horizon. "Those are cirrus clouds, and they're moving. Means the weather is about to change."

Alberto blinked twice, though his affable smile never faltered. "You are the weatherman, *sì*?"

"No. I'm *Hunter's* friend." Hunter might have been oblivious to Peyton's shifting affection, but Jake wasn't.

"Ah." Alberto shrugged. "Then I will wait for-a the weatherman to tell-a me to be afraid." He seemed casual, but his intense gaze held Jake's like they were in some kind of alpha male staring contest. The steely-eyed Alberto who'd taken down Greg Loomis lurked beneath the surface.

Jake took a step forward. "No need to be afraid." Except his squared-off shoulders and clenched fists suggested otherwise. When paired with his imposing height, it was the first time Izzy had seen danger in him.

"I have no fear of your-a . . . storm." Alberto matched his step.

"My dude," Hunter said, strolling casually between the two combatants as if he didn't notice the oatmeal-thick toxic male energy that had bubbled up between them, "if Jake says there's a big-ass storm coming, *trust me*, there's a big-ass storm coming. Bet you ten bucks it'll be all over the news by tomorrow."

"He's Italian, Hunter," Peyton said with a click of her tongue. "They don't use dollars."

Peyton had clearly missed the fact that Alberto paid for their lunch with two Ulysses S. Grants.

Hunter snorted. "He does if he wants to eat around here. Come on, Al. I'll show you around."

"Bene, grazie." Alberto smirked at Jake before following Hunter. "Can-a we take her out?"

"Sorry, dude," Hunter said. "Can't spare the gas the way prices are."

"But you have-a the keys, *sí*?"

Hunter once again patted his pocket. "Always, my dude!"

"You ever take-a her out alone?"

"It's a two-person job," Jake said. He watched Alberto closely.

Hunter cleared his throat, straightening his spine in the process. He looked like an actor about to go onstage. "Welcome to *Bodega's Bane*," he said with a sweep of his arm. "A forty-three-foot Delta charter powered by twin turbo CATs with up to three hundred and twenty horsepower, and certified for twenty-five plus two crew offshore."

Izzy's image of an actor preparing for a role wasn't far off. She'd heard Hunter give this speech so many times she practically had it memorized, and as Hunter pointed out the various features of the aft deck, she mentally ticked them off in her head: rear cabin door with tinted polycarbonate windscreens, standard fiberglass bait station, running lights with custom-made back plating. He was a salesman, hocking his wares, and Izzy wondered if this was part of the job of running a charter fishing vessel.

"The decking has an epoxy on it," Hunter continued, leading Alberto up the narrow side deck on the port side of the boat that hugged the cabin up to the wheelhouse door, "while keeping the original Delta grooving for improved footing when it's wet. We had it entirely refinished up in Coos Bay just a few years ago."

Alberto nodded as if he understood Hunter's word salad and slipped into the wheelhouse in front of his tour guide.

"We've got a three-hundred-and-sixty-five-degree view from the bridge, and the latest tech. Your plotter, fish finder, BIC units, Marine VHF radio set to the emergency—"

The wheelhouse door banged shut, cutting off Hunter's monologue, and Izzy felt the muscles in her arms and legs relax. She hadn't even realize she'd tensed up.

The instant Alberto and Hunter were out of view, Peyton marched up to Jake, smacking him on the arm. "What was that all about?" she hissed.

Jake flinched at the question. "What was *what* all about?"

"The pissing contest."

"I was just explaining meteorology."

"Uh-huh." Peyton put her hands on her hips. "Stop being a dick to the new guy."

Izzy rolled her eyes. "Didn't you spend most of the past week telling me not to be too nice to the new guy?" Her hypocrisy was staggering.

"That was before I met him."

Before you knew he was hot.

Hunter emerged through the cabin door onto the stern deck, finishing his tour with the cabin interior. "Fridge and freezer, standard galley with seating for eight. And that's about it."

"You-a no worry about-a the pirates?" Alberto asked, eyeing the interior of the cabin as he stepped through the open door.

Hunter busted out laughing. "Pirates. That's mad funny, dude."

"I think he's serious, Hunter," Izzy said, off of Alberto's quizzical look, and she wondered if pirating was still a thing that happened in the Mediterranean. Seemed like a stretch.

Alberto tilted his head. "You-a no need to protect the boat?"

"Nah, dude. All the fishing crews know each other."

"Ah, *sì.*"

"But my dad keeps a Glock nineteen inside. Just in case."

Alberto nodded slowly. "That issa good to know."

A breeze rippled across the inner reach, causing the flyaway hairs from Izzy's ponytail to whip around her face, tickling her nose. The boat rocked again, and Izzy felt a distinct chill in the air. More biting than usual. Though it was difficult to fathom this time of year, maybe Jake's prediction of a storm was dead-on.

"When did you say the storm was coming?" Peyton asked.

Jake gazed at the western skies. "Couple of days. Definitely by the weekend."

"I hope they don't cancel the bonfire." Peyton sighed, wrapping her bare arms around her body. Izzy wondered if she was wishing for a sweater.

"Bonfire?" Alberto said. "What is this?"

"You should totally come, dude!" Hunter clearly hadn't clocked Alberto as a threat to his relationship with Peyton, which was equal parts sweet and sad. "It's like the end of summer party to end all end of summer parties."

For the first time that day, Peyton readily agreed with her boyfriend. "Yes! You should totally come tomorrow night."

Alberto looked to Izzy, eyebrows high with a silent question. "I mean, it's a high school party," Izzy said with a shrug. "But we can go if you want."

"Awesome!" Peyton clapped her hands daintily. "Then it's a date."

Hunter slipped his arm around her waist. "Sweet." He pressed his lips to her cheek. "Shall we get outta here?"

Thankfully, he didn't seem to notice Peyton cringe.

FIFTEEN

IZZY COULDN'T SLEEP.

Not unusual. Her anxiety had teeth, and when it smelled blood, those canines sank in with a vicious bite.

What *was* unusual was the cause. Not the familiar lineup of triggers: *Why can't I figure my shit out? Why can't I speak up for myself? Why am I always so afraid?* Those concerns still lingered, simmering beneath the surface, waiting to pounce, but tonight's brain spiral had another cause.

And he was sleeping right downstairs.

It had been a quiet evening at home after Peyton dropped them off. Parker and Riley both had plans, and Izzy's dad was working late again, so it was only Izzy, her mom, and Alberto at dinner. He had been just as charming as the night before, though with fewer people to pull his focus, Izzy felt his attention much more keenly. She caught him smiling at her repeatedly during dinner and while they watched reruns of *Law and Order* afterward, and even noticed him wink as they ascended the stairs to bed.

Alberto Bianchi had caught Izzy off guard. She hadn't expected him to be so confident, so adult. Sure, he was technically a college student, but they were practically the same age, and yet Alberto, who was living halfway around the world with a group of strangers he'd just met, didn't appear to suffer from any of the insecurities that kept Izzy up at night. He was easygoing, charming, perpetually cheerful, but also alarmingly cool and surprisingly competent in the face of danger. And when he smiled at her, she felt as if she could do anything. *Be* anything. Even an art history major studying abroad.

Especially an art history major studying abroad.

Florence was looking more enticing every day.

And yet there was something about Alberto that made her . . . She wasn't even sure what word could describe the feeling in her gut. It wasn't nerves and it wasn't excitement, but there was another emotion tangled up in those two. Something that felt familiar. Something more like fear.

Was she afraid of Alberto? That was ridiculous. Despite his ruthlessness with Greg Loomis, who deserved it, there wasn't a mean bone in his body. Maybe the tinge of fear stemmed from Peyton's infatuation, as if Alberto's presence might spell the end of their friendship. Or maybe it was Izzy's reaction to his attention. She wasn't used to being noticed, to being told she was pretty, to having someone so focused on her, except . . .

Izzy rolled over and stared out the small dormer window beside her bed. The individual pieces of glass were narrow but double-paned to insulate the exposed attic from the elements, and the waning moon was large enough in the sky to be dissected by the metal frames. It was still ascending and the night was well lit, exposing fluffy, intermittent clouds that were sliding in from the west. The beginnings of Jake's predicted storm.

Was it really just two days ago that Jake had followed her home from the taco joint? That moment at her gate, his eyelids lowered, his body teetering so close to her own. She'd felt a sensation in her own body, similar to what Alberto provoked and yet different. The fluttering without the fear.

But maybe the fear was what mattered? Maybe it meant that she'd finally found something she wanted.

How fucked-up was it that actually *wanting* something was a cause of fear? One more item on the long list of things she was afraid of.

Izzy laughed as she sat up in bed. Shit. What *wasn't* she afraid of? That was a better question. She felt as if she lived on her tiptoes, creeping around and trying not to make a sound. And she knew exactly why.

She'd always known her mom was unhappy—it would have been impossible to miss those signs unless you were intentionally trying to ignore them (like Izzy's dad) or too wild to care (like her brothers). Izzy's earliest memories were of her mom crying. As the years went on, the sadness turned angry. The merest sound might set her mom off. A too-loud chime from one of the clocks, a clank of cutlery while unloading the dishwasher, an unexpected phone call. Even Izzy's signature swing move around the artichoke newel post had been born of necessity: the top stair creaked mercilessly, and her mom had snapped at Izzy a hundred times before she realized that if she got airborne and dropped down onto the second step, she could avoid that hazard altogether.

Izzy tiptoed. Adapted. Stayed quiet.

Somewhere along the line, she'd internalized that quietude. Not making a sound became not needing to. Her mom's sadness stemmed from her own disappointment in life, her unfulfilled dreams, her unheeded wants. Maybe if Izzy never reached for anything, she'd never feel the same disappointment.

If I don't want anything, I won't become my mother.

The thought jarred her, body and soul, and she threw her comforter aside and slid out of bed. She stomped over to the window, not caring if the floorboards squeaked or the thumping startled Alberto from his sleep. He wasn't going to save her. He wasn't the fix.

Izzy swung the heavy dormer out from the bottom until it stopped about a foot away from the frame, and she took a deep breath. The chill of the night braced her against the angry thoughts racing through her mind. There was something about the meaty tang of sea air that felt comforting. Outside her window, Old Town Eureka slumbered quietly. Contentedly. The ornate tower of the Carson Mansion dominated the landscape like a shepherd keeping an eye on his sleeping flock. The town didn't care about the storm brewing out at sea or the one that was already raging in Izzy's mind. Eureka took things as they came with a calm, measured patience. Just like Jake.

She squeezed her eyes shut. Why was her brain always returning to him? He'd bailed on her. She needed to let it go.

As she stood at the window with her eyes closed, Izzy heard a rhythmic sound. Not the muted ticking of the grandfather clock, but a sharper thud, drifting up from below. Like footsteps.

Izzy's eyes flew open; she scanned the darkness but couldn't see any movement. Old Town was completely still, but the rhythmic footfall got incrementally louder. It must have been someone coming up.

L Street was shrouded from her view, and as the noise faded, Izzy wondered who the hell would be out at that hour.

A faint click followed by the groan of a floorboard answered her question.

Izzy was well versed in every creak, shudder, and groan emitted by the hundred-year-old Bell house, and with three older brothers who had all, at some point in their lives, tried to sneak home after curfew, she knew the squeak from the fifth step on the main staircase as well as the sound of her own voice. Someone was coming up.

Izzy stood fixed at the window, not daring to make a sound while the footsteps reached the second-floor landing. The runner rug muted the creaking wood, but moments later, Izzy was sure she heard a door close. Whoever had been out was now tucked safely back inside. She glanced at the clock: just after one in the morning. Riley, coming home from one of his dates with Kylie. Gross.

Izzy was about to climb back into bed when a fragment of laughter interrupted her. It sounded like a giggle, wafted up on the breeze, followed quickly by a muted shush.

"Quiet," someone whispered. "They'll hear."

Izzy froze at the window. The house directly behind theirs was Miss O'Sullivan's Victorian Bed-and-Breakfast, owned and operated by Mr. and Mrs. Liang. Though the voice could have come from their house, every room was dark, and in the moonlight, Izzy could see that the casement windows facing her were all shuttered for the night.

Another giggle, louder this time. It sounded like it was coming from inside her room.

"Let them hear," another voice said. Not a whisper this time, and Izzy clearly recognized her mom's light soprano. "I don't—"

Her mom never finished the thought, and another sound took over. Like a slurping, followed by a deep moan.

"Fuck," Izzy said under her breath. It wasn't Riley coming home so late, it was her dad. She probably should have been grateful that her parents, despite their seemed estrangement, still cared enough about each other to get it on occasionally, but somehow it just made Izzy feel more alone.

Fingers in her ears like a three-year-old who thinks that by not hearing something it doesn't actually exist, Izzy turned back to the window. A cloud had momentarily passed between her and the moon, creating a glowing halo of moonlight around the puffy outline while the rest of the town was darkened. The cloud almost looked alive as it floated by, shimmering in the reflected light, and when the moon was revealed once more, the streets below her were lit up almost like it was dawn.

Out of the corner of her eyes, Izzy saw movement below. Something black, slipping through the blackness. She scanned the streets, wondering if she'd seen a huge dog or maybe a black bear that'd wandered down from the mountains. It took a few heartbeats before she saw the movement again, creeping toward her house.

Though the headlights were off, Izzy could distinctly make out the boxy shape of a black SUV driving up L Street in the dead of night.

SIXTEEN

BY THE TIME IZZY FINALLY DRAGGED HERSELF OUT OF BED THE next morning, the sunny skies and warmish temperatures from the day before had completely vanished. Last night's chill had not dissipated with the sun, and as her toes touched the frigid floorboards, she wished that she'd closed her window when she finally went to bed. She shivered, noting the time on the grandfather clock. Though the dark, gloomy skies made it feel pre-dawn, it was actually nine thirty.

Thankfully, the gloomy atmosphere hadn't permeated the house. As Izzy crept into the kitchen, desperate for some coffee, her mom greeted her with an enormous, glowing smile. "Good morning, sleepyhead! Would you like a bagel?"

Izzy blinked. "Um, sure."

Everything else in the house looked the same: Riley was glued to his phone at the window seat, Parker was in the laundry room, tossing all his running gear into the washing machine, and her dad was already gone. Pretty typical summer morning, except for her mom. It had been a long time since she'd seen her mom so happy. She floated over to the toaster oven, humming a tune as she slipped two halves of a three-day-old bagel onto the rack, then sashayed to the coffeepot.

"Cream, no sugar, right?"

She hadn't realized her mom even knew how she took her coffee. "Right."

Her mom's smile continued as she slid a mug in front of her daughter. "You've got to perk up, Izzy! It's a beautiful day."

Izzy glanced out the window just to make sure the weather hadn't changed since she'd come downstairs. Nope—still gross. Her mom's cheerfulness reminded Izzy of Peyton, walking up from the marina after a brief make-out session with Hunter. Sexy times made people oblivious to bad weather.

"Goddammit!" Riley shouted.

Parker poked his head in from the laundry room. "What happened?"

"Kylie bailed on me tonight." He tossed his phone onto the table. "Said something came up."

"I thought you said she's never up before noon?" Parker asked with a chuckle.

Riley scowled. "She texted late last night, I just saw the message now. Shit, my day is ruined."

"You're pissed because you won't get laid tonight?"

Riley scowled at him. "Wouldn't you be?"

Parker sighed, long and loud. "I can't wait until you go back to college."

"You'll miss me."

"When's your flight?"

"Monday morning," their mom said. Her voice practically tinkled with joy. "Ten o'clock."

"Ah, *Lunedi*!" Alberto's hearty voice drifted into the kitchen moments before his smiling face appeared. He was fully dressed, in jeans that reached his ankles and a tight gray-and-white-striped sweater. "Are-a we going somewhere?"

"Just Riley," Parker said, trailing through the kitchen on his way back upstairs. He grabbed a carton of coconut water from the fridge and a Luna Bar from the cookie jar. "Back to college, thankfully."

Izzy's mom patted her youngest son on the head. "I'm just ready to have the house to myself again."

"Um, I still live here," Izzy said, raising her hand. "Remember?"

Her mom smiled indulgently. "Of course, honey."

"Aren't moms supposed to be sad when their chicks leave the nest?" Riley asked, his foul mood deepening. He was his mother's son that way.

Alberto took a mug of coffee from Izzy's mom's hands. "Is *l'università* nearby?"

"If he didn't have to fly there, it would be too close," Parker said as he headed back upstairs.

Riley called after him, "I know where you sleep, dickwad!"

"San Diego." Izzy's mom answered Alberto's question as she placed a plate of poached eggs in front of him. Izzy had never seen her mom poach an egg in her life. "Far enough that he can't just drop in unannounced."

"Uh, thanks?" Riley said. He'd picked his phone back up and was typing furiously with his thumbs. Izzy wondered if he was trying to convince Kylie to un-cancel their date. That seemed like a very Riley thing to do.

Alberto dragged his stool up to the counter and leaned his elbows on either side of the coffee mug. His ever-present smile danced about his lips as he watched Izzy's mom closely. "Am I the sleepy-a brain this morning?"

"Sleepy*head*," her mom corrected, her bell-like tone still jingling with laughter.

"Ah, *sì*. Head, not brain. But-a my English, it issa improving!"

"Totally," Izzy said at the same time as her mom spoke.

"Totalmente."

At her mom's perfect Italian, Izzy was reminded of her own inadequacy in that regard. It had been three days and she'd yet to have a conversation with Alberto in Italian, which was entirely her fault because she'd been 100 percent avoiding it. But seeing the moment of secret joy between Alberto and her mom, Izzy suddenly wanted nothing more than to practice her Italian with him. Alone.

"I was thinking I should work on my Italian today," Izzy said.

"That's a wonderful idea!" her mom said. She took Izzy's bagel out of the toaster oven, slathered it with cream cheese, then placed it in front of Alberto. "You can do it while I take Alberto shopping. Poor boy needs some clothes that fit."

Izzy hadn't seen her mom this maternal since her sons still lived at home. It was nice, but she wasn't going to let her mom derail her. "I should practice *with* Alberto."

"Ah, *sì*," her mom said, nodding her head. *"Possiamo farlo insieme."*

Together? All three of them? No. *"Sola."* Izzy let her voice trail off. Other than *"ciao,"* she hadn't spoken any unsolicited Italian in Alberto's presence, and she fought against the wave of embarrassment simmering in her stomach. And fear. Always the fear.

Fuck the fear.

"Solamente Alberto ed io."

"Oh." Her mom was unable to hide her disappointment that Izzy wanted to practice only with Alberto. "Yes, of course," she said, turning her back on Izzy. "You kids should hang out. We can go to Target later."

"You can take me to Target," Riley said, raising his hand. "Got a whole list of shit I need before I fly out. And we should probably stock up on supplies before that storm rolls in."

Izzy's mom sighed. The joy was now completely gone. "Okay."

But for once, her mom's mood wasn't Izzy's main focus. She smiled at Alberto, forcing herself to make direct eye contact as she carried her coffee out of the kitchen. "I'm going to shower, and then after you eat we can . . ." Her voice trailed off as she walked through the dining room. A car was parked across the street, perfectly framed by the large living room window. It was a hulking black SUV.

The same one she'd seen crawling through the streets at one in the morning.

Alberto appeared at her side, his eyes following her gaze to the black car. He turned abruptly to Izzy's mom.

"*Scusa*, Elisabetta," he said. "What is thissa Target you say?"

"It's a store," Riley said. "A megastore. They sell everything."

"Big American shopping mall!" he exclaimed. "I would like-a to see this Target."

Seriously? "Now?"

"*Imediamente!*"

Izzy was about to protest, something she rarely did, but her mom was quicker.

"You can practice your Italian this afternoon," she said. "You have all day."

"But—"

"Riley's right. We need to grab toilet paper and batteries before the shelves are completely empty. You know how this town gets before a storm." Her mom grabbed the keys, vigor restored. "Meet me at the minivan in ten!"

"And the minivan—it issa out back?" Alberto said.

"All the way in the back," her mom replied.

"Eccelente." He practically skipped past Izzy up the stairs.

* * *

"I haven't had to sit in the back since I was in high school," Riley whined from the captain's chair beside Izzy. It was hardly a cramped backseat in the minivan, but Riley, already pissy about his canceled date with Kylie, had soured further when their mom offered Alberto shotgun.

Alberto had protested when Izzy's mom opened the door for him, but she was insistent, and when they pulled out of the driveway at the side of their house, he slouched so low in the front passenger seat that Izzy almost thought they'd left him behind. Once they were a few blocks from the house, he seemed to perk up.

"Imma so sorry to have-a your seat," he said, grinning over his shoulder at Riley.

Riley grunted a reply, and Izzy rolled her eyes. "He's just cranky because he got dumped."

"I did NOT get dumped," Riley said sharply. "Kylie just has to work tonight."

Her excuse might have been legit, but after the brief interaction Izzy had witnessed yesterday, where Kylie had practically thrown herself at Alberto, it seemed more likely that the bartender was actively hunting for another option. And had probably found one.

Which was just as well. The last thing Riley needed was an unstable ex like Greg Loomis gunning for him.

"How about some music, huh?" Izzy's mom suggested. It wasn't like her to even recognize tension in the car, let alone want to dissipate it, and Izzy liked that she didn't have to be the only one thinking about those things. For once.

"Sure."

Her mom pushed a button on the steering wheel and the radio came on. The Bluetooth must have still been connected to Izzy's phone from the other night, because the dulcet tones of *Murder Will Speak* filled the minivan.

"And so that's why they're calling him the Casanova Killer," Mags said.

"Again?" Izzy's mom asked, stabbing at the presets until the classical station came on. As if anyone in the Bell family listened to classical music. "Enough with the horrible murders."

"Sorry," Izzy said. She fumbled with her phone, switching off her Bluetooth so it wouldn't happen on the ride home.

"That's a stupid name," Riley said. He was still pouting, but not enough to stay quiet when he felt as if his opinion was warranted. "Not serial killer-y at all."

"It's because of how he kills his victims," Izzy explained.

"Which is?"

Ugh. Why did he have to ask? "He, um, strangles them while he's making out with them. Or, um, possibly during sex."

The car was silent for a moment while everyone processed that little nugget; then her mom sucked in a sharp breath. "Those poor women."

From the front seat, Alberto clicked his tongue. "Maybe they are not so poor?"

"They were murdered," Izzy said. "How can they not be victims?"

Her mom jumped in immediately. "I think this is a language issue," she said. "Alberto, poor can mean *povera, il contrario di ricca*, or it can be a term of pity, *come sei misero*."

"Ah, *sì sì*," Alberto said, nodding. "I understand. They were poor women." He paused, gazing out the window. "Even the rich ones."

SEVENTEEN

THE TRIP TO TARGET WAS ABOUT AS MUCH FUN AS IZZY ANTIC-
ipated. The store was mobbed: they had to wait ten minutes while Izzy's
mom stalked departing patrons just to find a parking spot.

Once inside, it was near pandemonium. Most aisles in the housewares
and grocery sections were picked clean, though Riley and Alberto were
able to nab the last package of name-brand toilet paper, a monster-size
box of batteries, and two flats of bottled water. Then Riley pouted his
way through the pilfered toiletries section, their mom picked out clothes
she thought might suit their Italian visitor, and Alberto marveled at the
bigness of everything American. Izzy pushed the shopping cart.

This magical shopping experience lasted twice as long as it should have,
partially because Alberto kept pulling Izzy's mom down random aisles

to ask questions about everything from the homogeneity of American clothing to why kitchen sponges were sold in packages of *una milliones*, and partially because half of Eureka was attempting to shop there at the same time.

As Hunter had predicted, everybody was talking about the storm. Local news had dubbed it the "Storm of the Century," which was less impressive than it sounded considering they were only a quarter of a way through the current century, but whatever. The inbound tempest was predicted to cause significant flooding, mudslides, wind damage, and even widespread power outages, and the greater Eureka area was taking no chances. Each register had a line ten people deep, all stocking up on paper goods and nonperishable food, and everyone was talking about what might happen this weekend when the storm surge rushed onshore.

Blind to the storm panic around her, Izzy's mom reveled in her role as tour guide, as if explaining Target to Alberto was the culmination of her life's work, while Riley, like a toddler in need of closer attention, kept trying to slip cases of beer into the cart when he thought she wasn't looking.

It was all sort of exhausting.

But her mom was energized by the entire trip. She chatted happily on the drive home, to Alberto, to Riley, and to Izzy, without expecting any specific interactions in return. By the time they got back, she practically danced through the kitchen door, Target bags dangling from both arms.

"Beth?" Izzy's dad called from the living room. "Is that you?"

Izzy was so unused to hearing her dad's voice coming from the living room of their house that she actually flinched at the sound of it.

"Yes, Harry," her mom said with something that resembled a sigh. She dropped her bags on the island and marched through the dining room. Izzy followed silently behind, curious.

Two strangers—a slim Black woman in her forties or fifties with her hair wound into a tight bun at the nape of her neck, and a shorter, portly white man whose blond-gray thinning locks hinted that he was about ten years older. They were both dressed in dark business suits, which gave them an official and somewhat ominous aura, though the friendly smiles they turned toward the newcomers to the Bell living room were disarming and guileless.

"These folks are here to ask you some questions," her dad said, rising along with the two strangers as Izzy's mom entered the room. He eyed the front door, contemplating an escape.

"Mrs. Bell? I'm Loretta Michaels," the Black woman said, extending her hand. "My partner and I are from the Bureau of Educational and Cultural Affairs, Exchange Programs division, and we're just checking to see how Alberto Bianchi is settling in."

Before her mom could answer, Izzy felt a sharp tug on her arm, yanking her none too gently back into the kitchen.

"Izz-*ee*," Alberto whispered, his lips close to her ear. "Will you-a show me your father's workshop?"

"His workshop?" She didn't realize Alberto knew her dad had a workshop on the property, let alone that he had any desire to see it.

"*Sì*." He nodded. "I would like-a to see it."

"Why?"

Alberto shrugged and flashed a half smile. "Because your father issa no there now."

"Oh."

Izzy felt that now-familiar tightening of her lower abdomen as she led Alberto through the kitchen into the backyard. Her body was quick to respond to his smiles, and though the excitement he caused in her wasn't necessarily unwelcome, it was alarming that he could play her so easily.

What kind of a stereotypically weak woman was she that a wink from a cute guy could send her into some kind of hormonal fugue state?

As they crossed the yard, the brisk wind buffeted them from the west. Izzy shivered despite her layered long-sleeve shirts and wondered if this was how serial killers marked their victims. Everyone described Ted Bundy as a handsome and charismatic man who used those qualities to disarm his victims. Would Izzy have fallen prey if Ted Bundy had the same smile as Alberto Bianchi? Maybe. She was lucky he was just a college student from Italy.

The old wooden door to her dad's workshop swung open easily at Izzy's touch. "It no lock?" Alberto asked.

"The latch is broken," Izzy replied. Then, suddenly self-conscious that her handyman dad hadn't bothered to fix the door to his own workshop, she quickly added, "He's been meaning to fix it, but he's been really busy."

"Ah, *sì*. He-a no home much."

She pointed to the window on the far side of the garage. "It's not a big deal unless the window's open. Then the door bangs back and forth with every gust of wind."

"I see."

Izzy took a quick inhale as she switched on the lights. She'd always loved the smell of her dad's workshop, a mixture of different woods and oils swirling around in bits of sawdust. That smell was connected to her dad's happiness.

But it looked as if he hadn't been working in the shop that morning, considering how tidy the space appeared. He always cleaned up at the end of the day, which was exactly how it looked now, even though it was well after noon. All of his projects were put away, his tools neatly stowed. The floor had been swept, but no new wood pilings were strewn about from a half-carved molding still mounted on the band saw. It was unusual for her dad not to start work before lunch, but Izzy hoped it meant that he'd been in another meeting, hopefully with the Pink Lady owners who had finally decided to put their multi-million-dollar bed-and-breakfast remodel into Harry Bell's capable hands.

Alberto followed her into the workshop, eyes wide as he scanned the space from the tool wall to the variety of work benches, and up to the garage door rails that spanned the ceiling. *"Mon dieu."*

"You speak French too?"

Alberto flushed. Was he embarrassed that he was multilingual?

"I think that's cool," she said quickly, hoping she hadn't offended him. "I mean, I can barely speak my own language half the time, let alone two others."

"My French issa . . . no so good," he said with a wicked smile. "I was with a French girl. Once."

"Oh." Was he trying to signal his disinterest in Izzy by mentioning an ex?

He lifted an eyebrow. "And I-a suspect that your Italian issa no so good."

Now it was Izzy's turn to flush. He'd guessed her secret, which was embarrassing, but at least he hadn't outted her in front of her mom.

"Issa okay." He took a step closer. "But my English, it is improved, *si*?"

"*Si.*"

"And-a do you know *how* it has improved?"

He'd spoken almost no Italian since he'd arrived, and he must have taken at least one English lesson with her mom, but as Alberto's blue eyes tore into her, she was unable to formulate those facts into a coherent response. "N-no," she managed.

Alberto lowered his chin. "Because of you."

That was not the answer she'd been expecting. "Me?"

"*Sì*."

"How?"

"Because I want to talk-a to you."

Izzy hadn't realized that she'd been moving backward, away from Alberto as he advanced, until her hip butted up against the miter saw in the far corner, below the open window. Part of her wanted to escape, climb over the table and through the window before Alberto could say anything else. But another piece of her wanted—desperately—to stay.

"Do I make-a you *nervoso*?" Alberto asked, catching her eyes as they flitted toward the open window. His voice was low, hardly above a whisper, and his light blue eyes were hypnotic.

"Everything makes me nervous."

He reached for her hand, lifting it gently to his lips as he'd done at the airport. She could feel her fingers trembling at his touch. "Maybe I can change-a your mind?"

Alberto drew her arm behind his back, effectively pulling her body closer to his own. He was in control, confidently focused on Izzy, and his attention made her feel special. *Wanted*. That was a new sensation.

"Izz-*ee*," he whispered in her ear. He pressed her hand against the small of his back and snaked his other arm around her waist. "I would like to—"

WHAM!

The sound of the door blowing open and smashing into the wall startled Izzy so badly she actually jumped away from Alberto, shuffling to the other side of the miter saw. A scowl flashed across Alberto's face. He swung viciously around, fists balled, as if he was ready to smash the door to splinters.

"It bangs when the window's open," she reminded him.

"I see." Alberto made a guttural sound in his throat, like a tiger warning off a potential threat, though when he turned back to Izzy, he was all smiles again.

But the spell was broken. "We should get back," she said.

"No!" Alberto shouted.

His reaction was so startling, Izzy froze and was suddenly cognizant of the fact that Alberto stood between her and the door.

"I mean, not yet, Izz-*ee*."

"Izzy?" Her dad's voice in the backyard. "You in there?"

"Here!" she cried, a confusing wave of relief washing over her. What the hell was going on in her brain?

"Gonna help me with that fireplace molding?" He chuckled as he stepped inside. Then his eyes shifted from Izzy to Alberto. "Everything okay?"

"Yeah, sorry." Izzy stepped around Alberto toward the door. The chilly breeze felt sobering, as if she'd been awoken from a dream. "I was just giving Alberto a tour of your workshop."

Her dad's eyebrows hitched in surprise. "You're interested in restoration, Al?"

Alberto's smile deepened. "*Sì*, Signore Bell. *Mi nonno*, he restored his old-a olive farm."

"I thought your grandfather lived by the sea?" Izzy asked.

Alberto laughed. "My *other* grandfather."

Duh, of course. Why did she even need to voice that question out loud?

If Izzy's dad was momentarily suspicious about what his teenage daughter and the hot Italian college student were actually doing unsupervised in his workshop, those thoughts evaporated from Harry Bell's mind at the prospect of a kindred spirit with whom he could discuss pointed-arch door surrounds and where to source period-appropriate ceramic tiles. "Did he do his own plaster work?"

"From a mold?" Alberto said with a quick wink at Izzy. *"Sì, sì."*

He guided Alberto over to the corner of his workshop near the window. "Then feast your eyes on this baby. An authentic Joachim Jungwirth mold. I know his stuff didn't show up in California, but look at the detail on this scrollwork."

Her dad's shoptalk faded in the background as Izzy caught movement through the open door. She poked her head out in time to see Loretta Michaels and her coworker walk slowly toward the front gate. Loretta turned back and waved, and Izzy heard a click as the front door latched shut.

The moment the door was closed, Loretta dropped her arm and her smile. Her entire demeanor changed. Her head swiveled around, searching the Bell property, though for what, Izzy didn't know. She instinctively ducked back inside the garage, into a pocket of dark shadows beside the door from where she could just see the two visitors in the yard. Loretta spoke to her partner with hand signals, pointing to him, then the car. He nodded and hurried through the gate to the black SUV parked across the street.

Was it weird that a foreign-exchange student agency would send two representatives into the middle of nowhere in a giant, tinted-window assault vehicle? It seemed weird. Certainly not the kind of car you could rent at Hertz. They must have driven up to Eureka. But from where?

While her partner was grabbing something from the car, Loretta sidled down the length of the fence toward the garage, seeming to admire the overgrown hedges. She glanced at the garage once or twice, then quickly pivoted back toward the gate. With her back to the garage, she signaled to her partner, now inside the SUV with the rear passenger window rolled halfway down.

Izzy felt her stomach tighten as she saw an object rest on the lip of the open car window. She opened her mouth to shout a warning, assuming that the object was a gun of some kind, but it would have been a gun with a muzzle about six inches wide. She was staring at a camera lens, taking a quick series of snapshots.

The photography session ended as quickly as it began, and the camera disappeared from the window into the car. Without a word, Loretta swiftly crossed to the SUV and climbed inside, and the car pulled away.

EIGHTEEN

PEYTON WAS EARLY TO PICK THEM UP FOR THE BONFIRE THAT night.

Peyton was never early.

She also got out of the car and rang the doorbell.

She never got out of the car and rang the doorbell.

Izzy was still up in her room when she heard it, trying to decide what to wear. On the one hand, the dark clouds clustered on the horizon meant that a warm coat and beanie cap might be the most appropriate outfit, especially with the "Storm of the Century" lurking to the west, ready to pounce as far south as Half Moon Bay and as far north as Oregon.

But the massive storm was still forty-eight hours away, which meant tonight's bonfire was happening. Freezing cold weather or not.

Izzy really should have busted out her winter wardrobe. Except she wanted to look cute. Parkas and "cute" rarely went together.

She finally settled on jeans and boots and a long-sleeve Henley shirt in emerald green that brought out the orange overtones in her hair. It didn't exactly put her minuscule cleavage on display, but by leaving the top two buttons open, it did reveal more skin than most of her wardrobe. Her wool, navy-blue beanie cap didn't look too heinous, and the parka . . . She decided to ditch it in favor of her down-filled puffer vest. Which she would carry unless it got really cold.

A second ring at the doorbell followed by the buzz of an incoming text on her phone meant that no one had bothered to answer the door.

"I'll get it!" she called out as she hurried down the stairs from the attic. It appeared no one was home to hear her, though the door to Alberto's room was open as she whizzed by. She looped an arm around the wooden artichoke at the top of the stairs and swung around it with more energy than usual. She missed the second step where she always landed, and her boots caught on the lip of the third. Izzy would have gone careening headfirst down the stairs if she hadn't been able to grip the handrail at the last moment. She wrenched her shoulder but was able to stop her forward momentum.

Izzy was standing on the staircase, panting, railing still gripped beneath her white-knuckled fingers, when a head appeared over the banister.

"Izz-*ee*? Are you okay?"

"Yeah," Izzy said, mortified that Alberto had witnessed her clumsiness. Again. "I just slipped."

"You might have been-a killed," he said, his voice flat.

Just like my mom always says. "I'm okay." She straightened up, smoothing down her shirt, and avoided looking at Alberto as she trotted down the stairs. "I think Peyton's here."

"Um, yeah!" Peyton said, the moment Izzy opened the door. "Been here forever."

If Izzy had been wrestling with the cute-versus-practical dilemma, Peyton hadn't even considered the latter as an option. She wore a pair of white high-waisted leggings, running shoes, and a red strappy cropped top that looked more sports bra than overgarment. She'd barrel-curled her chestnut-brown hair into long spiral tendrils that fell over each shoulder with the kind of precision that could only have been carefully staged, and her false eyelashes and cherry-red lips made her look like she was about to get glamour shots taken.

"Aren't you gonna be cold?" Izzy said, eyeing her friend from head to toe as she sidled through the doorway.

Peyton rolled her eyes. "Okay, *Mom*." Then she looked over Peyton's head toward the staircase, and her face lit up. "Are you ready?"

Izzy knew the question wasn't for her, even before she heard Alberto's footsteps on the creaking floorboards.

"*Ciao*, Peyton!" Alberto's voice rang out from behind her. "*Buona sera!*"

Alberto bounced into the foyer, smile broad. He'd done his hair, molding the front up into something similar to Riley's signature pompadour, and was wearing some of the clothes Izzy's mom had picked out for him at Target, a pair of flat-front, straight-leg jeans and a sapphire-blue sweater that hit right at his hip bone. The serious reaction to Izzy's near accident on the stairs had been replaced by his usual cheerful self except the wattage was dialed up, like he had so much positive energy pinging around inside he might actually explode. He clasped Izzy by the shoulders with one arm, Peyton with the other, and hugged them to his sides. "It is a beautiful evening, *sì?*"

"*Sì!*" Peyton cooed, batting her fake eyelashes as Alberto released them from his embrace.

"Except for the massive storm rolling in," Izzy said with a tight smile. "Won't you be cold on the beach?"

Peyton's eyes never left Alberto's face as she reached out and lightly touched his arm. "We can always snuggle up for warmth."

"I'm sure your boyfriend will love that," Izzy said, both as a reprimand and as a reminder. Why did Peyton have to horn in on Alberto? Wasn't the doting love and affection of one guy enough for her? "Where *is* Hunter?"

"Meeting us there." If Peyton felt shame at Izzy's barb, she didn't show it. "Shall we go?" Without waiting for an answer, she swiveled her hips toward the door and sauntered out into the darkening evening.

Izzy sighed. She couldn't compete with Peyton's aggressive sexuality. Even if she'd possessed an outfit like the one Peyton had on, and had the guts to wear it, she'd have looked like a little girl playing dress-up in mommy's clothes. Whereas Peyton looked like a woman. A worldly, commanding, experienced woman. There was no comparison.

The sun still hung above the horizon, but the gathering of dark storm clouds over the ocean blocked the orange-red rays and made the evening darker than it should have been. A gust tumbled sticks and dry maple leaves across the walkway, and Izzy was thankful she had the good sense to at least bring the vest with her. But the cold didn't seem to bother Peyton, who continued her catwalk strut to the car.

Alberto closed the door behind him and fell into step beside Izzy, his eyes locked on Peyton's bouncing glutes. Once again, Izzy felt the hopelessness of trying to compete against her friend.

"She is beautiful tonight," Alberto said quietly as they passed through the gate.

See? No competition. "Peyton's always been the pretty one."

"I was-a no talking about Peyton."

She found that his eyes were now fixed firmly on her face. His gaze was intense, stark blue eyes boring into her own as if he were trying to read her innermost thoughts, but while Izzy expected the hot blush to push up from her chest to her neck and face, the embarrassment didn't appear. She was either getting used to Alberto's attention or was immune to it.

"Alberto, you're in the front," Peyton said as she climbed into the aged Explorer. Alberto winked at Izzy, then hurried around the front of the car. Though she appreciated the clandestine nature of his flirtation with her, Izzy secretly wondered if maybe he was trying to have it both ways.

Much like Izzy's mom on the drive to and from Target, Peyton chatted nonstop en route to the beach, only pausing for the occasional breath as she cited the entire known history of Eureka High School bonfire parties. "They used to do them at Samoa Beach, but years ago a bunch of yabbos set off fireworks and started a wildfire in the beach grass, so now the fire department is paranoid, which blows." A quick breath. "And then they used Mad River Beach for a while, but the city voted to put up a gate that closes after sunset, and you do not want to get your car stuck in that lot. Trust me."

If Peyton had ever been to a bonfire at Mad River Beach, let alone gotten her Explorer impounded after parking in a restricted lot, she must have gone without Izzy *and* never spoken a single word about the experience. Which was unlikely.

"Moonstone Beach is the prettiest and the most romantic, but some of the local weirdos up there call the sheriff's department every single time, so now we use the beach behind Ma-le'l Dunes, which at least isn't so far to drive home. We park in the gun club's lot, and since nobody lives over there, nobody complains. Plus it's a pain to get down to the beach, so the cops don't usually bother us unless shit gets crazy."

Alberto's head turned sharply. "Cops?"

Peyton waved him off. "Just the sheriff's department. They're, like, not even real cops."

"Say that to their faces," Izzy muttered under her breath.

"Issa what we are doing against-a the law?" Alberto asked. He swallowed, visibly nervous. Not a usual reaction from the uber-confident Italian.

"Nah." Peyton laughed. "High school parties are, like, totally the norm around here. Don't you have them in Italy?"

"*Sì, sì,*" Alberto said. "But no, eh, cops."

"Don't worry about it," Peyton continued. "Unless things get out of hand, they'll leave us alone."

Alberto nodded to himself, slowly turning to look out the passenger side window. "Then we keep-a things in hand. Tonight."

NINETEEN

DESPITE THE NOTICEABLE LACK OF CARS IN THE GUN CLUB'S parking lot, at least fifty people were gathered around the blaze, which had been set up a sensible distance from the blanket of flammable beach grass and tufts of coyote bush that surrounded the rolling dunes. The sun had disappeared completely, taking with it whatever glow had permeated the encroaching clouds, but the moon was out, peeking through breaks in the overcast skies. The oscillating moonlight was bright enough for Izzy to distinguish individual faces, and as they tramped across the fine sandy dunes, Izzy recognized people in the crowd.

Including Hunter and Jake, who hung back from the bonfire, waiting. Hunter's face was buried in his phone, but Jake spotted them immediately.

He stood like a huge statue, hands shoved into his pockets, thick hair only partially contained beneath his ever-present knit cap. He tapped Hunter on the arm to alert him to their presence, and Izzy realized that she'd chosen a navy-blue hat exactly like the one Jake always wore.

"Babe!" Hunter said, jogging across the uneven terrain as gracefully as was humanly possible. Which wasn't very. He stopped shy of embracing Peyton. "Aren't you going to freeze to death?"

Peyton remained at Alberto's side, leaning closer to him than was appropriate, and when she spoke, her voice was as cold as her manner was detached. "I'll be fine."

"She will cuddle," Alberto said with a laugh, nudging Peyton with his shoulder. "To keep-a the warmth."

It was meant jokingly, and Izzy suspected Alberto was even poking a little bit of fun at her friend, but as Hunter's eyes trailed from Alberto's shoulder to Peyton's bare arm, his face clouded. "Dude, don't talk about my girlfriend like that."

Alberto held his hands up in front of him, palms out, a signal of surrender. "I do not know-a what I say. Did I give the offense? Izz-*ee*, can-a you translate?"

Izzy felt her stomach drop. He'd already called her out on her horrible Italian. Why make her put that lack of skill on display?

"*Non lo so*" was all she could think to say. *I don't know.*

Which wasn't entirely true. She knew that Alberto's words on the surface shouldn't have made Hunter territorial, but Peyton's overt flirting had certainly put him on high alert.

"Ah," Alberto nodded his head. "Too many brewskis, *sì*?"

"Sure." Izzy, who rarely drank, was just about ready for a brewski herself. She tugged on the sleeve of his sweater. "Let's find the stash."

She moved quickly across the dry sand, half dragging Alberto behind her. Her boots felt like they were made of cement as she trudged across the dunes, and she was happy when she made contact with the more compact wet sand, recently smoothed and shaped by the retreating tide.

"Imma so sorry," Alberto said at her side. "I did no want to upset the Hunter."

Izzy snort-laughed at the idea that the usually laid-back Hunter was *actually* a hunter.

Alberto's eyebrows pinched over his nose. "Did I make the goof?"

"No, no!" Izzy said. "I was just laughing at the idea that Hunter could actually hunt and kill anything."

"Ah," Alberto said. "Yet he is a fisherman, *sì*? That is a hunt."

Izzy had never really thought of fishing as a hunt—more like an exercise in patience and dumb luck. "I guess you're right."

She looked over her shoulder toward Peyton, who stood opposite Hunter, her hands animated as she emphasized whatever argument she was making, and though the crash of waves drowned out the details of their conversation, Izzy could guess the basics.

Jake, to the credit of his manners, had disappeared.

"All men, we like-a the hunt." Alberto's eyes turned glassy as he focused on the ocean, which pulsated with the retreating tide. "Some just enjoy the catch more."

Izzy really hoped she was missing something in translation again, because suddenly Alberto sounded 100 percent creepy. "Um, okay."

He gripped her arm. "*Basta*, Alberto. I did it again, *sì*? The offense?" His smile was so warm, his eyes so full of genuine concern, Izzy laughed, this time at her own foolishness in thinking he was creepy. She had to remember that English was his second language, and if she'd been trying to navigate a new home and new friends in Italy, she'd probably have offended an entire town by now.

"You're fine," she said, hoping he believed her. "Come on. The stash is usually this way."

Alberto trudged by her side as they rounded the bonfire, and Izzy sensed heads turning to follow them. Taking stock. She wondered how many of them were confused that a hot guy like Alberto was talking to a nobody like her. Normally, this thought would have crushed her under the weight of a thousand nameless and nebulous anxieties, but instead of hunching her shoulders and wishing that no one would notice her, Izzy straightened up and tried not to give a shit.

The "stash" of alcohol at underage beach bonfires usually resided a good fifty yards from the actual conflagration, literally stashed in the sand and camouflaged by a strategically placed collection of dried seaweed and driftwood. Tonight's location was behind the hollowed-out remains of a rotted redwood trunk, grayed with age, which shielded the hastily dug hole from view. A green tarp covered a mix of hard cider and beer, and though Izzy didn't know the difference, she confidently grabbed a bottle, whose green label sported a Granny Smith apple, and hoped for the best.

Alberto cocked an eyebrow. *"È buono?"*

"Non lo so," Izzy replied, and this time it wasn't a lie.

"Is that all the *italiano* you know?" In the moonlight, Izzy found his piercing blue eyes fixed upon her. She couldn't tell if his question was born from curiosity, derision, or both, but for some reason—perhaps from the ease of their conversation or the realization that Alberto might, in fact, be flirting with her—the language poured out of her with shocking ease.

"Parlo bene l'italiano. E tu?" I speak Italian quite well. Do you?

She hadn't meant the question to come across so confrontational, and for a nanosecond as she was locked in Alberto's gaze, she thought she saw his eyes harden, the muscles in his square-cut jaw bulging at the joint below his ears, but the awkwardness only lasted a moment before he threw back his head and laughed with abandon.

"Ah, the humor again, Izz-*ee*."

Said literally no one ever. Izzy Bell wasn't known for her lightning wit. But she was thankful he'd taken her outburst as a joke. "I try."

He screwed off the top of his hard cider and tapped the neck to hers, which seemed very un-Italian. "To the American humor!"

"Hey, you're the one who made the Hunter is a hunter joke," she said, cheers-ing him with her bottle.

"I try," he said, repeating her own words.

"You should stop apologizing for your English" she said as Alberto sipped his cider. "It's really quite good. Idiomatic."

"Idio . . ." He shook his head, not understanding.

"Id-i-o-ma-tic," she said. "Fancy way of saying you speak the language as if you'd been doing it all your life."

The eyebrow lifted again, slowly this time. "Really?"

"Yeah." Izzy took a sip to hide her smile. Was this flirting? She was pretty sure this was flirting. "I like the hair," she said, pushing her luck. The lack of soul-crushing fear made her giddy.

Alberto patted his pompadour gingerly with his free hand. "*Sì?*"

"Looks good. Even if it reminds me of my brother."

"You think I look-a like Riley?"

Izzy snorted. "Just the hair. Thankfully."

Alberto nodded slowly and fell silent. He gazed out at the dark sea. "I dream-a, you know."

"Don't we all?"

"I dream-a of running away."

Izzy had just started to take another sip of her cider and ended up choking on it, sputtering droplets all over her hand. "From Eureka?"

"No."

"From Italy?" It seemed impossible that the place she'd contemplated escaping *to* was the same place he wanted to escape *from*.

"*Sì.*"

"Why?"

"My hometown, it issa small. The people are also small. The minds are small." He stepped in front of her. "Even at *l'università*. I need new start."

The words could have come from her own mouth.

"Does that sound . . . How do you say? Silly?"

Izzy was afraid to blink, afraid to look away, lest this moment evaporate like a misty fog on a warm morning. Peyton didn't understand. Izzy's family didn't understand. Her mother understood but not really, since she was part of the problem. And Jake, who *had* understood, had bailed. Now, this beautiful boy with the piercing blue eyes was standing in front of her, seeing the thoughts inside her head.

A new start. A new life. Alberto understood. He *knew* what it was like to run away. And he'd come all the way to Eureka to do it.

"No," she croaked, her voice knotting up in her throat. She swallowed, and spoke again, just loud enough to hear over the crashing waves. "No, that's not silly at all."

"Ah, *sì*." His lips crinkled into a thin smile. Not the broad, luminous one he usually wore but something deeper, more knowing. "When first-a I see you, I think-a, *she* will understand. *She* will—"

"Alberto!" Peyton's cry cut through the intimacy of the moment like a hawk screeching down toward its prey. Izzy turned to find her friend teetering toward them in her stark white leggings, attempting to cross the uneven beach terrain like a runway model. She looked like a spindly-legged newborn foal just learning to walk, and she stumbled as she reached them, clinging to Alberto's arm for balance.

"I found you," she said, maintaining physical contact with him despite how quickly she regained her balance. Izzy wondered if the fall had all been for show and silently cursed herself for not thinking of it first. "Why are you hiding way over here? The party's by the fire."

"Is that where Hunter is?" Izzy asked.

Peyton narrowed her eyes as she shrugged. "We had a fight." She pawed at Alberto's chest. "He's such a child sometimes."

Her words slurred ever so slightly, and she swooned as she clung to Alberto, so much so that he had to loop an arm around her waist to keep her from flopping onto the wet sand. They'd only been at the party for, like, fifteen minutes—how much booze had Peyton chugged? And where had she gotten it? Izzy's stranger danger kicked in, and she worried that Peyton might have accepted a roofied drink from some rando.

Peyton giggled in Alberto's arms, as if to confirm Izzy's concerns.

"What were you two talking about, huh?" Peyton continued. The words were innocent, but the tone was confrontational.

"Izz-ee, she shows me the stash," Alberto said, gesturing toward the hollow log.

"Huh," Peyton traced a line from Alberto's bottle to Izzy's with the tip of her index finger. "I've never seen you drink before."

Was Peyton trying to infantilize her? Pointing out her lack of drinking was a stupid way to do it, because not drinking certainly wasn't something she was ashamed of. "Yeah, that's because I don't."

Peyton raised an eyebrow, upping the ante. "Showing off?"

"Being hospitable." Peyton was making it really difficult to be her friend.

Peyton turned her focus back to Alberto, one hand drifting down his chest to his abdomen. "I can be hospitable."

Izzy fought back a pang of jealousy and immediately reprimanded herself. She should be more concerned that a drugged and drunk Peyton was about to do something incredibly stupid that she'd pitifully regret in the morning. Maybe she should take Peyton home.

"Okay," she said, unzipping her vest. She looped it over Peyton's shoulders and tried to maneuver her away from Alberto. "Let's get you back to the car before you catch a—"

"I'm fine, *Mom.*" Peyton shrugged off the vest, leaning into Alberto as if he'd protect her. "I want Alberto to meet some people. Not stand over here all night talking to you."

"What the actual fuck, Pey?" Peyton could be flighty, occasionally self-absorbed, but this viciousness had never reared its ugly head before, and Izzy deserved an explanation.

But she wasn't going to get it tonight.

"Come on." Peyton grabbed Alberto's hand in both of hers and backed toward the fire, pulling him away. "Let's have some *fun.*"

Neither of them looked back.

TWENTY

IZZY SHOOK THE SAND FROM HER VEST AS SHE WATCHED Peyton and Alberto struggle across the beach until they emerged from the darkness into the lively, dancing glow of the bonfire. She couldn't hear, but she could see Peyton shouldering into group conversations to introduce Alberto to a bunch of Eureka High School students he'd literally never see again, and she realized with a pang of shame that *she* should have been the one doing that, instead of hiding at the back of the party.

She'd tried to stop her friend from throwing herself at Alberto, but it was difficult to control Peyton when she was set on a thing. She was exactly like Izzy's mom that way. Her mom had decided she wanted Izzy to fulfill her lost dreams in Italy, and so that's exactly what she was going to do. Peyton had decided she wanted Hunter, and she got Hunter. Now she wanted Alberto, and she was probably going to get Alberto. Peyton was sexy; she knew how to seduce the way that girls who've had actual sexual experiences innately understood. It wasn't just the way she dressed but the way she made Alberto the center of her universe, the focus of her attention.

Even the way Peyton moved her body: sinuous, rhythmic. Every step was a wordless declaration that her body was something you wanted to touch. Meanwhile, Izzy was wearing sensible layers, a pair of hiking boots, and only a thin application of mascara and lip gloss on her face. She felt like she'd brought a trike to the Tour de France and was trying to pedal up a mountain with the pros.

She turned away from the bonfire, away from the warmth and the noise and the light, and trudged up the nearest dune. When she reached its crest, she sat down, swiveling her half-full bottle into the sand before hugging her knees to her chest. Peyton and Alberto had been swallowed up by the growing crowd and blinding glow of the flames. Even her friend's bright white pants were lost in the press of bodies. Izzy knew she should probably be down there, attempting to prevent her friend from blowing up her life, but she was tired of the fight.

Maybe deep in the darkest part of her soul, Izzy kinda-sorta wanted to see Peyton's world fall apart. For once to see her friend stumble. Hunter was, in the words of Izzy's dad, a "good egg," and considering how many douchebags existed in Humboldt County, let alone the world, Izzy thought you should probably count yourself pretty lucky if you were happy with one of those good eggs. Izzy felt bad that she'd ever disapproved of her friend's relationship with him, although it wasn't really *Hunter* she disapproved of, but the idea of marrying a guy you fell in love with when you were in high school.

Or college, like my mom.

Izzy winced. Again, her mom's life, her mom's choices, were influencing her own. Was she running away from her problems instead of facing them head-on? Even if she were running toward Alberto instead of away from her hometown, it was still just running, wasn't it? All part of the same fear, the same gnawing anxiety that woke her up at night and wrapped itself around her thumping heart. The same fear that had banished her from the bonfire the moment alpha-dog Peyton had dragged Alberto away.

It wasn't even that she wanted Alberto, necessarily; it just felt nice to be the most important person to somebody. Peyton already had that, with Hunter and with her mom. Izzy literally had no one.

Tears welled up in her eyes. *Shit.* The sad girl crying at the bonfire was not a good look as she started senior year. She turned her head aside and was swiping at her damp cheek with the back of her hand when she heard a familiar voice.

"Hey."

Jake stood halfway up the dune. His hands were still shoved deep into the pockets of his jeans, and unlike everyone else at the bonfire, he still didn't have a beer.

"Hey," she said, relieved to hear no trace of her recent emotional break in her voice.

"Do you mind if I join you?"

"No."

Jake's smile was tight. "Good."

He stepped lightly up the side of the dune with a spryness that belied his size and nestled down beside her in the sand. Close, but not oppressive. Like he wanted to talk but didn't want to pressure her.

Except he didn't say a word. They sat in silence, with the background noise of the surf, the fire, and the party ebbing and flowing from across the beach. Though she was still angry at the way he'd abandoned her, her feelings had softened a little. Thinking about their lost connection no longer ignited her anger, it just made her sad.

"Your new roommate's pretty popular down there," he said at last, nodding toward the bonfire. "How's that going?"

"Good, I guess. My mom's happy." She hated the casual conversation. It felt so forced.

"And that makes you happy," he said, not even phrasing it as a question. He knew her better than that. "Or at least lets you breathe a little."

"It does." She paused, wondering if he had anything else to say, but when he fell oddly silent, she felt the need to check in with him as well. "How are things with your dad since you got back?"

"Same," Jake said with a shrug, his eyes fixed on the dancing flames in the distance. "Still against college. Still thinks I need basic training after I graduate to toughen me up."

"You work on a fishing boat. How is that not tough?"

Jake snorted. "Tell that to the sergeant."

"Maybe I will."

"I would pay cash money to watch you tell off my dad."

Izzy smiled, practically against her will. She hated how easily she'd fallen back into this comfortable space with Jake, and yet it *was* comfortable. And comfort*ing*. She didn't want to let that feeling go. "How much we talking?"

He looked at her sidelong. "I've got a shiny quarter just burning a hole in my pocket."

"Nah," she said, waving him off. "That'll run you at least a twenty."

"I thought you were just flush with money." He turned his whole body to face her, a playful smirk on his face. "When you refused to let me buy you lunch."

"I'm not just going to let some guy I *barely know*," she said, eyebrows arched, "buy me lunch. What would people think?"

"That we're friends."

"Are we?"

It was the kind of challenging comeback she often thought of and never said, but judging by the way Jake's face had gone slack, she realized why she never spoke those things out loud. She hated seeing the hurt she'd caused.

Jake took a slow breath, steadying himself. When he spoke, the playfulness was gone from his tone. "You're right. I owe you an explanation."

Izzy felt her pulse quicken. She'd wanted him to explain, to apologize, to say something that would allow her to not hate him anymore, because she needed this easy banter with him so much more than the pain she'd been carrying around for weeks. Then Izzy's thoughts flew to Tamara, the super-accomplished college student he'd met at Monterey who happened to go to school, like, ten minutes away from where they were sitting. Suddenly, Izzy didn't want to hear another word.

"You don't owe me anything."

"Of course I do."

Izzy fidgeted in the sand. "Look, it's fine. Life happens, right? You were doing your thing, and I was . . ." *Doing nothing? Desperately waiting for a reply? Wondering what I'd done to make you disappear?* Izzy thought. "I was busy too."

"I wasn't too busy. I was avoiding you."

Ouch. Was every single person in her life going to stab her in the gut today? Was this her Ides of March?

Izzy pushed herself to her feet, dusting sand from the back of her jeans. "There's such a thing as too much honesty."

"Wait!" He shot up beside her. She thought for a second he was going to grab her hand, but he didn't. "Please."

"What?"

"I just . . ." He paused, puffing up his cheeks as he blew air through pursed lips. Then he slid the cap from his head and ran fingers through his dark curls. He glanced at her, furtively, like he didn't want her to catch him doing it, then pulled his hat back down over his forehead.

"Izzy," he began, then paused again. His reticence was infuriating. "I need to tell you—"

"Ooooooo!" A collective cry rose from the bonfire, cutting off whatever Jake was about to say. Down at the bonfire, an eerie silence had descended on the group, and though she was too far away to see specific faces, Izzy could tell that a circle two or three bodies deep had formed to the left of the fire. Above the roar of the angry ocean, Izzy caught staccato bursts of shouting.

"A fight," Jake said. "I should see what's going on."

Before he made it three steps down the dune, the circle of partygoers broke open, and two people emerged from the center, a guy and a girl. He was dragging her toward the parking lot.

Izzy had just registered Peyton's stark white pants when she heard Hunter's voice. "Come on, Peyton. We're leaving."

"Fuck off!" Peyton tried to shake her wrist free from his grasp, her movements unsteady and erratic, but he held firm.

Izzy raced down the side of the dune, Jake close behind. She wasn't sure what she could do to help, but she sensed that things were about to get ugly.

"You've had enough," Hunter said. He was pissed, a rarity for Hunter, for whom laid-back seemed to be an understatement. "And so have I."

They hadn't gone five steps when Alberto appeared at Peyton's side, clamping his hand over Hunter's. The crowd collectively sucked in a breath.

"I think Signorina Peyton can make her own mind."

TWENTY-ONE

HUNTER STIFFENED, SHOULDERS SQUARE. IF ALBERTO WAS trying to intimidate him, it clearly had the opposite effect. "Back off, dude."

"No, *dude*," Alberto said in disturbingly perfect English vernacular. "You back off." Then he began to pry Hunter's fingers from Peyton's wrist.

"I'm warning you . . ."

"What are you going to do?" Alberto asked. "Kill me?"

That was enough for Jake. He sprinted forward, the crowd parting as he advanced and making room for the fight everyone sensed was on the horizon.

"Hey!" Jake barked in an authoritative tone that Izzy had never heard before. His drill sergeant father bleeding through. "What's going on?"

"This is not your business." Alberto said to Jake. He never took his eyes from Hunter, but Alberto's grip on his hand relaxed slightly. Enough for Hunter to shake him free.

"He's been all over her," Hunter said, pulling Peyton behind him. "She's clearly drunk, and she needs to go home."

Alberto arched an eyebrow. "With you?"

"Yeah," Jake said. "With her boyfriend, as opposed to the stranger."

Alberto turned his pale blue eyes on Jake, who was more his equal in size. "You no trust me?"

"No, I don't." Jake never blinked, never faltered, and Izzy sensed that the marquee fight had shifted from Alberto versus Hunter to Alberto versus Jake.

They stared at each other in silence while the crowd whispered, and more than once Izzy thought she heard her name among the muted voices. Should she step in? Take control? They weren't fighting about her, but Alberto was living in her house—didn't that make him her responsibility?

Before Izzy could decide what to do, the beach was suddenly illuminated. For a split second, Izzy thought the police had arrived with spotlights and this whole confrontation would be over. But then she realized that the light was coming from higher up. A break in the clouds had revealed the moon, whose beams hit the circle like a theater's spotlight.

"What the hell is this?" Hunter held Peyton's arm up in the moonlight. Dangling from her wrist was a bracelet. Unlike her mom, Peyton wasn't much for jewelry, and the delicate gold chain with some kind of charm wasn't one that Izzy had seen before. She must have gotten it recently, but judging by the look of rage on Hunter's face, it hadn't come from him.

"It's nothing," Peyton said, wrenching her arm from Hunter's grasp. She hugged it to her chest possessively. "Just a gift."

Even if her eyes hadn't involuntarily darted to Alberto's face when she said it, Izzy would have known the bracelet came from him. Her stomach knotted in jealousy and shame. How stupid had she been to think she and Alberto had a connection? She was just a speed bump on Alberto's road to Peyton.

But her disappointment was nothing compared to Hunter's. His face contorted in pain as he staggered away from his girlfriend, visibly shaken.

"Dude, seriously?" he said, voice quivering with pent-up emotion. "You're going to throw away everything we have over this Italian clown?"

Instead of being offended, Alberto merely smiled at the insult, but Peyton's face fell, her eyes wild with fear. Clearly she'd never contemplated the consequences of her flirtation with Alberto.

"Hunter, no," she said, sounding more sober than she had moments before. "I didn't mean—"

"Yeah, you did, Pey," Hunter said, cutting her off. He stormed back to her, arm raised, and for a moment Izzy thought he was going to strike her. But his hand darted toward her wrist, ripping the charm bracelet away. It snapped, releasing into his hand, and then with one fluid movement, Hunter launched the bracelet into the darkness of the sand dunes.

There were tears in his eyes when Hunter turned back to Peyton. "This relationship is—"

Before Hunter could get the last word out of his mouth, Alberto rushed him, T-boning him from the side. The two bodies went sprawling into the wet sand, sending chunks of it flying into the crowd that surrounded the escalating argument like inmates around a prison-yard brawl. Alberto rolled on top of Hunter, pinning him to the sand, and punched him viciously in the face once, twice. Again and again.

The crowd yelled and hollered, some egging them on, some begging them to stop, while Peyton shrieked above the chaos, a wordless cry of terror. Izzy was rooted to the ground, unable to move or help or look away from Hunter's pummeled face. She could hear the squishy crunch from each impact of Alberto's fist, only partially drowned out by Peyton's screams. Everything around her slowed down—even the flames from the bonfire felt as if they flickered in slow motion—and the beatdown might have continued for ten seconds or ten hours for all she could tell.

Alberto's face had hardened, his blue eyes cold and focused. It was the same look she'd seen when he defended Kylie at the restaurant, the same detached efficiency with which he'd taken Greg Loomis to the ground and slowly, mercilessly, pressed on his windpipe. Then, he'd seemed like James Bond. Now, he just looked like a psychopath.

Suddenly Jake was on top of Alberto, pinning his arms as he tried to pull the Italian off his best friend. Alberto writhed beneath Jake's grasp, rage burning in his eyes as he tried to get back to his prey. Peyton had come to her senses, and with tears dragging black trails of mascara down her cheeks, she collapsed beside Hunter in the sand, weeping on his chest.

"Stand down!" Jake barked at the still-struggling Alberto. "He's had enough."

Alberto didn't respond, but his body stilled. His face relaxed from demonic rage back to his more normal and affable countenance.

Hunter, who at first had seemed unconscious, was able to sit up with some help from Peyton, who fawned over him through her heaving sobs, kissing the bloody pulp of his face with a pitiful devotion that made Izzy both sad and jealous. Two guys from the crowd helped him to his feet, and in the embers of the neglected bonfire, Izzy could see the extent of the damage: deep gashes over his nose and left cheek, an eye that had already swollen shut, and two cuts on his lower lip.

The party was over. A few responsible people kicked sand onto the fire, extinguishing the last of its flames, while others trudged over to the stash to retrieve the remains. Though he'd released Alberto, Jake still physically stood between him and Hunter, who was staggering back to the parking lot, leaning on Peyton.

"Imma sorry," Alberto said through an embarrassed smile. His hair flopped back into his face as the force of the fight overcame the structural integrity of his hair gel. "My Italian temper, it issa hot."

"Uh-huh," Jake said, having none of the apology. He fished a pair of keys from his pocket and handed them to Izzy. "Take my truck. Get him home."

She appreciated his ability to make decisions in a crisis. "Okay."

"*Grazie.*"

Jake ignored Alberto, focused on Izzy. "And we'll discuss all of this tomorrow."

* * *

The drive home felt as if it took twice as long as it had to get to the Ma-le'l Dunes just a couple of hours earlier. She and Alberto didn't speak, but unsaid words still filled the cab of Jake's pickup, crowding them from all sides. Questions and worries and pregnant statements that didn't necessarily have answers.

Izzy wondered how well she really knew the guy sitting in the passenger seat. She had thought she did. Thought that he understood her in return. That they had a true connection. Then the charm bracelet he'd given Peyton, and the fight. Alberto had seemed like an entirely different person. Was it just a matter of "lost in translation," or was she really that bad a judge of character?

She thought maybe he'd say something, try to explain his actions or defend himself, but as they drove, the silence deepened until it felt almost impenetrable, and if Izzy wanted answers to any of her questions, she didn't feel strong enough to break through the soundless wall between them.

Alberto didn't appear to sense the tension. Psycho James Bond had vanished, replaced by his usual affability, and he looked out the window, inspected his cuticles, brushed sand off the sleeve of his sweater as if nothing unusual had happened.

Maybe that's just how Italians are?

Izzy thought back to a scene from *A Room with a View*, where Lucy faints after witnessing an argument between two Italians escalate to a stabbing incident. Not that an old British movie based on an even older British book was the litmus test for all Italians in the twenty-first century, but it was her only frame of reference, and as such, Alberto's violent outburst might not have been so out of character if it had happened in Florence instead of Eureka.

Holy shit, she sounded like one of those interviewees on *Murder Will Speak* who had been the girlfriend or coworker or roommate of a serial killer, talking about how he was *basically* normal except for the fact that he wet the bed once a week. Or he was obsessed with lighting fires in the backyard. Or, to complete the Macdonald Triad, neighborhood pets seemed to disappear after he moved in. As if these were just slightly outlandish behaviors instead of clear signs of a dangerous and psychopathic mind. Was she actually trying to justify Alberto's violence?

She eased Jake's pickup to a stop in front of her house and cut the engine, finally daring to break the silence. "Are you okay?"

"*Sì, sì,*" Alberto said. He rubbed his palm over the knuckles on his left hand, which were raw and bloody, either from his own blood or from

Hunter's—she wasn't sure. "Imma sorry if I embarrass you."

That's what he's sorry about? "I'm not embarrassed. I'm worried about Hunter."

Alberto shrugged. "He will be fine."

"And Peyton?"

"Ah, the Peyton." He sighed, shaking his head. "She should feel-a much guilt."

"Why should she feel guilty?" *You're the one who beat the shit out of her boyfriend.*

"Because she flirt with me. She take-a the bracelet from me." He shrugged again. "She want-a the Hunter to be jealous."

Which probably wasn't entirely untrue, but it still made Izzy uncomfortable that Alberto took no responsibility for what had happened. He viciously attacked someone at a party, and if Jake hadn't been there to break it up, who knows what would have happened. Shouldn't that give him pause?

"I hope Hunter doesn't file charges," she said with a sigh, hoping that might impart the gravity of the situation. "With the police."

"He no do that," Alberto said with a curt shake of his head. "He no want people to know."

Izzy opened the door and climbed down. "His dad might feel otherwise." She imagined Mike's rage after getting a look at his son's face. He'd be on the phone to Eureka PD in seconds.

The house was brightly lit as she and Alberto approached the front door, unlocked per usual, but it was deathly quiet when they stepped inside.

"Hello?" Izzy called out. The metric ticks from a half-dozen clocks were her only response. "Anyone home?"

"Finally!" Footsteps pounded down the stairs as Parker double-timed his way to the ground floor. "Don't you check your phone?"

"Okay, Zoomer," she said, fishing her phone from the pocket of her vest. There was no reason to check your phone when there was no one who'd message you. But she immediately saw that she'd been wrong. She'd missed a dozen phone calls and even more texts, all from her mom.

"What happened?" she said, a cold chill making her fingers tingle. She could sense their mom's panic without listening to or reading any of the messages. Images of wine and pill bottles flashed into her mind. "Is Mom okay?"

"She's fine," Parker said, "but—"

"Dad?"

"Dad's working," Parker said, twisting his lips. "I guess."

"He's not in his workshop?"

Parker arched a brow, staring at her as if she'd just made the stupidest comment of the year. "Um, no."

"Then where's Mom?"

Parker sighed. "She's with Riley. At the police station."

"What?" Izzy cried. Whatever she'd been expecting, this wasn't it.

"The police?" Alberto said, almost at the same time.

"Yeah, they wanted to ask him some questions, and mom insisted on going with him."

Why would anyone want to ask Riley questions, least of all the police? "Why?"

"It's about his girlfriend. The bartender . . ." He snapped his fingers, grasping for her name.

"Kylie," Izzy said.

"Yeah." Parker took a deep breath. "She's dead."

TWENTY-TWO

IT WAS ALMOST DAWN. NOT THAT IZZY COULD TELL FROM THE dark sky outside her dormer window. Heavy clouds crowded upon each other, stretching as far as the horizon, a warning that the Storm of the Century was almost upon them, and the only reason Izzy knew it was five o'clock in the morning was because the grandfather clock in the corner of her room told her so.

Izzy hadn't slept. She sat up with Parker in the living room until well after two while he binged the new season of *Only Murders in the Building*. A questionable decision, given the news of Kylie's death, but Parker was a scientist, and his left-leaning brain had always compartmentalized emotions in a way Izzy envied. Nothing to be afraid of if you kept your feelings at arm's length.

Alberto had discreetly excused himself to bed soon after they'd gotten home while Parker filled Izzy in on what he knew. Which wasn't much. He'd been downstairs helping their mom clean up from dinner while Riley packed upstairs. The knock at their door had been sharp and unapologetic, as were the three officers who stood on the porch when Parker answered.

Riley was wanted for questioning in regard to the death of Kylie Fernández, whose body had been discovered earlier that evening. He wasn't being arrested or charged with anything, but he needed to accompany the officers to the station, they told him, whereupon they handcuffed him "for his safety and theirs" and led him out to a waiting squad car.

Izzy's mom had shifted into Mama Bear mode, peppering the officers with questions as she followed them outside. Because Riley wasn't a minor anymore, she wasn't allowed to accompany him in the squad car, so she'd hopped in the minivan and raced off behind them.

The texts and voicemails her mom had sent over the next hour had confirmed both what Parker knew and what Izzy suspected—that Riley was being questioned, not arrested; that her mom's mood was manic; and that Kylie's death was being investigated as a homicide.

Izzy's mind immediately flew to Greg Loomis, Kylie's ex who had threatened her at Woodley's. He seemed like the right brand of entitled, emasculated white dude who would murder his ex-girlfriend simply because she refused to get back together with him, and she hoped that the police were questioning him as well. Definitely a better suspect than her sex-obsessed yet slightly prissy brother.

She told her mom as much during one of their thirteen conversations over the next few hours. Parker's phone never so much as lit up from a text.

"Greg Loomis," her mom had repeated slowly, as if she was writing down the name with pen and paper.

"Yeah, he's a fisherman, I think," Izzy said. "Alberto, Pey, and I saw him threaten Kylie at work."

"How's Alberto?" her mom asked, ignoring the rest. "I hope he's not disturbed by all the police activity."

"No." *But he will be if Hunter's dad presses charges.*

"Good." She let out a slow breath, then launched into a fast-paced monologue. "I'm going to make your father call Bob Hanneman. He does real estate law, but it's better than nothing, and since they're old high school buddies, I'm hoping he'll be cheap. Or free."

"Where *is* Dad?"

"I don't know!" her mom had snapped, more viciously than the question warranted.

Parker's reaction to the same question made it seem as if no one in the family actually believed their dad was working at eleven o'clock on a Friday night.

"Mr. Hanneman will protect Riley," Izzy had said, calm and confident. She actually had no idea if her dad's friend was a capable attorney or not, but it was what her mom needed to hear. "Everything's going to be okay."

"Do you really think so?"

"Of course!"

Her mom had sighed. "I can't imagine what the neighbors must think, seeing my Ri led away in handcuffs."

"Insider trading," Izzy had joked, forcing a laugh. A snort from the other end of the line meant that her attempt at levity had worked. She doubled down. "Or maybe jaywalking. I hear they're cracking down on—"

"Your dad's here," her mom had interrupted, sounding more annoyed than relieved. "I'll call you back."

Izzy hadn't heard another word for an hour.

Well, not from her parents, at least. She had gotten a few texts.
From Jake.

Home from ER. Hunter needed eighteen stitches.

Peyton's sleeping it off.

How are you?

They were the first texts he'd sent her in weeks, and she was actually relieved to have someone to talk to while Parker binged Hulu.

Riley's at the police station for questioning.

A girl he dated was found murdered.

Jake's response had come immediately.

Are you there alone? I'm walking over.

Which could have seemed creepy but actually felt kind of sweet. Something Peyton would have done. Once.

Parker's here.

She almost added "And Alberto" but decided against it because of their standoff. The next reply came slowly, as if Jake had typed, deleted, and retyped it several times before he settled on a single word.

Good.

Another pause.

Want to make sure you're OK.

She wasn't. But that wasn't exactly new.

I will be.

She thought about texting him back to prolong the conversation but wasn't sure what to say. Instead, she followed Parker upstairs and tried to sleep, with no luck. She just lay there, listening for any sound that might be her parents and her brother coming home. Finally, just after five o'clock, she heard the front door open.

Izzy raced down to the second floor and found her dad trudging up the stairs. He looked exhausted. Not just from the day but from life. He couldn't meet her eyes when he passed her on the landing.

"Were you at the station? Did you see him? Did you get a lawyer? Are they coming home?" Izzy asked, not even pausing for a breath between questions. She was desperate for information, even though she suspected her mom would be the first to have any.

"Yes. No. Yes. And eventually." Her dad yawned, as if it were just a normal day. "I'm tired, Izzy. Can we talk tomorrow?"

"Um, sure."

He kept his eyes glued to the carpet runner as he skulked to his room.

It was another hour before Izzy heard the front door creak open again.

"Mom!" Izzy cried as she swung around the artichoke at full speed on her way downstairs. The old wood newel groaned under the stress.

"Slow down, Izzy," her mom scolded in a weary voice. "How many times do I have to tell you that you're going to snap that thing in half one of these days? Fall downstairs and break your neck?"

Izzy threw her arms around her mom's neck and squeezed. "About a million times."

Behind them, a red-eyed Riley sank into the sofa, elbows on his knees, head in his hands. His fingers trembled as he sucked in a ragged breath. It was the first time she'd ever seen his unflinching self-confidence crumble.

"Ri, are you okay?"

"No," he said honestly. He looked up at her, then swallowed twice. "No, I'm not okay."

"I'm so sorry."

"I can't believe it," he shook his head, voice quavering. "I can't believe she's gone."

"Your brother's not being charged with anything in the death of that woman," her mom said.

"Fuck, Mom!" Riley exploded. "Her name was Kylie, and I cared about her and now she's dead and they think I might have . . ."

For the first time in Izzy's life, her mom let the use of a four-letter word go unchecked in her home. "They think nothing of the sort." She sat down beside him on the sofa and scratched his back, just as she'd done when they were children. "If they did, you'd be in jail right now."

Izzy had listened to enough murder podcasts to know that just because they let her brother go didn't mean they'd crossed him off the suspect list, but it was a good sign.

"Besides," her mom continued, "once they pick up that Greg Loomis, I'm sure it will be case closed."

"You told the police about what happened at Woodley's?" Izzy asked. She wasn't sure which image from that afternoon haunted her more: the wild look in Greg's eyes when he confronted Kylie or the cold one in Alberto's as he stepped on Greg's throat.

Her mom nodded. "He was already on their list, but they were having trouble tracking him down."

"He'd better hope the cops find him before I do," Riley said.

Izzy lowered her chin to hide a smirk. While she appreciated the emotion behind the threat, Riley would be no match for the burly Greg in a fight. If Riley even knew how to fight. Which she was pretty sure he didn't.

"Did they tell you what happened?" Izzy asked, changing the subject.

Riley shook his head. "They only asked questions. Where I'd been. When I'd seen her last. Over and over."

"You told them how she'd dumped you?" Izzy asked. He flinched at her characterization of his last interaction with the victim, and Izzy immediately regretted her choice of words. "I mean, canceled your date?"

Riley nodded. "Showed them the texts. They seemed really confused. And I'm not sure if that made me look better or worse."

"It made you look truthful," Izzy's mom said. "And that can only be a good thing."

Riley didn't look so sure. "I hope so."

He yawned, wide but silent, which triggered the same reaction in Izzy. Their mom jumped to her feet, her energy unaffected by a sleepless night.

"Riley, I'm going to make you some tea. Izzy," she pointed to the stairs, "get some sleep."

Izzy wasn't about to argue. She didn't want to answer questions about the bonfire.

As she started up the stairs to the second floor, Izzy heard a creak on the floorboard above. It was a creak she knew well, the top step of the staircase, the one she'd learned to avoid by swinging around the newel post. She thought maybe Parker or her dad was coming down to check on Riley, but as she ascended, she caught movement from the corner of her eye.

Then the door to Alberto's room gently clicked.

TWENTY-THREE

THE HOUSE WAS QUIET AGAIN WHEN IZZY WOKE UP. NOT THE pregnant, uncomfortable silence of last night, when all the lights had been on with only Parker home, but the serene midday stillness of an empty house. No creaking floorboards, no muffled voices drifting up through the vents, nothing.

She wanted to roll over and bask in the glorious solitude, but a buzz from her phone reminded her that real-life shit had gone down with both her family and her friends last night, and sticking her head in the sand was not going to be an option. She picked up her phone and found a slew of texts.

The first two were from her mom: one to let Izzy know that her dad was taking Riley to meet with Bob Hanneman, with Parker tagging along for moral support, the second to say she was driving Alberto to urgent care to get his hand looked at after his fall on the beach last night.

Fall on the beach. Okay, that was a lie she could live with. Sorta. She didn't need her mom knowing that the guy living under their roof had an explosive temper.

At least not yet.

The next texts were from Jake, to say that he'd walked over to get his truck with his spare key and had checked in on her, but her brother had said she was still asleep. Izzy's smile surprised her. *I guess I'm not angry at him anymore.*

The most recent message was from Peyton, a tearful frownie face followed by two words:

I'm sorry.

Izzy wasn't sure how to respond, so she simply sent a heart in return and tucked her phone into the pocket of her pajamas. They could all wait for actual responses while Izzy took advantage of an empty house to make herself some lunch and eat in exquisite quiet.

She was only two bites into a microwaved slab of her mom's chicken enchilada casserole when the doorbell rang.

Normally, Izzy would have played possum. Odds were good it was a delivery that would simply be left at the door. Besides, girls who opened the door to strangers while they were home alone became victims profiled on *Murder Will Speak.*

But what if it was Jake? He might be worried since she hadn't texted back and have driven over to check on her again. Her heart rate quickened as she hurried through the dining room to the front door.

The bell was just ringing for the second time when she peeked around the lace curtains that covered the stained-glass window beside the door. Standing on the front porch were the two representatives from the Exchange Programs division of the Bureau of Educational and Cultural Affairs.

Shit. Had they heard that Riley had been questioned in regard to a murder? Probably. And now they were coming to remove Alberto from their home.

Would that really be so bad?

Izzy couldn't say that it would be. Without waiting to think it through, she unbolted the door and swung it wide.

"Can I help you?" she said, trying to sound as if she had no clue what was going on.

Instead of launching into a litany of hosting regulations that the Bell family had violated, Loretta reached into the inner pocket of her jacket and removed a thin billfold, flipping it open just like they did on TV.

"Miss Bell, my name is *Agent* Loretta Michaels."

Agent? "From the Bureau of Educational and Cultural Affairs," Izzy said. She didn't even look at the ID.

"Not that bureau," Agent Michaels said with a wry smile. "This is my partner, Agent Stolberg."

Izzy blinked at Agent Michaels's billfold, which clearly read "Federal Bureau of Investigation."

The FBI? She'd never seen a real FBI identification before, and though this could have been a fake, Izzy was swayed by the authority in both Agent Michaels's demeanor and her voice.

"What's going on?" she asked, her body tense.

Agent Michaels peeked past Izzy, as if ascertaining they were alone. "I know you're the only one home, but may we come inside?"

They know I'm home alone. Had they been watching the house?

This all made Izzy incredibly uneasy. She started to close the door. "I'm sorry. I'm not comfortable letting you in."

Agent Michaels gripped the edge of the solid oak door before Izzy could close it all the way. She didn't push it open but held the door ajar with one arm. "Your family could be in danger."

"From what?"

"From a very insidious man."

A very insidious man wasn't particularly specific, but it gave Izzy pause enough that she loosened her grip on the door, allowing Agent Michaels to swing it open again.

"May we come in?" she asked, but this time she didn't wait for Izzy to answer, stepping over the threshold, her partner close behind. Izzy had to admit her curiosity was piqued, and since the only other choice was to forcibly remove two FBI agents from her living room, she decided to hear what they had to say.

Agent Michaels didn't make her wait long. "We're investigating a series of crimes in both the Los Angeles and San Francisco areas," she began as she sat down on the sofa, "and believe the suspect may have recently moved north."

Los Angeles *and* San Francisco.

It couldn't be.

Mags and Amelia *had* said there was evidence he'd moved north.

Could it be?

"The Casanova Killer?" The words raced out of her mouth before she could stop them, and though Agents Michaels and Stolberg were as stony faced as the best poker players on the planet, the latter's eyelids fluttered at the mention of the serial killer's nickname.

Agent Michaels wasn't willing to confirm or deny Izzy's question. "We are tracking a suspect wanted for questioning in a series of murders."

Izzy felt the back of her neck go clammy. She didn't need an official explanation. She already knew why they had come to her house. "You think it's Alberto."

Again, neither agent denied her statement.

"The agency is following hundreds of leads," Agent Stolberg said. "This is one of them."

"Alberto's only been in this country for a couple of weeks." It felt surreal to be defending the foreign exchange student in her house from accusations of murder. "The Casanova Killer's been active since last fall."

Agent Michaels's left eyebrow lifted a millimeter. "Been following the case?"

Admitting that she was obsessed with a sexually deviant serial killer would be a bad look. "I, uh, like true crime."

"I've heard that's popular with your generation," Agent Stolberg said, unable to suppress the tinge of disdain in his voice. Izzy wasn't entirely sure which generation she belonged to, but she knew a dis when she heard it.

"It's literally all over the news, you know. It's not some morbid fascination." Well, not *just* some morbid fascination.

Agent Michaels cleared her throat. "Regardless of his name, we have reason to believe that a possible suspect in a recent string of murders might have been on a flight from San Francisco to Arcata on the night of August sixteenth." She still watched Izzy closely. What was she looking for? "You were at the airport that evening."

Though it wasn't a question, Izzy nodded meekly in response.

"Eyewitness accounts describe the suspect as tall, five foot eleven to six foot one, with medium brown hair and greenish or hazel eyes."

Izzy blew a long stream of air through pursed lips as a wave of relief washed over her. Other than the height, that didn't describe Alberto at all.

But apparently Agent Michaels wasn't done yet. "Though we have reason to believe his appearance could be altered."

"Oh."

"Several passengers meet the general description, and we're following up with all of them."

"Oh!" Then this wasn't specifically about Alberto, they were just checking in on all the tall men who got off that plane. Seemed legit. "You don't *actually* think Alberto is the Casanova Killer."

Again, Agent Michaels's eyebrow quivered. "We are considering a range of suspects at this time."

A new thought flashed into Izzy's mind. One that might exonerate her brother completely. "Is Kylie Fernández one of his victims?"

"We are not at liberty to discuss the details of an ongoing investigation," Agent Stolberg said with all the enthusiasm of a child reciting a math formula in school.

That was a "yes." "So my brother isn't a suspect."

Agent Stolberg took a deep breath. "We are not at liberty to discuss—"

But his partner cut him off. "No, he isn't." Agent Stolberg shot his partner an annoyed look, but she ignored him. "We believe Kylie Fernández was already dead before your brother received her text."

"Oh." Izzy felt a wave of relief. Riley wasn't a suspect, and once the FBI found their Casanova Killer, he'd be completely off the hook. That was a good reason to offer an assist. "What do you want from me?"

"Have you noticed anything unusual about your houseguest?" Agent Stolberg said, finally getting to the point. He didn't share his partner's epic patience.

Izzy snorted. She was pretty sure all Italians were a little unusual.

Agent Michaels pounced. "Why did you laugh, Miss Bell?"

"I . . . I'm sorry." Izzy felt her face flush. "Alberto's European. They're all a little unusual."

"Anything more specific?" she pressed.

"Like an explosive temper?"

Agent Michaels tilted her head. "Perhaps. Though that's circumstantial."

"What should I be looking for?"

Agent Stolberg flattened his lips, pressing them into a wrinkled line. "Serial spree killers don't usually wear a shirt advertising their crimes."

"Would it make it easier for you to catch them if they did?" Izzy quipped. Agent Stolberg was clearly the Bad Cop in their professional role-play, and Izzy was already tired of his condescension. They wanted to ask her questions, and she was doing them a favor by answering. He could park the snark outside.

The joke made Agent Michaels crack a smile, at least. "Nice one."

"Thanks."

"But though that would help, we have other, less obvious clues to look for."

"Like?"

"Like do you remember where Alberto was Thursday night between the hours of ten and midnight?" Agent Stolberg asked. He smiled at Izzy, like a cat who had just cornered a mouse. Who was the suspect, Alberto or her?

She shrugged. "Home? There's not a lot to do around here at night."

Agent Stolberg leaned closer. "But you can verify his whereabouts?"

"He doesn't wear a GPS," she blurted out. His question was ludicrous. "Why can't you just check the dates on his passport? If he arrived in the US after the Casanova Killer's spree began, then he's not your suspect."

Now it was Agent Stolberg's turn to snort. "You watch too much TV. We can't just waltz into his room and go through his things."

Izzy rolled her eyes. "Then get a search warrant or something. Isn't that what you guys do?"

"It's not that easy for us." Agent Michaels sighed, her first show of emotion.

Izzy didn't see why not. If they honestly thought Alberto was a serial killer, searching his stuff was the easiest way to either exonerate or convict him. Except he was a foreign national. So maybe the rules for these things were different. Was that why they were pumping Izzy for information?

Instead of explaining, Agent Michaels fished her phone out of her jacket pocket. She opened her photo album, scrolled through a few pictures, then turned the screen up to Izzy.

"Have you seen any jewelry that might match this? We believe the killer took several pieces from the body of Daniela Margolis."

Izzy recognized the name immediately. The third known victim, Daniela Margolis, had met the Casanova Killer at a busy bar in downtown Los Angeles several months ago. The bartender who served them gave one of the better descriptions of Casanova's MO. He'd joined Daniela at the bar, sitting several stools away with people between them. She was alone, and after making eye contact and some wordless flirtations back and forth, he'd gradually moved closer to her as others vacated their stools. They'd talked for a few minutes at the noisy, packed bar before Casanova had apparently suggested they leave. He paid both tabs in cash and left with Daniela a little after midnight.

Her roommate initially reported her missing forty-eight hours later. Three days after that, her remains were found in a dumpster in the garage of her apartment building. She'd been strangled and sexually assaulted, either before, during, or after her death.

Now Izzy was staring at a close-up photo of an ear. There was no blood anywhere, no signs of violence or trauma other than that the blond-highlighted hair and darker roots that surrounded the ear were tangled and knotted. But the ear and the skin of the victim's skull and neck were an unnatural shade of brownish-gray, almost as if this photo had been shot in sepia, except for one bright yellow piece of jewelry dangling from the lobe: a gold heart on a loop.

"Her roommate described a matching bracelet the victim always wore. It was not recovered from the crime scene."

Missing jewelry wasn't mentioned in any of the *Murder Will Speak* episodes about the Casanova Killer, but the authorities would have been tight-lipped about evidence. And Izzy couldn't hide her surprise at seeing the heart. She hadn't really been close enough to Peyton on the beach, but she remembered a flash of gold reflecting the bonfire flames and the sense that she was looking at a single-charm bracelet. Could it be the match to this earring?

"What?" Agent Michaels asked sharply. She hadn't missed a single emotion that had flashed across Izzy's face in the last ten seconds. "Do you recognize it?"

Izzy shook her head. "No," she said truthfully.

"You're sure?"

She wasn't. "I'm sorry."

Agent Michaels stared hard at Izzy for longer than was comfortable, and Izzy fought the overwhelming urge to look away by reminding herself that she hadn't done anything wrong and that there was no evidence linking Alberto to these heinous crimes. The idea that she had a serial killer sleeping in her house was outright ludicrous.

Wasn't it?

"Okay, then." Agent Michaels stood up, followed immediately by her partner. She whipped a business card from her pocket and dropped it on the coffee table. "If you think of anything, please call."

"I will," Izzy croaked as the agents filed out. She stood in the doorway until they got into their black SUV and drove away.

TWENTY-FOUR

IZZY SLOWLY CLOSED THE DOOR, THEN PRESSED THE SMALL OF her back against the cool, sturdy wood, breathing deep and slow until the sound of blood racing through her veins faded from her ears. As soon as her heart rate calmed, she whipped her phone out of her pocket and texted Peyton. She needed to know what that bracelet looked like.

How are you?

Thankfully, she didn't need to wait long for an answer. Peyton began typing immediately. She must have been on her phone already.

Hungover.

Did you get my text?

I'm really sorry about last night.

While Izzy appreciated Peyton's contrition, she was pretty sure Hunter deserved it more. Thankfully, it seemed like whatever spell Alberto had cast on Peyton was wearing off.

I know.

I'm glad you're feeling better this morning.

Then, before Peyton could respond, Izzy asked the question burning a hole in her brain.

The bracelet Alberto gave you.

Do you remember what it looked like?

She could have just asked Alberto. If he was as innocent as she kept telling herself he was, then the bracelet was just some trinket he picked up in San Francisco and had absolutely no connection to Daniela Margolis or the Casanova Killer. Yet the idea of confronting him about it tied her stomach up in knots. What if she were wrong?

It took Peyton forever to answer, which meant she'd either gotten distracted or she wasn't sure how to respond. And when a text did arrive, it wasn't what Izzy wanted to see.

Can we not talk about it please?

I know.

He's the last person you want to think about right now.

I'm sorry.

But it's important.

I SAID I DON'T WANT TO TALK ABOUT IT

All caps. Peyton was done talking about Alberto.

Izzy sighed. Hunter had also been up close and personal with that bracelet, but it felt too soon to ask him, especially after he spent the night in urgent care getting stitched up. There was one other person who might have caught a detailed look at the charm before Hunter launched it into the sand. Someone who'd also been completely sober. That was about as reliable as a witness could get.

She quickly opened Jake's last text.

Question.

Did you get a look at the bracelet Peyton was wearing last night?

The one Hunter chucked into the dunes?

Like Peyton, Jake began typing his response almost immediately.

Not really.

There was a charm on it, I think.

Gold maybe?

Ugh. Not enough.

Could it have been a heart?

She knew the question was leading, but she needed closure.

Maybe? I honestly don't know.

Why?

Why, indeed. That was an explanation she'd prefer to give in person.

I'll tell you later.

I'm free now.

I'd like to see you.

We didn't finish our conversation.

I have something I really need to tell you.

Izzy didn't have time to deal with Jake's guilt. Or his admission that he was dating someone else. She eyed the staircase. There was something she needed to do right away, while Alberto was gone.

It's not that easy for us, Agent Michaels had said.

It wasn't that easy for the FBI. But what about for Izzy? She had a unique position in the investigation of the Casanova Killer: if he was truly living in her house, Izzy could search his things without legal ramification.

Like every other door in the Bell house except Izzy's attic, there was no lock to Alberto's room. His door was closed, but as Izzy twisted the handle it gave easily, swinging open into Riley's old bedroom.

It was the first time Izzy had been inside since Alberto's arrival, and though he'd been with the Bells for several days, he'd hardly settled in. His single duffel bag sat on the easy chair in the corner, puffed up as if all of Alberto's clothes were still inside. The furniture was exactly where Riley had left it, which wasn't too out of the ordinary since there wasn't much in the room to begin with, but even the desk chair sat pushed into the old writing desk beside the window, as it had been when Alberto arrived.

The bed was meticulously made, not a single piece of dirty laundry had been flung onto the floor or over the back of a chair, and the room was spotless. No dust, no dirt, no cobwebs, no fuzzballs. It was as if the bedroom had been professionally cleaned and then hermetically sealed.

Izzy looked around aimlessly. She wasn't sure what she was searching for, or even if she was searching for any *thing* in particular. It was more like a feeling she couldn't kick, a simmering unease in her gut. Would she find the Casanova Killer's smoking gun just casually tossed over the back of a chair in the room directly below her own? Unlikely. But maybe the lack of evidence might just prove—both to herself and to Agents Michaels and Stolberg—that Alberto Bianchi was exactly who he said he was.

Fingertips vibrating with a mix of anxiety and fear, Izzy hurried across the room to the duffel bag, making careful note of its exact position on the chair. Years of listening to true crime podcasts and streaming police-procedural-series reruns had primed her to keep track of details. She started to unzip the bag when a sunbeam glistened off a single strand of Alberto's sun-streaked hair that lay over the top of the handles.

Human hair got everywhere. It was one of the easiest pieces of DNA evidence for crime scene investigators to bag and tag, and was instrumental in solving more cases than most laypeople were aware, so it could have just been a coincidence that this single golden strand had fallen where it had, dislodged from Alberto's head while he was getting dressed that morning. Yet looking around the polished oak floorboards, she didn't see another one like it.

Izzy plucked the hair between her forefinger and thumb, then carefully laid it on the nightstand before sliding the zipper noiselessly open.

Inside, the clothes were neatly folded, as carefully arranged as the room, shirts and shorts in one pile, socks and underwear in another. She slipped her hand into one of the two side pouches. It was empty, but the other side held a flat object about the size of a small notebook. Alberto's Italian passport.

Izzy's whole body relaxed as she stared at the *Unione Europea Repubblica Italiana Passaporto*. A regular old EU passport. This would prove Alberto Bianchi was still in Florence, Italy, when the Casanova Killer began his spree. She flipped open the back end, where all the pages of entry and exit stamps would be, and found exactly what she was looking for: a United States entry stamp in red ink with the date Aug. 11.

She smiled as she gazed at Alberto's exoneration, laughing at her own silliness in thinking for even a moment that her Italian exchange student was actually a serial killer, and casually opened the first page to Alberto's passport photos. Then her stomach dropped.

The ID photos looked as if someone had taken a razor blade to them. Harsh scrapes to the iridescent laminate didn't cut all the way through but marred parts of both the main ID picture and the overexposed version on the opposite page. You could still see Alberto's face, and a stranger would be able to identify him by his hair, the shape of his jaw, and those piercing blue eyes, but parts of the nose, mouth, and cheeks had certainly been damaged. Holding the photo at arm's length, she couldn't actually see Alberto's face in it.

This passport belonged to Alberto Bianchi. That was clear beyond a shadow of a doubt, but could Izzy swear that this passport belonged to *her* Alberto Bianchi?

No. She could not.

While Izzy was still processing this information, she heard a deep creak from the staircase. The fifth step from the bottom, and whoever stepped on it was heavier than Izzy's mom. Or Parker or Riley. More like Alberto's size. If so, she'd have only seconds to get out of the room before he saw her.

Izzy shoved the passport back into the inner pocket, zipped the duffel bag, then hurriedly placed it in the exact position she'd noted when she entered the room, squarely centered on the chair with the corners poofed up so the bag almost looked as if it were inflated. She started to leave, then remembered the hair.

Realizing that she wouldn't have time to get out of the room before Alberto saw her, she made a rash decision. She darted back to the night-stand, gingerly picked up the hair, and laid it back in place over the zipper, then crawled onto Alberto's bed and flopped back against the pillows, pretending to be asleep.

A heartbeat later, the door swung open.

It was a violent movement, one that almost felt as if it was meant to startle a potential intruder, and Izzy didn't need to fake her shock. Her heart was even pounding as she sat up and found Alberto glaring down at her.

The look on his face made Izzy want to recoil into her own body. His eyes were sharp, nostrils flared in rage, and when he reared back his arm, she almost thought he was going to hit her. It was the same look she'd seen on Woodley's patio as he loomed over Greg Loomis and then the next day illuminated by the flickering bonfire while Alberto pounded the shit out of Hunter in the sand, but Alberto's rage only lasted an instant this time before it was replaced with a wide-eyed, opened-mouthed gasp of surprise.

"Izz-*ee*! What are you-a doing inna my bed?"

Izzy blushed for the second time that hour. She was thankful that her pale skin made her emotional reactions so transparent: they were helping sell her innocence.

"Sorry!" she squealed, hopping to her feet. "I was waiting for you and . . . I guess I just fell asleep."

"Waiting for-a me?" Alberto's eyes darted to the chair that held his duffel bag, resting on it for half a second before returning to her face. "Why?"

She could have told him the truth, detailed the visit by Agents Michaels and Stolberg, shared her own momentary suspicions that he might, in fact, be the most wanted man in all of North America. Alberto Bianchi the Florentine exchange student might have gotten a good laugh over being mistaken for a serial killer. But after discovering that damaged passport, the same fluttering unease that had inspired Izzy to search Alberto's room in the first place was now screaming at her to keep her damn mouth shut.

"To talk." She let her eyes fall to the floor, highlighting her embarrassment. "About Peyton."

Jealousy seemed like a plausible reason that Izzy would be camped out in Alberto's bedroom, and he bought the excuse right away, smiling broadly as if her reaction was expected.

"You are angry with me, *si*?"

"Not *angry*," Izzy said coyly. She was channeling Peyton, using all the body language tricks and vocal intonations in her friend's arsenal. They'd already succeeded in seducing Alberto once, maybe the tactics would work again for Izzy? At least long enough for her to get out of that bedroom.

"Jealous."

"Maybe." She glanced up at him from beneath lowered lashes.

"Ah. Women are so predictable."

Izzy fought the urge to roll her eyes. "I thought we had a connection."

Alberto stepped toward her, eyelids half closed. "Oh, my Izz-*ee*. We do have the connection, you and I."

"And Peyton?"

"She issa nothing."

Despite the situation, a little petty piece of Izzy thrilled at hearing him say it. How fucking pathetic was that?

"Peyton is a silly-a little girl playing silly-a little girl games," Alberto continued. His face hardened, jaw clenched, and he spoke through his teeth. "And silly little girls need to learn a lesson."

Izzy didn't like the edge to Alberto's voice, or the fact that his accent seemed to slip for a second. "I shouldn't have come," she said, attempting to shoulder her way past him. "I'm sorry."

Alberto looped an arm around her waist and spun her back around. He pressed his body against hers, and while holding her with one incredibly strong arm, he brought his other hand to her face, tracing her chin with his thumb. "No, Izz-*ee*. I want you to-a stay."

Izzy swallowed. There was something hypnotic about staring up into Alberto's unnaturally blue eyes. She felt her body relax into his, her weight being taken on by his strong frame, and all her concerns about who and what he was seemed to melt into a puddle on the floor.

"Is this what-a you wanted?" His fingers trailed up to her cheek before slipping around the back of her neck. As they snaked into her loose hair, his thumb pressed against her throat. Not hard, but with enough pressure that it triggered her fear response. Izzy stiffened, and she rocked back on her heels, disentangling herself from Alberto's embrace.

"I . . . I don't know." Which wasn't entirely a lie. Though it should have been.

"Ah." Alberto straightened up, eyes wide and laughing again. The seducer was gone. "Maybe *that* issa the problem."

"Maybe." Izzy forced a smiled as she backed out of the room, then turned and walked calmly to the attic door.

But all she really wanted to do was run.

TWENTY-FIVE

FOR THE FIRST TIME IN HER LIFE, IZZY LOCKED THE DOOR TO the attic.

The dead bolt was a remnant of an earlier time, when the attic had been used for storage, long before her dad had renovated it for Izzy, and though the lock had always existed, she'd never before felt the need to use it. Riley had been the dramatic one, always blockading Parker out of their shared room with theatrical piles of furniture when they were kids. Parker would respond with a mathematical formula and a roll of blue painter's tape, dividing the room into equal portions. Which was about as dramatic as Parker ever got.

Their anger was always short-lived: by the time one of her parents coaxed the barricader out of the room, or peeled up the blue tape, the fight was over. Izzy had always been as afraid of Riley's outbursts and Parker's levelheaded retaliations as she was of her mom's erratic moods, and her placating personality meant that she'd never fought with anyone in her home, and thus never needed to lock anyone out.

Until now.

Her heart was still racing as she sat down on the edge of her bed; the rush of blood made her dizzy. She took a deep breath through her nose, held it for a three count, then blew the air out through her mouth. Again. And again. Izzy repeated the deep breathing until her pulse returned to normal and her anxiety stilled.

Now she could think.

Was Alberto the Casanova Killer?

Logically, it made no sense. She'd seen his passport with her own eyes. Defaced or not, Alberto wasn't even in the country during the majority of the murders, and Agent Michaels admitted that they were merely following up on a variety of leads. This could all have been Izzy's murder podcast–soaked mind getting carried away with circumstantial evidence.

And yet . . . she couldn't ignore the menace she'd just felt in Alberto's room. Whether her impression of him had changed since the incident at the bonfire, or she was finally seeing him without a hormonal haze affecting her judgment, it was difficult to say, but what if the affable, smiling version was just an act and this angry, rage-filled person was the real Alberto? He didn't have to be a killer to still be a danger to her family.

The damaged passport. What could have caused that other than intentional vandalism? And if so, why would Alberto want to slice up the face on his only form of identification?

Because it's not really him.

How hard would it have been? Izzy and her family had never met Alberto, and they'd only seen a few photos. If someone about his size and about his age were to steal his passport . . . it wouldn't be that difficult to impersonate an Italian foreign exchange student. Especially one who had managed to not speak more than a few words of Italian since he'd arrived at their house.

No wonder his accent felt so over the top: it was an act. A bad Chico Marx impression. His pants were too short because they weren't *his* pants at all.

But what about the real Alberto Bianchi? If theirs was an imposter who had stolen luggage and a passport, wouldn't their true owner have gone to the authorities immediately when he realized he'd been robbed?

Not if he was dead.

Izzy's fingertips began to buzz again, a mix of horror and excitement as the pieces came together in her mind. Another unsolved murder in the Bay Area, not a woman but a male body fished out of the San Francisco Bay. Jake had mentioned it at lunch, and Mags and Amelia had dropped a reference to it into a recent *Murder Will Speak* episode.

Izzy dug her phone out of her pocket and pulled up her favorite podcast. She didn't even bother to pop in earbuds but let the episode play through the phone's speaker.

"And did you hear about this other body they pulled out of the Bay?" Mags said. "Totally unrelated to the Casanova Killer. Body was male, but here's the fucked-up part: the face had been removed and the tips of the dude's fingers chopped off."

Amelia whistled. "That's seriously fucked-up I hope it was portmortem?"

"*He* hopes it was portmortem." Then they both laughed, which was probably more charming the first time Izzy listened to it but now felt ominous. "But it sounds like an attempt to prevent a positive identification of the body. Local authorities have declined to comment."

Izzy stopped the playback before it shifted to another topic. *An attempt to prevent a positive identification of the body.* That would track with Alberto's mutilated passport. He'd killed the real Alberto and then taken his place on the flight to Eureka. *Regardless of his name, we have reason to believe that a possible suspect in a recent string of murders might have been on a flight from San Francisco to Arcata on the night of August sixteenth.* Agents Michaels and Stolberg weren't tracking several suspects, Izzy suddenly knew—they were only tracking one. Alberto.

Yet they hadn't arrested him, hadn't even taken him in for questioning. Why? If they suspected that Alberto was an impostor, why leave him free on the streets, where he could possibly kill again?

They must not be sure. A DNA sample should prove Alberto's guilt or innocence. The girls had discussed that too. Izzy scrolled back to an earlier episode, beginning playback a few minutes in, after the sponsors.

Amelia, the legal expert, was mid-sentence. "—and according to the web page for California's attorney general, 'As of January first, 2009, adults arrested for any felony offense are subject to DNA collection.'"

"So they could just, like, arrest someone for a DUI and swab his cheek?"

"Not that simple. DUIs are categorized as misdemeanors. They'd need to arrest a suspect for something more serious."

Mags snorted. "Like murder and sexual assault?"

"Well yeah, but then they'd need an actual suspect and probable cause, and they're desperate not to fuck that part up because who wants to release a notorious serial killer on a technicality? Even if they had an idea of who this guy was, they'd need direct evidence connecting him to one of the Casanova Killer murders, and so far there just isn't any."

"Any loopholes?" Mags asked. "Any chance this guy is killing every other week because he feels like he can't be touched?"

"There's always an element of egotism," Amelia said. "But what loopholes do you mean?"

"Like, could he be in the government? Or a foreign national? I got rear-ended by a consulate car once, and my insurance company basically told me I was shit out of luck because they had no jurisdiction."

"If they force a DNA sample and they're wrong, it would be a diplomatic nightmare."

Izzy paused the playback. Holy shit. No wonder the FBI was so cagey. They weren't positive enough about Alberto's identity to arrest him. They'd probably been in contact with Italy already in an attempt to get some identifying factors from the body they pulled out of the Bay, but that would take a while.

Which is why they'd come to her. If Izzy could supply the FBI with even a shred of evidence, they could arrest Alberto immediately without endangering the case against him. And every day the Casanova Killer was a free man, there was the possibility that he would kill again.

Had killed again? Izzy thought of Kylie, how she'd flirted with Alberto at lunch the other day, even slipping him her phone number on the check. Was that the same day she dumped Riley? If not, it was soon after. Either way, she needed to tell Agent Michaels.

Whose business card was still downstairs on the coffee table.

Where Alberto could see it.

Izzy bolted out of bed and down the stairs. When she reached the main staircase, she looped her left arm around the artichoke newel as she'd done a billion times before and swung her body to make the 180-degree turn down the stairs.

Only unlike the other billion times, the newel post didn't hold her weight. She felt something give as she spun around, and then instead of the stairs beneath her feet, she was airborne, falling.

Then everything went black.

TWENTY-SIX

"IZZY? IZZY, ARE YOU OKAY?"

She could her hear name being called, faint and muted, as if the voice came from far away. Yet Izzy felt a hand gripping her arm, fingers digging into her flesh with fierce desperation.

"Izzy?" Her mom.

"Don't move her." Riley's voice now.

Ragged breaths tickled her face, and as she forced her eyelids to open, she saw her mom hovering upside down, with Riley below, a hand on their mom's shoulder.

"Izzy!" Relief in her mom's voice. Why?

"Yeah?" she managed. She blinked, trying to get her bearings, and realized that she was lying on her back, head down, on the staircase.

Her mom placed a hand behind Izzy's neck, supporting her weight. "Are you hurt?"

"Don't think so." She wiggled her hands and feet, then turned her head from side to side. Other than a rapidly growing headache and some sore joints, she was fine. "What happened?"

"That goddamn artichoke," her mom spat viciously as she helped Izzy sit up. "How many times have I told you not to mess with that thing?"

"The artichoke?" Izzy looked up toward the oblong vegetable at the top of the staircase. Or where it used to be. An empty spot at the corner of the railing was all she found. Below her, over Riley's shoulder, she located the wooden decoration where it had rolled to a stop against the front door. It had completely snapped off the top of the newel post.

"That's impossible," she said, eyeing the splintered base.

"*Cosa c'è?* I hear boom!" Alberto's head popped over the upstairs railing. "Is everyone—" He gasped at the sight of Izzy on the stairs. "Izz-*ee*! Are you oh-kay?" He articulated each syllable as if he were speaking to a small child.

"Fine," Izzy said, waving him off. "Just an accident."

He sucked in a breath through clenched teeth. *"Uno sfortunato incidente."*

The over-the-top concern in his voice gave Izzy pause. His brows were knitted with worry, and his hands were clasped together as though in prayer. It was a theatrical pose, practiced and staged, and suddenly Izzy was pretty sure Alberto had something to do with her *sfortunato incidente.*

"An unfortunate incident," Izzy repeated slowly.

Alberto met her gaze. "Very unfortunate."

"Very avoidable," her mom said, pushing herself to her feet. Now that Izzy had proved to be unharmed, her mom was going to lay in. "How many times have I told you not to swing down the stairs like that?"

"A million and one, since this morning," Izzy said with a tight smile.

Her mom marched down to the living room. "This isn't funny, Izzy."

"I'm not laughing, Mom," Izzy said, following. Her eyes darted to Agent Michaels's white business card on the coffee table.

"You could have been killed!"

Riley sighed. "Don't you think that's a little melodramatic?"

"Said the son mixed up in a murder," her mom snapped.

"Whoa," Izzy said as her brother backed away. "That's not fair."

But her mom doubled down. "Isn't it? I told him not to mess around with girls like that."

"Girls like what?" Riley was braver once he'd put some physical distance between himself and his mom. "Bartenders? Virgos?"

"Sluts," Alberto said, coming down the steps.

"Don't talk about her like that," Riley said. He wasn't as tall as Taylor or as nimble as Parker, and Izzy was relatively sure that her smooth-talking brother had never been in a fight in his entire life, but as he stared up at Alberto, jaw set and head lowered, Izzy felt like Riley was ready to throw down. His feelings for Kylie must have gone deeper than she thought.

Alberto patted Izzy on the shoulder as he brushed passed her. She shuddered at his touch. "Imma just translating for your mama."

"I know exactly what she meant," Riley said. "I was being sarcastic."

"Leave him alone, Riley," their mom said, taking Alberto's side.

Riley threw up his hands. "You're defending him?"

"Alberto is just trying to help."

"Is that really what you think?"

Izzy's mom sucked in her cheeks, then made a clicking sound with her tongue before she spoke. "What are you implying?"

Riley shook his head. "You know, whatever. Do what you're going to do, Mom. I'm out of here in two days anyway." He stormed off through the dining room.

"Ri?" Izzy's dad's voice drifted in from the kitchen, just before the back door slammed shut behind Riley's exit. Her dad wandered into the living room, wiping his hands on a towel. His eyes slowly trailed from his wife to Alberto, who still loomed behind her, to the carved artichoke at the bottom of the stairs. "What happened?"

"Your handiwork almost killed our daughter," Izzy's mom said, upper lip curled into a sneer.

"My handiwork?" Her dad strode across the room to the artichoke, lifting it gingerly. "That's impossible."

"Impossible that the great Harry Bell might not be so great after all?"

"Mom!" What the hell had gotten into her? Izzy had seen her mom angry, depressed, desperate, but just as with Peyton in recent days, she'd never witnessed the nastiness.

Her dad remained cool, though to Izzy's dismay, he took the bait. "The great Harry Bell that pays all the bills around here?" Once again, he went right to the sexist power play.

"You mean all the past-due ones?"

"I don't see you writing a check."

So much for their sexy times the other night. They were at each other's throats again in less than forty-eight hours.

"Scusi, signora." Alberto bowed at the waist like a butler taking leave of the lord and lady of the manor, and backed toward the front door. "I will leave-a you alone."

"Rimani, Alberto," her mom said, telling Alberto to stay. *"Per favore."*

But he merely shook his head and slipped outside.

"Be home for dinner!" she called after him. "Taylor and his fiancée are coming to meet you!"

Family dinner? So nice of everyone to let Izzy know.

Alberto didn't respond, and the instant the front door clicked, Izzy's mom turned vicious.

"Look what you did."

"Made the Italian freeloader uncomfortable?" Izzy's dad shrugged. "Big whoop."

"The money we get for that freeloader kept the goddamn power on last month."

Izzy knew they weren't well off, but she had no idea that things were so bad the utilities were getting shut off. How was that possible when her dad was working literally all day and night? "Guys!" she cried. "Enough."

Izzy's mom whirled on her. "You're not the adult here."

"Aren't I?"

Her mom's face deepened to an explosive fuchsia. "Go to your room."

Without a word, Izzy turned up the stairs, only too happy to comply. She was tired of placating her mom and shielding her clueless dad from them. Let them deal with each other for once.

"Apple doesn't fall far from the tree," Izzy's dad said with a snort.

"Maybe if you were here more," her mom hissed, "instead of 'working' . . ."

Her voice trailed off, but Izzy didn't want to hear anymore. She raced upstairs to her room, shutting and locking the attic door for the second time that day.

And Alberto wasn't even home.

* * *

Izzy watched at her window until she saw her dad slip out the laundry room door with the newel post cradled in one arm and retreat to his workshop. His body language was more defeated than pissed off, which didn't surprise Izzy after a fight with her mom.

She crept downstairs to retrieve Agent Michaels's card, tucking it into a pocket on her phone case. The clank of pots and pans indicated that her mom was working in the kitchen, so as silently as possible, Izzy opened the front door and followed her dad to his workshop.

He was in the attached bathroom, bent over the sink, splashing water on his face.

"Dad?"

He straightened up, dabbing at his chin with a towel that looked as if it hadn't been washed in months. "I'm sorry you had to see that."

"It's okay." Though witnessing her parents fight wasn't a highlight of her week, it wasn't even the worst thing that had happened to her that day, and she'd already put it out of her mind.

His watery eyes met hers in the mirror. "No, it's not."

"Have you had a chance to look at the artichoke?" Izzy asked, changing the subject. She had bigger issues to deal with than her parents' shitty marriage.

"Not yet." He dropped the towel in the sink and backed out of the bathroom. As he ambled over to the broken bits of the newel post on his worktable, two beads of red bubbled up on his clean-shaven chin.

"Why are you shaving in the garage?"

"Better lighting."

She didn't understand how the unpermitted half bath her dad had tacked onto his garage workshop could have better lighting than the main bedroom's en suite bathroom upstairs, but before she could press that point, her dad had picked up the rounded artichoke finial in one hand and tossed it up in the air. It flipped upside down before he caught it mid-fall, angling the base so Izzy could get a good view.

"The dowel screw snapped," he said pointing to the hole in the bottom of the finial. Izzy could see the nub of a metal screw flush with the wood.

"I thought it was one carved piece," Izzy said.

"Nah." He pointed a callused finger at a metal nub in the middle of the artichoke's base. "It's just screwed on."

"Is it normal for one to break like that?"

Her dad shrugged. "It's an old house."

"So it could just have been a fluke." Was her gut instinct that Alberto was involved in this mishap wrong?

"What else could it have been?"

"I don't know," Izzy said absently. She took the artichoke from her dad's hand and walked to the window. Though the afternoon light was muted by the thickening clouds, it provided enough illumination to see the broken screw. She ran a finger over the divot of the hole and felt smooth metal. "If it had broken off," she mused, rubbing the spot slowly with her index finger, "wouldn't the screw be jagged? Uneven?"

"It might." He peered over her shoulder, and Izzy caught an unfamiliar wisp of aftershave. Since when did her dad start wearing cologne? "Huh. Yeah, that looks like a clean break."

Too clean. "Could it have been cut?"

"It does look that way." Her dad laughed. "But why would anyone want to cut through the screw?"

"I don't . . ." She was about to say "I don't know," except she did. She knew exactly why someone would want to sabotage the structural integrity of the newel post at the top of the stairs: to cause an accident. There was only one person in the Bell house who routinely swung around that finial, and there was only one person in that house who might want to do her harm.

"Alberto," she breathed out loud.

"The Italian kid?" her dad asked, as if there was another Alberto floating around. "Why would he deface our staircase?"

Izzy's theory was bananas, but she needed to tell someone. Her mom was already in a mood, Riley and Parker were MIA, and talking to Peyton about Alberto had already proved to be impossible.

You know you can tell me anything.

Her dad was her best chance. She turned to face him squarely, artichoke still gripped between her hands. "You know those foreign exchange people who came by the other day?"

His eyebrows bunched together. "Yeah."

She paused and inhaled slowly, settling her butterflies. "They're FBI agents."

He stared at her for a second before an enormous grin tugged at his cheeks. "Good one, kiddo. You had me for a sec."

She slid Agent Michaels's business card from her phone case and held it up in front of him. "Dad, I'm serious."

"Okay," he said, stifling a laugh. "Sure. Let's pretend that's real."

"Pretend?"

"The FBI was here because . . ."

"Because they've traced the Casanova Killer to Eureka," she said quickly, dropping her voice instinctively. Just in case anyone else was listening. "And Alberto is their number one suspect."

"That goofy kid?" her dad said, laughter erupting from him despite his efforts to suppress it. "Who tells stories about chicken wings and wears his pants a size too small? You think *he's* a serial killer."

When he put it that way, it sounded ridiculous, but Izzy couldn't shake the feeling in her gut.

"Yeah."

"You've been listening to too many of those murder podcasts, Izzy."

She wouldn't let it go until he'd heard all her arguments. "He fits eyewitness descriptions, except for his hair and eye color, but those are easy to change. He never speaks Italian with me, hasn't taken any English lessons with Mom, his clothes are all too small like you pointed out, and, Dad, at the bonfire last night he got into a fight with Hunter and—"

"Peyton's boyfriend?"

Izzy paused, surprised her dad actually remembered the name of her best friend's boyfriend considering they'd only met once. "Yeah."

"Is Peyton okay?"

"Yeah." Why did her dad suddenly care about Peyton?

"Good." His eyes darted to one of the old mantel clocks that lined the shelves on the far side of the room. "Look, I know having Alberto here was your mom's idea, and I know you're only going along with this Italian Scheme to please her." He spoke hurriedly, as if he had someplace to be. "So maybe this FBI stuff is just a way to get out of doing something you really don't want to do?"

Izzy blinked. "You think I'm imagining all of this because I don't want to go to Italy?"

He shrugged, noncommittal.

So much for *you can tell me anything.* "I'm accusing someone of murder, Dad. Not faking the stomach flu."

But her dad was no longer paying attention. He grabbed his jacket from a peg on the wall and sidestepped her to reach the door. "I'm late."

"You need to listen to me." Izzy wasn't going to let him run away this time.

"This is crazy."

She grabbed his arm. "Dad, stop!"

"Enough with the crazy, Beth!"

"Beth?" Izzy froze. Though she and her mom technically shared a first name, her dad had never mistakenly called her by her mom's nickname.

Not once. But in a heated moment trying to extricate himself from a conversation he deemed "crazy," he'd called her Beth.

His eyes darted away from her face, ashamed. "I meant Izzy." He turned back to the door.

"Don't go, Dad." If there was ever a time his family needed him, it was now, with a potential serial killer living beneath his roof. Izzy was desperate for him to believe her.

Her dad paused mid-step, and she saw his shoulders sag, either from defeat or shame, she wasn't sure. "Sorry," he said without turning around.

The door banged open with the wind, allowing him an easy exit, and without another word, he was gone.

Izzy stood rooted in place long after her dad had left the workshop. What was she going to do? If she couldn't talk to her own parents about Alberto, who could she turn to?

Jake.

If he thought her theory was bananas, then she'd drop the whole thing. But if not, she was calling Agent Michaels immediately. Izzy whipped out her phone.

> Hey, can we meet up?

As always, Jake's response was swift.

> Thought you'd never ask. ☺
> How about the Grind?
> I can swing by and get you.

Izzy didn't want to be anywhere near her house, even for the ten minutes it would take Jake to drive to her, but thankfully the Grind wasn't far.

I'll walk.

A pause before Jake's next response.

Okay. Be there in 15.

She smiled as she shoved her phone into her pocket, then stepped out into the backyard. As she did, she saw a curtain drop over Alberto's now-empty window.

TWENTY-SEVEN

WALKING THROUGH THE WEIRDLY DESERTED STREETS OF OLD Town might have been even more unnerving than sharing a house with a serial killer.

Not that Eureka was midtown Manhattan or anything, but it had its own brand of hustle, especially during the summer when the historic neighborhood was flooded with tourists, capped off in August with an influx of college students and their families as Humboldt State started its academic year. It was also the kind of town where, despite the weather, people walked. They walked to shops, they walked for exercise, they walked their dogs. Hell, in a week, Izzy would be walking to school every day with dozens of other students. But today the streets felt oddly abandoned. Tourists had canceled their reservations or headed home early. The Storm of the Century had turned Eureka into a ghost town.

She was inclined to roll her eyes at the media drama over this storm: anyone who had grown up in the area was heavily acclimatized to overcast skies and endless days of rain. But Izzy had to admit that there was a rare ferocity to the wind whipping off the coast that made her shiver beneath her hoodie. Fierce gusts propelled microdroplets of seawater that stung at her face and neck as she marched steadily into its full-frontal assault. She secured the zipper at her neck and pulled her hood low over her eyes to protect herself from the onslaught. Though there weren't many tall trees this close to the coast, the bushes and sycamores shuddered from invisible blasts of sea air, and even the power cables rocked back and forth between their poles.

By the time she got to the Grind, Izzy wished she'd let Jake pick her up.

Even inside the café, the storm was looming large. Two baristas were busy hauling sandbags from a storage room to the main eating area, and huge sheets of plywood leaned against the far wall, ready to be nailed into place over the storefront windows.

"They're calling it the 'Storm of the Century,'" a barista said, tracing the path of Izzy's gaze. As if anyone on the northern coast of California hadn't heard about it yet. The barista's dimples deepened, and her teeth flashed brightly against her dark skin as she smiled, but Izzy felt that her lightheartedness was forced. She was definitely more worried about this storm than she wanted to be.

"Are you expecting it to flood this far up?" Izzy asked. Her own house wasn't at much higher of an elevation than the coffee shop.

"No idea," the barista said. "But I'd rather be safe than sorry."

"Smart."

"I even brought in extra help." The barista nodded to the two other employees, still dragging sandbags in from the back. "Well, that, and I didn't want to work alone with a freaking serial killer on the loose."

"Serial killer?" She knew? Had word of Agents Michaels and Stolberg gotten around?

Her brown eyes grew wide. "Didn't you hear about Kylie Fernández?"

"Oh yeah." Izzy faltered. She wondered if people considered Riley a possible suspect. "Do they know who did it?"

"No, but *I* heard it was the Casanova Killer."

Suddenly, Izzy wished she had flipped on the local news in the last twenty-four hours. "I thought he was down in Los Angeles."

"His last victims were in San Francisco," the barista said. "Though the authorities won't confirm that. Have you ever listened to *Murder Will Speak*?"

"Occasionally."

"They did a cool breakdown proving that at least two unsolved murders in the Bay should be attributed to him." The barista leaned over the counter and dropped her voice, as if everyone within earshot didn't already know her news. "My boyfriend's cousin's girlfriend is an artist—she's got a panel down on the waterfront, the one with the peace mosaic?"

Izzy nodded, realizing with a cold wave of nausea that the last time she'd passed the graffiti wall was in the car with Alberto on the way to the marina, where he'd met Kylie.

"Anyway," the barista continued, her lowered tone forgotten. Probably not the first time she'd told this story that day. "So she gets called in sometimes to do sketch work for the police, and she worked with one of Kylie's coworkers the other day who might have seen her with a guy the night she was killed. And *she* said that there were two dudes in black suits at the station, working with the sheriff."

Izzy wondered if Agent Michaels would be secretly delighted that she had been referred to as one of "two dudes."

"They *must* have been FBI agents, and the *only* reason they would be here is because of the Casanova Killer."

Probably not the *only* reason, which the barista should know if she was even a casual fan of *Murder Will Speak*, but her boyfriend's cousin's girlfriend might have just sketched a portrait of Alberto.

"What did the guy look like? The one your friend sketched."

The barista's face was all dimples again. "Tallish and good-looking, just like the Casanova Killer. Young too. She said that was a surprise."

"Anything else? Should we be on the lookout for a blond dude with blue eyes?"

"Definitely a white dude," the barista said with an eye roll. "Isn't it always?"

Izzy nodded. "Good point."

"But she did say his hair was kinda poofy on top."

Poofy. Like a pompadour.

Was she describing Riley?

Izzy had to take a steadying breath to keep her voice from shaking when she spoke again. "And do they think this is the murderer?" She wasn't willing to take it on Agent Michaels's word that Riley wasn't actually a suspect.

But instead of nodding enthusiastically, the barista just flipped a long braid out of her face and shrugged. "No idea. Now, what can I get you?"

Izzy ordered in a daze, choosing whatever her eyes happened to fall upon as she stood at the register trying not to freak the hell out. A sketch artist had done a portrait of Riley based on an eyewitness who had seen him with Kylie. But that was a couple of days ago, probably the reason Riley was picked up for questioning. And since they hadn't arrested him yet, there was a good chance that this was old news and Riley wasn't actually a suspect anymore.

Izzy had calmed down by the time she paid for her double cappuccino and raspberry muffin; then a gust of wind accompanied another patron through the door.

"I'm guessing you won't let me pay for that," Jake said, leaning against the counter beside her.

Izzy shoved her phone back into her pocket. "Too late."

"Damn it."

"You can get round two."

He grinned at her. "Deal."

"Just so you know, we close at four thirty," the barista said with a nod to the clock on the wall. It was already four. "But you can sit in the courtyard out back as long as you'd like."

"Thanks, Terry," Jake said. Damn, was he on a first-name basis with everyone in town?

He ordered an iced coffee, a ballsy move with plunging temps outside, and a matching raspberry muffin, then grabbed both of their drinks and led Izzy through the side door to a small outdoor seating area. Surrounded on three sides by the café and a two-story office building, the courtyard was filled with potted ferns and umbrella trees, which offered more of a buffer from the wind than Izzy would have expected. Once the foliage was paired with a couple of space heaters mounted on the overhang of the roof, it was pleasant enough out there to unzip her hoodie.

"Thanks for meeting me," she began awkwardly as she tested the temperature of her cappuccino. The sides of the mug hinted at molten hot, so using her finger, she made a little hole in the thick foam to let the espresso beneath cool off.

"Of course." Unburdened by the temperature of his drink, Jake took a long sip of his iced coffee. He drank it black—no sweetener, no milk or cream—and there was something about the simplicity of his order that matched his personality. Jake was a straight-to-the-point kind of guy. Not in a brusque way like Peyton or a know-it-all way like Riley, but just calm, rational, no bullshit. If there was anyone who might see the truth in her theory, it was him.

"I'm going to preface this story by saying that I know I listen to too many murder podcasts, but I'm not making things up." Her dad's words from half an hour ago still haunted her.

"Okay."

"That said, if you think I'm off the deep end on this, I want you to tell me."

Jake nodded slowly. "I'll do my best."

"Your best to tell me I'm bananas?" she said with an arched brow.

His small grin signaled he knew she was teasing. "I'll do my best to usher you into the padded room gently."

"Fair." Izzy took a deep breath. She'd already been shot down once today, but if there was even the teensiest chance that she was right, she needed confirmation. "Here goes."

The story tumbled out of her, beginning with the moment Alberto greeted them at the airport. Her recitation was succinct and to the point, and all the small inconsistencies that nagged at her seemed so obvious now. The clothes that didn't fit, the reticence to speak Italian, the fucked-up passport, even the over-the-top accent that reminded Izzy of Riley when he was being a dick about her Italian lessons.

By the time she got to the afternoon lunch at Woodley's, Jake seemed invested. "Kylie slipped him her number on the bill for lunch. She and Peyton were flirting with him like crazy."

Jake's left eyebrow inched upward as he tilted his chin down. "They weren't the only ones."

Izzy could feel the heat in her cheeks at Jake's reminder of her own flutterings for Alberto. If he was the Casanova Killer, then it was an apt name—that guy's ability to charm women was impressive.

"And right after that, Kylie broke her date with Riley. Maybe she was seeing Alberto instead?" The idea that a murderer was sleeping just below her own bedroom made goose pimples pucker up on the skin of her forearms. The feeling of his thumb pressed against her throat . . .

Jake's hand shot across the table to hers, grasping it firmly. "Are you okay?"

"Y-yeah."

"You looked like you were going to be sick."

The heat of her embarrassment moments ago had been washed away by an icy panic. She'd been right there in Alberto's arms. She'd felt the pull of his magnetism, and the danger of his menace. At least thirteen other women had felt the same push and pull but had made the wrong choice and were now dead, their limp, defiled bodies shoved into closets, under beds, and into crawl spaces to be found by unfortunate friends and family members. Strangled, all of them.

How close had Izzy come to being next?

"Izzy, you're okay." Jake squeezed her hand, ripping Izzy from her nightmare. "I'm not going to let that guy hurt you."

She nodded mutely, eyes downcast. It was nice that he was being protective, but what good would Jake be against an experienced killer?

His hand lingered, softly cupping hers. "I . . . I need to tell you something."

Her eyes flitted up to his face. Jake shifted in his chair, his body suddenly agitated, the calm confidence fallen away. He looked nervous, and he couldn't meet her gaze.

For an instant, Izzy recalled the moment in front of her house when she'd thought Jake was about to kiss her, and her stomach tightened. He'd been so kind since he'd been back, their banter on the beach bordering on flirty. Was there even a chance that Jake had feelings for her?

No.

The familiar voice of fear was in her head, reminding her of Tamara, the Humboldt State student Jake had met at his summer internship.

She's definitely cooler than you are. Probably hotter too.

It was much more likely that Jake was about to tell Izzy about her, and Izzy, already feeling like she had no one else to turn to, wasn't ready to hear it.

She slipped her hand out from beneath his. "I can't."

Jake winced as if in pain. "Can't what?"

"I . . ." Izzy knew she was being a terrible friend, preventing Jake from sharing his feelings with her, but she was too overwhelmed, too terrified of losing him. She'd wait until after the Casanova Killer business was over, then plaster a fake smile on her face and listen to whatever Jake wanted to tell her.

Just not now.

Before she could say as much, the door to the café opened and the barista stuck her head outside. "Wanted to let you guys know that we're closing up." Her eyes landed on Jake, who looked pained. "You okay, Jake?"

"Yeah," he nodded, forcing a tight smile. "Fine."

"Okay. You can stay as long as you'd like. The courtyard entrance is always open."

"Thanks," Jake said.

"At least the streets are safer," the barista said as she picked up Izzy's empty mug.

"Safer?" Izzy asked.

"Didn't you hear? They arrested the Casanova Killer."

Jake turned his head sharply toward her. "What?"

"Can't believe he'd been a local all along. You know my sister went to school with him?"

Izzy felt the world fall away around her. She certainly wasn't talking about Alberto. Had Riley just been arrested for murder? "Who was it?" she managed.

"Greg Loomis."

TWENTY-EIGHT

IZZY FELT LIKE AN IDIOT.

How could I have been so wrong?

Greg Loomis, Kylie's menacing, toxic ex. She'd completely forgotten that he'd been on Alberto's flight from San Francisco. They were about the same height, but unlike Alberto, Greg had brown hair and hazel eyes. According to the local news report Jake pulled up on his phone, the police received an anonymous tip, and when they searched his apartment, they found a piece of jewelry identified as belonging to Kirsten Deschamps, the last suspected victim of the Casanova Killer, a French teacher who had been found dead in her Oakland apartment by a roommate just nine days ago. The only other information they learned was that Greg had been turned over to the FBI and was being transported back to San Francisco.

Maybe Izzy's dad had been right: too many murder podcasts. She'd seen facts and evidence where only coincidence existed. What if she'd actually called Agent Michaels and shared her suspicions about Alberto? The poor guy would have been dragged into a murder investigation half a world away from his home, in a country where he had no friends or family to support him. And it would have been all Izzy's fault.

"It was a good theory," Jake said when he dropped Izzy at her house. "I mean, it still is."

"Past tense is fair," she said with a sigh.

"Greg hasn't been convicted yet."

"A technicality."

"I'm just saying . . ." He rested his arm against hers, their skin lightly touching. "Trust your gut. It told you that guy was menacing, and after what we witnessed at the beach, I don't think you're wrong."

Izzy knew Jake was being kind, but she still felt foolish. "Thanks."

"Can I see you tomorrow?"

The question was so abrupt it caught Izzy off guard. "Isn't there a massive storm rolling in?"

Jake shrugged. "Not until tomorrow night. I still need to talk to you."

He wasn't going to let this go. Her stomach dropped at the idea of having to pretend she had no feelings for Jake while he told her about his crush on another girl, but it was probably better to rip the Band-Aid off quickly and be done with it than to let hope linger. "Sure."

Jake's face softened, and Izzy realized that he'd tensed up, waiting for her answer. "I'll text you."

"Okay."

He smiled at her for a hard second as she slid out of the truck, and he was still smiling when she closed the passenger door. But for Izzy, the anxiety over this future conversation with Jake lingered. She didn't hear him pull away until she was safely inside, whereupon an aggressive aroma from the kitchen pushed all thoughts of Jake aside. It smelled like an entire garlic plant had given its life for the meal Izzy's mom was preparing.

It wasn't that her mom didn't cook Italian food—pasta was a staple in a house with three boys—but spaghetti Bolognese was child's play compared to what was laid out in the kitchen. Occupying most of the island was a full antipasto platter: a gorgeously arranged display of heirloom tomatoes, sliced fresh mozzarella, rolled prosciutto, marinated olives, and julienned basil leaves, all drizzled with what looked like a balsamic reduction. Beside it, a bowl of garlic bread covered by a towel explained the pungent aroma, and on the stove, a pot almost as tall as Izzy's mom filled the kitchen with steam, hinting at the boiling pasta water within.

Izzy's mom whizzed from stove to oven to refrigerator like a honey bee preparing for winter and hardly glanced in Izzy's direction when she entered.

"You're back." She pointed to a set of oven mitts on the counter. "Can you rotate the chicken parmigiana?"

Though all she really wanted to do was slink up to her room and avoid human contact for the next twelve hours, Izzy recognized her mom's manic energy and did as she was told. The cookie sheet of perfectly crispy chicken breast fillets smothered in homemade marinara, mozzarella, and the titular Parmesan cheese looked like enough food to feed Taylor's entire fire battalion, though it was just him and his fiancée, Martina, a fifth-grade teacher who'd moved north from Sacramento a few years ago, joining for dinner.

"I like Martina," Izzy said absently as she rotated the pan 180 degrees.

"You'd rather spend time with her than your own mother?" her mom snapped. She was primed for a fight, her anxiety ratcheted up to an unhealthy level over this stupid dinner.

"Answer me!" her mom said while Izzy was still trying to decide whether an answer was even necessary.

Izzy sighed. "That's not at all what I said."

"But you meant it."

"No, I didn't."

"You did!"

"Shit, Mom! Stop it."

"Four-letter word!" Her mom slammed a metal colander into the sink with a loud crash. "Watch your mouth!"

Izzy was tired of walking on eggshells, tired of being her mom's favorite target. She knew why: Izzy was the only one in the family whose reaction to such abuse was consistent and predicable. She never fought back, never escalated, always forgave. Izzy's approach was to soothe the savage beast inside her mom. She'd let her mom rant and rail until the initial onslaught of her attack ebbed, and then Izzy would apologize and fawn over her, which always put Izzy's mom in a good mood.

But for some reason, tonight Izzy just didn't feel like playing along.

"Mom, I love you, but I am not responsible for keeping you in a good mood, and I will not be your punching bag." She closed the oven gently, laid the mitt on the counter, and marched through the doorway.

* * *

Izzy half expected to hear her name screamed through the house before she reached the top of the stairs, but her mom had fallen silent. Maybe Izzy's uncharacteristically fearless response and calm conviction had stunned the fight out of her, or maybe she was so worked up that the words got all jumbled in her brain to the point where she couldn't say anything at all. Either way, Izzy had half an hour to herself before she heard her dad calling her through the vent system.

"Izzy, this is your dad." As if she might not recognize his voice. "Your presence is requested in the dining room. Over."

Her dad's insistence on using the vent system like it was a ham radio was equal parts endearing and hokey, but even though she was still angry at him for running out when she needed to talk, Izzy was thankful to hear his voice instead of her mom's.

Taylor and Martina had arrived and were already seated side by side in the middle of the dining room table. Parker and Riley were helping their mom in the kitchen, and Alberto was deep in conversation with her dad.

"So the vents, they are like-a the telephone?"

Izzy's dad laughed. "Yep! Discovered it a couple of years ago, and now we don't have to run upstairs when we need her."

You could just text me like a normal family.

"These vents, they connect all the house?"

"Every room. Old heating ducts, hooked up to the furnace in the basement."

"How old?"

"Fifty years, at least," her dad said, taking a sip of wine. His face was already turning red. "They say you're supposed to replace them after twenty-five, but I say, if it ain't broke, don't fix."

"And as a firefighter," Taylor said with a smile, "I say the buildup of dust and other materials is a fire hazard." He was shorter than his younger brothers, but broad where they were wiry. The same build that had gotten their dad a football scholarship to a Division II college. All of the Bell Boys shared the same pale skin, medium brown hair, and brown eyes, but Taylor's temperament was a midpoint between Parker's introversion and

Riley's emotional exhibitionism with a dash of their dad's naïve cheerfulness, and his presence in the house had always been a calming influence.

"*Pfft,*" Izzy's dad said with a dismissive wave of his wineglass. "Whoever heard of a fire in a heating vent?"

Taylor was about to respond, but he was interrupted by Parker and Riley, who pushed into the dining room with the tray of antipasto and bowls of salad.

"You'd best grab a plate," Izzy's dad said to Alberto. "These boys eat fast."

Izzy waited to take a seat until Alberto had chosen one, then sat at the opposite end, beside her dad. Even if he wasn't the Casanova Killer, Izzy still wanted some distance from Alberto. Being near him made her nervous.

"Damn, Dad," Riley said as he sat down next to Izzy. He sniffed the air, then waved a hand in front of his nose. "Did you bathe in that stuff?"

Izzy's dad shifted in his chair. "In what?"

"Dior Sauvage. Christmas gift from Park and me, like, four years ago. Can't miss those amberwood notes."

"Oh yeah," Parker said as he loaded his plate with vegetarian antipasto offerings. "I remember that. Didn't think you'd ever used it."

"Of course I have," her dad said.

Izzy's mom focused on her husband. "Special occasion, Harrison?"

The only time she used her husband's full name was when she was angry, though Izzy couldn't figure out why her dad's cologne usage would suddenly set her off. The tension at the table was unbearable as Izzy's parents' eyes locked in an epic showdown. Unsurprisingly, her dad flinched first.

"One of your special dinners is occasion enough, Beth."

"Agreed!" Taylor said. "You really outdid yourself, Mom."

Izzy's mom smiled demurely. "Thank you, Tay."

At her elbow, Alberto poured her a glass of water.

"And when do you guys leave for school?" Martina asked Riley and Parker, seated directly across from each other. She was petite like Izzy's mom, though with black hair and brown skin. Unlike Izzy's mom and her ever-present updos, Martina always let her long waves hang freely down her back, which Taylor liked to caress when he thought no one was watching.

"Another two weeks for me," Parker said, "but Ri's out Monday morning."

"If the storm doesn't close the airport," Riley added with a sad shake of his head.

Izzy's dad reached for a piece of garlic bread. "Tay, how's the storm prep down at the station?"

"Good," Taylor said with a noncommittal shrug. "We trained for swift water rescue last winter, so I feel like we're ready. Coast Guard's closed the harbor—no boats in or out as of sundown tonight. And the sheriff's department is shutting down Highway 101 in both directions along the coast and all routes through the mountains."

Alberto sat up in his chair. "*Scusa*, they are closing *all* the roads? Even inland?"

"Yep," Taylor nodded. "In case of mudslides after the fires this summer."

"Feels like the media is blowing this out of proportion," Izzy's mom said, ignoring the water at her elbow and pouring herself a glass of wine. "We had a nor'easter every winter back in Connecticut when I was a kid, and I don't remember them closing down all of Mystic."

"Global warming," Parker said. "Warmer air holds more moisture, and as the Pineapple Express pushes north, we'll see more of these super-storm events."

"Another reason I'm ready to get the hell out of here," Riley said with a tight grin.

Between Kylie's death and being a suspect in her murder, Riley couldn't really be blamed for never wanting to come home.

Parker smiled wryly. "We'll miss you too."

"You fly direct, *sì*?" Alberto asked. "Eureka to San Diego?"

Riley nodded. "I'm lucky they haven't canceled the route yet."

"And then how do you-a get to the school?" Alberto pressed. "A friend picks-a you up, maybe?" Why was he so interested in Riley's travel plans?

"Uber," Riley said. "My buddy Tito's on the same flight, so we'll split it."

Alberto looked disappointed. "Ah, I see."

Izzy felt her phone buzz in the pocket of her jeans and silently slipped it out, keeping it in her lap as she read the message. She didn't even realize she'd been hoping it was from Jake until she saw that it wasn't.

HEY

Peyton's all caps text meant she was worked up about something.

Hey.

WANTED TO WARN YOU
HUNTER'S DAD WANTS HIM TO FILE CHARGES AGAINST ALBERTO

A few hours ago, Izzy was planning to turn Alberto over to the FBI, but now, she was worried about the police getting involved.

PROBABLY

Izzy's thumbs hovered over the keypad as she struggled with a response. For some reason, she wanted to warn Peyton about Alberto, even though her Casanova Killer theory had proved to be erroneous. There was still something dangerous about him, and though Alberto's beatdown of Hunter was probably enough to cool Peyton's jets, she wanted to make sure her friend didn't put herself in harm's way.

Alberto's temper . . . be careful.

Izzy expected a follow-up, like "I'll keep my distance" or "you be careful too." but neither came. And once again, when faced with a conversation she didn't want to have, Peyton had stopped texting.

As she shoved her phone back into her pocket, Izzy noticed that the conversation at the table had drifted onto something other than Parker and Riley's travel plans, and Izzy really should have been prepared when the words "Casanova Killer" came up.

But she wasn't.

"I'm so glad they caught him," Martina said with a shiver. "Terrifying to think that sicko was right here the whole time."

"Sicko?" Alberto said, eyebrow raised. "I do not understand this-a term."

"A deranged personality," Izzy's dad said.

"Deranged?"

"Not in their right mind."

"Il pazzo," her mom translated.

Alberto's blue eyes grew wide. "You think-a this killer, he is the madman?"

"No," Izzy's mom said quietly.

"Definitely," her dad said. Then he snort-laughed, covering his mouth with a napkin as he sputtered bits of garlic bread across his plate. "Al, did you know that Izzy here actually thought it was you?"

Izzy felt her stomach drop to the floor.

"Me?" Alberto said, drawing out the syllable as if it were a musical note. "A deranged killer?"

Izzy's dad laughed again, a hearty guffaw, as he reached for more wine. "I mean, the cops were close, right? When they brought Riley in. All in the same house." He slapped his hand on the table, laughing hysterically at his own supposed joke.

Izzy's mom tittered nervously. "That's absolutely ridiculous." Her eyes narrowed on her daughter. "And insulting."

"Not *that* ridiculous," Taylor said. True to form, he was always trying to negotiate peace.

Taylor was the golden child, and hearing him contradict her made Izzy's mom fidget in her seat. "Of course it's ridiculous, Taylor. How could it not be? Alberto's a guest in our house, in our country. We can't go around accusing him of horrible things without any evidence."

"It is okay, Elisabetta," Alberto said softly, nodding to Izzy's mom. "I am not offense."

"You should be," her mom said, leaving his incorrect grammar unchecked for the first time. "Taylor, I demand that you explain yourself."

Taylor smiled, calm as ever in the face of his mom's agitation. "After what happened to Kylie Fernández, the police are taking all violent crimes more seriously. Including last night with Hunter Bixby."

"Is he pressing charges?" Riley asked, turning to Izzy.

The words from Peyton's text were still fresh in her mind. "His dad wants him to."

"Man, the cops are gonna love this house," Parker said. "First you, then him. We'll all be under surveillance soon."

"What are you talking about?" Izzy's mom asked.

"I assumed Izzy told you," Riley said, laying his fork down dramatically beside his plate and tenting his hands smugly over it so his fingertips just touched. "But I'm delighted to do the honors. Our Italian friend here turned Hunter's face into hamburger meat last night at the bonfire."

Izzy watched her mom process the information. She blinked slowly, like a cat, reached for her wineglass, then seemed to second-guess herself and took a sip of water instead. Whatever Alberto had told her about his messed-up hand, it certainly wasn't this.

"So Hunter is going to file assault charges?" Izzy's mom said at last.

Riley shrugged. "Guess so."

"That is unfortunate." Her mom sighed, then abruptly pushed her chair away from the table. "Chicken parmigiana, anyone?"

TWENTY-NINE

THE SOFT CLICK OF A CLOSING DOOR WOKE IZZY UP.

It was one of those sounds humans were wired to hear, a twenty-first-century Darwinian throwback to a time when humans needed to sleep with one eye—or ear—open if they intended to survive the night.

Unlike her early human forebearers, Izzy had no known predators. She didn't need to sleep with a guard dog or dig a moat around her house for protection, but the soft click of a door latch engaging against a metal strike plate was so familiar, and so unfamiliar in the middle of the night, that the signal of encroaching danger roused Izzy from a dead sleep at a quarter to three in the morning.

She lay perfectly still, waiting for the creak of the third stair from the bottom—her bedroom's own form of a Nightingale floor—as someone's body weight gradually lowered onto it, but as the seconds of silence crept by, Izzy began to wonder if the sound of a door closing was from someone coming in or going out.

She wasn't sure which was more disturbing.

Confident there was no one else in her room, Izzy sat up and switched on her nightstand lamp. As the lack of noise indicated, she was alone in her small attic room, had probably been so since earlier that night when she'd crawled up to bed after helping her mom clean up from dinner.

Izzy closed her eyes, a dull headache forming at the back of her skull. Tension, probably, mixed with fear and anxiety. She wanted to stay in her room forever, or at least until Alberto returned to Italy in three months. The look on his face when Izzy's dad joked about her Casanova Killer theory had been a mix of anger, resentment, perhaps even a tinge of fear, and he'd avoided her completely for the rest of the evening, excusing himself to bed before dessert. Izzy didn't blame him, and understood if he wanted nothing to do with her for the rest of his stay. But they couldn't avoid each other altogether, and though Izzy was loath to bring up the subject of her bogus theory, she recognized that Alberto deserved an apology.

The throbbing at her temples intensified, and Izzy pushed herself out of bed to grab some Advil from her dresser. The moment she was upright, the room spun around her, and she had to brace herself against the headboard to keep from tumbling over.

She panted as she slipped into her UGGs. Why was she short of breath? Why was her room so hot? She felt the desperate need to open a window for fresh air, and her knees shook as she wobbled across the room to the nearest dormer.

Izzy knew she felt weak, and when she tried to push the window open, it wouldn't budge. The window and the wall blended together, overlapping images swirling around as if her eyes were two lenses that couldn't come into focus. Struggling to stay on her feet, she ran her fingers across the windowsill, tracing nubby, cold metal bits sticking up from the wood. Her brain couldn't process this new information. They felt like nailheads. . . .

Had someone nailed her window shut?

Unable to stand any longer, Izzy dropped to the ground. Her mind was sluggish, her decision-making impaired, but in the same way that her primordial human alarm system had woken her up at the sound of the door closing, something deep inside urged her to get the hell out of that room. She army-crawled across the floor toward the stairs, her fingernails clawing at the minute gaps between floorboards to help drag her body toward safety. By the time she reached the top of the stairs, she was fighting the urge to close her eyes and go to sleep, a move she knew could be fatal.

Her hand groped for the top step, then Izzy half slid, half tumbled down the flight, collapsing in a tangle of her limbs against the attic door. She lay still for a heartbeat, her breaths a bit less shallow, and the brain fog began to clear. Whatever was poisoning the air in her room hadn't dispersed fully into the stairwell. Yet. She had time to escape.

Izzy uncoiled her body and grasped the doorknob, hauling herself to her feet. It turned easily in her hand, and she felt an intense wave of relief, knowing she was moments away from safety. But when she pushed her body against the door, it didn't budge.

Straightening up, Izzy rattled the door back and forth, and she could hear the latch still engaged. Wrenching the knob spun it endlessly round and round without any friction whatsoever. The mechanism inside was broken.

Accident or sabotage?

The thought hit her like a sledgehammer on the side of her still-throbbing head. At dinner, Alberto had looked as if he wanted to murder her. The same way he'd looked at Hunter before he attacked. Someone had been in her room. Someone had nailed the windows shut. Alberto could have done that when he went to bed early while everyone else was still in the dining room, talking and laughing. No one would have heard a thing.

For the second time that day, Izzy wondered if Alberto was trying to kill her.

And if he was, did that mean the FBI had arrested the wrong suspect?

The second question could wait. Izzy had to get the hell out of her bedroom before whatever poison that had permeated the air farther up in the attic made its way down to her. She banged against the door with balled fists and screamed as loud as she could.

"Help! Help me!"

She waited, still pounding and kicking the door, but heard nothing in response.

"Mom! Dad! HELP!"

Her voice was getting weaker, her strength draining away, and the stairwell was beginning to feel warm. She was running out of time, and the solid wood construction her dad loved so much was literally thwarting her attempts to wake anyone up. Her voice couldn't be heard through multiple closed doors, and striking the thick oak door with her bare fists wasn't making enough noise to wake anyone up. What was she going to do?

Break a window? The dormers were small, the framing between panes solid. She might be able to smash a couple of the small rectangular panes, but she probably wouldn't be able to bust out the entire window. A pane would be enough for her to be able to breathe untainted air, but then what? Scream into the night and hope someone heard her while murderous gas permeated the rest of the house, killing her family?

No. She had to bust down the attic door. And to do so, she was going to need a battering ram.

Or a big-ass grandfather clock.

When her dad and Taylor moved the clock into her room years ago, they'd removed the internal weights, stabilized the glass door by stuffing the compartment full of blankets, and swathed the entire cabinet in plastic wrap before lugging all hundred and fifty pounds upstairs. Izzy didn't have that kind of time. She would only get one shot to topple the clock, slide it a couple of feet to the top of the stairs, then shove it down. Just a minute or two before she lost consciousness. She'd need to make it count.

Izzy eyed the top of the stairs. The soft orange glow from her bedside lamp lent a cheery mood to the death zone above, even as her breaths were becoming shorter again, more labored.

Now or never.

Izzy panted shallowly four or five times to get all the air out of her lungs like she'd seen divers do on the Discovery Channel, then took a deep, full breath, held it, and sprinted up the stairs.

She'd never particularly cared that her attic room was small and slightly cramped—the dimensions had always felt cozy, not confining—but tonight she was particularly thankful for the small space. The clock stood just to the left of where the stairs opened up onto her floor and clear of the banister that surrounded the aperture. All she had to do was topple the clock onto its face, then shove it forward a couple of feet over the stairwell until gravity took over and pulled the monstrosity down with it.

Still, the clock weighed a hundred and fifty pounds, and Izzy wasn't entirely sure she could move the damn thing at all. She just had to hope her strength—and her lungs—held out.

Thankfully, the clock didn't sit flush against the wall due to a rather thick baseboard that ran the circumference of her room. She was able to wiggle her right arm behind the cabinet, all the way up to her shoulder, and with one twist of her body, she scooted the clock far enough from the wall that she could wedge her hip into the gap.

With half her body jammed into the newly made crevice, Izzy pushed the giant cabinet with one hand while using her other elbow for leverage against the drywall. The clock screeched across the hardwood, inching its feet toward the stairs, but Izzy needed the damn thing to fall on its face. She shimmied farther up the back of the clock, soles of her UGG boots providing some traction in the tight space as she tried to get high enough, and tried again.

Her center of gravity raised, Izzy pushed against the solid-oak backing, and she felt the clock begin to tip forward. Her lungs burned and the muscles in her back and arms felt as if they were ripping away from bone, but with a guttural cry, Izzy channeled all her remaining strength into her upper body and heaved.

She felt the clock tip onto its front legs. It hung there for one excruciatingly long second where Izzy was convinced it would fall back toward the wall, crushing her in the process; then, as if an unseen hand gave a teensy little push, the eighty-year-old clock toppled forward.

The door shattered on impact, glass crunching beneath the oak cabinet as it crashed to the floor. Izzy landed on top of the prostrate clock with a heavy thud that forced the remaining air out of her lungs. She took a reactionary breath, forgetting the air was literally poison, and her head swirled. But her task was only half finished. She still had to push the clock to the edge of the stairs.

Her limbs were heavy, her movements sluggish and clumsy as she pushed herself off the clock, feeling for the wall behind her. Shards of broken glass cut into her palms and knees, but she could barely feel them. Every sound and sensation was muffled by a veil, like it was happening to someone else's body.

Focus. Izzy shook herself, trying to throw off the malaise. She slid her butt to the floor and dragged her legs in front of her, planting each foot deliberately against the bottom edge of the clock. Once again, she used the wall for leverage, and flexed her quads.

The sound of wood scrapping against broken glass was like nails on a chalkboard, but it was the most joyous noise Izzy had ever heard. The clock was moving, and the progress spiked her adrenaline, allowing her body one last burst of strength. A final kick and the clock was as far away from the wall as she was going to get it.

And yet it didn't career headfirst down the stairs toward the locked door as Izzy had hoped. The top half of the clock wasn't heavy enough. She needed to add weight.

Izzy's eyelids felt leaden, the effort to keep them open requiring more energy than she had left. She crawled onto the clock, arms wobbly with the effort. She slumped forward and felt her cheek pressing against wood. Unsure of her surroundings, all she could do was claw at the wood while her wheezing breaths became increasingly sparse and ineffectual. The pounding inside her skull had intensified, muddling her thoughts. She couldn't recall why she was inching her way across this cold wooden surface, or why she was moving at all when what she really wanted to do was close her eyes and sleep. . . .

As her eyelids drooped, Izzy experienced a moment of weightlessness. She wasn't sure what was up and what was down, though she had the impression that her body tilted forward, a sensation of movement, like she was diving off a cliff.

But instead of the give of a water landing, Izzy felt the ground beneath her shudder while a shrieking crash cut through the muddiness of her brain. She rolled forward, and her head smashed into a hard surface. The impact knocked her from her dreamlike state, and her eyes flew open.

It took her a heartbeat to recognize her surroundings. The floral-striped wallpaper, the family photos on the wall, the shattered grandfather clock on its side beneath her. She was in the hallway.

Bedroom doors seemed to open simultaneously, and images of her mom and her brothers racing toward her were the last things Izzy saw before she passed out.

THIRTY

IZZY'S TEMPLES WERE STILL POUNDING WHEN SHE PEELED open her eyes again. She was expecting to see the living room of the Bell house, swathed in the warm glow of the table lamp beside the sofa, but the room in which she lay was painfully white and lit from what felt like a billion LEDs that stabbed mercilessly at her pupils with every furtive blink. An oxygen cannula rested below her nose, the tubes wrapped around the sides of her face. White walls and ceiling tiles, beige chairs, and the gentle beep from a large machine beside her bed signaled that she was at the hospital.

She was alive, and she needed to tell someone what had happened in her room.

"Hello?" she croaked. Her vocal cords were sandpaper rubbing against each other, and her abdominal muscles ached. Had she been vomiting? That would explain both, but she didn't remember any of it.

Another beep was followed by the gentle sound of an engine engaging. A cuff on Izzy's left arm began to constrict, taking her blood pressure. Someone must be around, monitoring all these devices. "Hello?" she repeated, more forcefully.

Nearby, a toilet flushed, then a door in the corner opened, revealing her mom. "Izzy?"

"Hey, Mom."

"Izzy!" Her mom flew to the bed, scooping her daughter into her arms. "I'm so glad you're awake."

There had been a gulf between them lately, ever since Alberto arrived, and it was good to feel that distance vanish.

"What happened?" Izzy asked.

Her mom stroked her hair. "You're going to be fine, just fine. We got you here in time."

In time. "In time for what?"

"You have carbon monoxide poisoning." Her mom's voice shook. "You were minutes away from a coma when you crashed out of the attic."

Carbon monoxide. Izzy didn't know much about it, only that it was known as the "silent killer" and there was a carbon monoxide monitor in every room of the house. Why hadn't it gone off? And how had her room been flooded with deadly gas?

"The dryer vent was clogged," her mom continued, squeezing her hand. "Just like Taylor warned. Someone ran a load of laundry and flooded the basement with gas, which then seeped into the vents."

"How?"

Her mom shook her head. "Bad luck. There was a buildup of lint inside the venting duct, plus a plastic bag had accidentally blown over the outside hood. Taylor examined it himself."

Accidentally on purpose. "Is everyone else okay?"

"Yes," her mom said, tearing up. "The damper in your room was the only one open."

How convenient. "There was something wrong with my door," Izzy began, hoping she could get her mom to understand this wasn't an accident.

Her mom clicked her tongue. "Your father's handiwork, no doubt. And your carbon monoxide monitor was unplugged." Izzy noted the hint of parental blame creeping into her mom's tone. "You could have died."

Should have died. Izzy was pretty sure that had been the plan. Someone had come into her room after she went to sleep and dismantled the lock in such a way that Izzy couldn't open it from her side. After unplugging the CO monitor and tampering with the windows earlier when everyone else was still eating dinner downstairs. This was no accident: someone had tried to kill her.

And there was only one someone who might want to see her dead.

"Was it Alberto's laundry?" Izzy asked.

Her mom laid her head on Izzy's shoulder. "Hm?"

"In the dryer. Whose clothes?"

"Yes, Alberto's, I think." Her mom sat up suddenly. The softness in her brown doe eyes had hardened, shifting from relief to suspicion in a heartbeat. "Why?"

She should have told her mom the truth. That's what parents were for, right? The absolute unburdening of one's soul to an ear that would at least be sympathetic if not understanding. But Izzy's dad had already laughed off her suspicions, and that was *before* an arrest had been made in the case, and the abject rage on her mom's face the previous night at dinner when her dad had teased Izzy about it was a big red warning flag. Her mom would not be an objective audience.

"Nothing," Izzy said, averting her eyes. Not because she didn't want her mom to know she was lying, but because she didn't want her mom to see her disappointment. "No reason."

"Well," her mom said with a heavy exhale. "How about I see if we can spring you out of here?"

"Sure."

Her mom cupped Izzy's face in her hand. "I'm so glad you're okay."

"Me too."

Then she flitted out of the room to track down a doctor.

Izzy slumped forward, her hospital gown gaping open in the back. Alberto's clothes in the dryer, clogged ducts, and a plastic bag that just happened to get looped around the exterior dryer vent hood accidentally so as to create an airtight seal. The same night that her dad spilled the beans about Izzy's Casanova Killer suspicions. If she hadn't woken up from the sound of the door closing, she might not have woken up at all.

Izzy reached toward her pocket to retrieve her phone, then remembered that she wasn't wearing any clothes. Her pajama bottoms, long-sleeve shirt, and the UGG boots she'd slipped on earlier were in a pile on a chair, but when she examined them, she didn't see her phone among her belongings. It must still be at home, along with Agent Michaels's business card. Shit.

She scanned the room, looking for any means of communication, and her eyes fell on her mom's purse.

The wires and cords attaching Izzy to her monitors were just long enough for her to reach the bag, where her mom's cell was tucked into the front pocket. Thankfully, she knew the password.

She might not have Agent Michaels's business card, and calling the police with her story was going to elicit the same reaction it had in her parents, but she did have one relative whom the authorities would listen to. If she could just find him.

Izzy scrolled down to Taylor's cell phone first. She was pretty sure her eldest brother would answer a call from his mom, but after six rings, it kicked to voicemail.

She tried Martina next, hoping Taylor's fiancée had a good enough relationship with Elizabeth Bell that she'd willingly take her call, but instead of ringing several times, the call went straight to voicemail. Martina's phone was off.

Thankfully, Izzy had one more place to try.

"Humboldt Bay Fire Department," a male voice droned on the other end. He sounded like he'd answered the phone the same way for eight hours straight. "Is this an emergency?"

Yes. "I need to speak to Taylor Bell."

A pause on the other end. "Martina?" He sounded confused.

"No, his sister, Izzy."

"Taylor has a sister?"

Being invisible kind of sucked. "Yes, please just tell him that I need to talk—"

"Taylor's out," the voice said, cutting her off. "You wanna leave a message?"

Of course this wouldn't be easy. "No. Just tell him I called?"

"Sure." He wouldn't. "Stay safe."

Izzy hung up. She could try the police department and drop Agent Michaels's name, but she doubted they'd believe her. *No one* believed her.

No one but Jake.

All she needed to do was remember Jake's phone number.

Izzy closed her eyes and tried to picture Jake's contact info on her phone. A series of digits came into focus, but Izzy wasn't sure if they were actually his number or just wishful thinking on her part. And even if she *had* the right number, would he pick up a call from a strange phone?

There was only one way to find out. She just prayed Taylor's info about the closed harbor was correct and Jake wasn't out on *Bodega's Bane*.

"This is Jake," he said, picking up after a few rings.

Izzy sighed, grateful he answered. She probably wouldn't have. "Hey, it's me."

"Izzy?" Jake switched over to a video call immediately. His curly hair was an unruly mess, corkscrewing straight up from his head, and he squinted against the gray morning, much as Izzy had done half an hour ago. "I didn't recognize the number."

"My mom's phone. Sorry I woke you up."

"No, no. It's cool." He stretched his free arm over his head, and Izzy immediately noted that his arms and shoulders were bare. Despite the seriousness of her call, she felt the desire to see more.

Jake blinked his eyes open, finally adjusted to the light, and smiled at her. "So what's . . ." His voice trailed off as he seemed to take note of what she was wearing. "Are you in the hospital?"

"Yeah."

"Holy shit." He sat straight up, gripping the phone with both hands. Izzy caught a peek of chest hair against his smooth brown skin. "Are you okay? What happened? Which hospital?"

"Saint Joseph's, and I'm fine. Now."

Jake clenched his teeth. "Alberto?"

Izzy glanced at the door. Her mom was nowhere to be seen, but she dropped her voice and spoke quickly regardless. "I think so. Carbon monoxide poisoning from a blocked dryer vent. I'll explain when you pick me up."

The phone jostled and his bedroom whirled in the background as Jake hurriedly got out of bed. "Who's with you?"

"My mom."

"We have to tell someone."

"I know." She was out of her league dealing with a serial killer, but with a suspect in FBI custody already, Izzy was going to need proof to get anyone to take her seriously.

Thankfully, she knew where to find it. Sorta.

"Don't rush," she said to Jake, swinging her legs over the side of her hospital bed.

"The hell I won't." He was jumping around, trying to pull on a pair of pants with his free hand.

"I need you to do something for me first."

"Anything."

Izzy arched an eyebrow. "You wouldn't happen to know anyone with a metal detector, would you?"

THIRTY-ONE

BENEATH THE OVERSIZE FLANNEL SHIRT SHE'D BORROWED from Jake, medical tape tugged at Izzy's forearm as she traipsed across the Ma-le'l Dunes. The nurse had told her to keep it on for an hour to prevent bruising from her blood draw, but she was done. She reached up into the sleeve and peeled the tape away from her skin. As if in protest, the adhesive caught a few strands of arm hair, ripping them from their roots. Izzy sucked in a breath through clenched teeth.

"You okay?" Jake asked, glancing down. He had his uncle's metal detector slung over one shoulder, and he reached his free arm toward Izzy in case she needed a steadying hand.

"Just exfoliating an entire layer of my epidermis." She held up the offending bandage before stuffing it into the breast pocket of his shirt. "Don't say I never gave you anything."

He grinned. "I'll treasure it."

A gust of wind whipped across the beach, pelting them with tiny bullets of wet sand. Izzy wrapped the flannel shirt around her body, holding it taut with both arms. "Thanks for the loan."

"Looks cuter on you anyway," Jake said with a nod. Always practical, he'd dressed in layers, which was good, since she was only wearing the leggings, pajama shirt, and UGGs she'd had on when she passed out in the hallway. He'd offered the warmest layer he had, leaving himself with a long-sleeve Henley and puffy vest, and though she should probably have stopped back at the house to change, she wasn't ready to face Alberto. With any luck, she and Jake would find the evidence they were looking for, Agents Michaels and Stolberg would authorize Alberto's arrest, and Izzy could sleep easy in her bed by the time the massive storm rolled in that night.

They trudged the rest of the way in silence, the thunderous crash of waves making conversation difficult. It had been less than forty-eight hours since the bonfire, but already the encroaching storm had changed the topography of the beach. Seaweed, kelp, and driftwood carried by the tide had been pushed twelve feet farther up the beach than where the waterline had previously been, sloshing close to the charred remains of the fire. Part of the pit had already caved in—the result of a rogue wave, no doubt—and the hollow log that had camouflaged the booze stash had been dragged back toward the ocean.

Izzy shivered, her UGGs wet and caked with sand. The folly of her plan nagged at her. Would they really be able to find a small bracelet in this expanse of beach and dunes? She had a vague idea of which direction

Hunter had chucked the thing, but it had been dark, the weather had changed the landscape, and now, staring at the roiling ocean on one side and the undulating waves of beach grass blanketing the dunes on the other, finding a needle in a haystack seemed like a simpler task.

If Jake was feeling the same sense of futility, he didn't show it. With a good-natured grunt, he heaved the metal detector off his shoulder, laying it carefully on the beach, then strode over to a spot on the far side of the bonfire pit.

"I was standing about here," he said marking an X in the sand with the toe of his boot. Then he took three measured strides toward the water. "I'd say Hunter was here."

Izzy guesstimated her own position from that night and tried to remember exactly what had happened. "He held her arm up in front of the fire. I saw a glint off the bracelet."

Jake moved forward. "About here?"

"To your right."

He took a baby step. "Better?"

"Little more." He moved slowly, stopping abruptly when Izzy held up her hand. "There. That's where Peyton stood."

"I wish I'd gotten a better look at it," Jake said, shaking his head. "Could have spared you last night."

"You couldn't have known it might be evidence of murder," Izzy said. She took a large side step to her right, trying to triangulate Hunter's position with her own. When she closed her eyes, she could see his face illuminated by the flickering orange flames, a glint of metal dangling from Peyton's wrist. "He ripped the bracelet off with his right hand, turned, and threw." She pointed over her left shoulder. "That way."

"All right." Jake fished a set of keys from his jeans pocket, weighing them gingerly in the palm of his hand. Then he unhooked a single key and tested the weight again. "This seems about right. Shall I?"

Izzy swept her arm toward the dunes. "I hope it doesn't unlock anything important."

Jake winked. "Me too." Then, with a quick breath, he launched the key into the air.

The wind caught it, propelling it toward the dunes, before it dropped into the beach grass over an outcropping. Jake and Izzy hurried toward the spot. She was afraid to blink in case she lost its exact landing position. It took a few moments of peering into tufts of vegetation before Izzy caught a glimpse of silver, half buried in the sand.

"This it?" she asked, holding up a single house key.

Jake was by her side in an instant. "Yep. Looks like I can go home tonight after all."

"Should we start here?"

He shook his head. "The wind wasn't as strong Friday night."

"Then this should be the farthest edge of our search radius." Izzy gazed out over the expanse of grass and sand. Even after narrowing it down, the task seemed gargantuan.

"Agreed." Jake flipped a switch on the metal detector, sparking it to life.

Beachcombing was a tough job. Not only was the device heavy, but there was so much metal debris buried in the Ma-le'l Dunes, she'd have thought they were adjacent to a recycling plant. The electronic buzz seemed to alert them to a new find every thirty seconds, and after an hour, Izzy and Jake had amassed a substantial collection of bottle caps, aluminum can pull tabs, keys, fishing lures, pennies, a Hot Wheels race car, and a fabric-covered furniture button that looked like it came from an old sofa.

They worked in silence, occasionally commenting on their odd finds, until they'd covered a significant portion of the dunes. Suddenly, Jake stopped and turned his eyes toward the ocean.

"What's wrong?" Izzy asked, shivering through her damp clothes.

"We were sitting here." He paused. "At the bonfire."

Izzy recalled that she'd wandered away from the party, away from Peyton and Alberto and the drama that was just beginning to unfold. She'd picked the highest dune, close enough to the fire that she wasn't utterly consumed by the darkness, but far enough away that the individual voices and conversations of the party morphed into ambient white noise.

She'd liked the spot, liked the solidarity of it if she were going to indulge in a good ugly cry, and even now it felt like a solid vantage point. She hadn't minded when Jake had joined her there.

Until he started talking.

"I've been trying to tell you something," he said now. The metal detector lay behind him on the downslope of the dune, and Jake's eyes were no longer fixed on the horizon, but on her. "Ever since I got back."

Jake had been trying to explain why he'd ghosted her over the summer. She vividly remembered his last words that night at the bonfire: *I was avoiding you.* She'd jumped to her feet and rushed off, not wanting to hear what came next. She still didn't. "You don't need to explain."

Once again, Jake shook his head. "Please, Izzy. Hear me out."

Izzy felt the dank panic of loneliness begin to swallow her whole. She didn't want to hear that Jake thought she was getting too close to him, and so he kept his distance "for her sake." She didn't want to hear him say that he'd been doing them both a favor, because he clearly didn't feel the same way about her that she did about him. And she certainly didn't want to hear that he was in love with Tamara, the fellow intern he'd met in Monterey.

She felt her throat catch, and she turned away. She wasn't sure when she'd fallen in love with Jake, but now as she stood there on the dunes in this green-and-blue flannel shirt that smelled deliciously like his bodywash, she felt her heart breaking. Whatever she'd felt for Alberto had sprung to life and died as quickly as a match is struck and burned through. But her feelings for Jake were deeper, more grounded, and the last few days had reminded her of how much she loved being near him. She couldn't watch him walk away. Not again.

"Izzy, will you look at me?" Jake stood right behind her, his body so close she could feel his warmth through her wet and matted clothes.

"Don't," she breathed, unable to suppress a sob.

"Don't what?"

Was he trying to torture her? She swung around, fists balled at her side. "Don't let me down easy, okay? Don't tell me that you're doing it for my own good. Don't tell me how awesome Tamara is and that I'd like her, because I can tell you right now that I won't."

She stared squarely at his chest, unable to look him in the eyes, but instead of confirming all her worst fears, Jake gripped her by the shoulders and laughed.

"What's so funny?" Izzy asked, looking up. She was calmer now that she'd blurted out all the words.

"You think I'm in love with Tamara."

She blinked. "Aren't you?"

"Oh, Izzy." He smiled, his body suddenly calm, and he relaxed his grip on her shoulders. "I've been trying to tell you, to let you know. The reason I disappeared over the summer . . ."

Jake swallowed, and his chest heaved as his breaths came faster upon each other. Almost as fast as her own.

"Izzy." His voice was now a whisper that she felt more than heard over the wind and surf.

"Yes?" Her body ached to be near him. *Please.*

One hand drifted up to her face, cupping her cheek. "Izzy, I'm in love with *you*."

Her heart was pounding so ferociously, she wasn't entirely sure she heard him. "What?"

"I love you." He cleared his throat, his voice more confident as he stroked her cheek with his thumb. "I knew it before I left for Monterey. I waited for your texts every day, hoped to catch you at night so we could chat back and forth, checked my phone if I woke up at two a.m. in case I'd missed a message from you."

"You love me." Izzy didn't believe her ears. She needed to repeat the words out loud, giving Jake time to refute them.

"Yes." His gaze faltered. "But you kept talking about leaving, this plan to go to Italy and never come back. I'd never see you again, so I tried to protect myself. I should have told you the truth and not just vanished. It was a douche move."

"It was," Izzy said, and this time it was her turn to laugh. "It really was."

Jake reared back. "Now what's funny?"

"Maybe you had to disappear. It hurt so badly. I tried to ignore it, but I missed you." She smiled into his deep brown eyes. She never wanted to blink. "And then I saw you on the boat last week, and I knew . . . I knew why I wanted to punch you in the face."

Jake raised an eyebrow. "Yeah, you did look like you wanted to rip my ears off."

Or kiss you. "I didn't think I'd ever feel this way."

"Yeah?" His body inched closer.

"I love you too."

Jake bent his face to hers, his lips hovering an inch away. She could feel his breath on her face, the pounding of his own heart in syncopation with hers, a hormonal drumline beating out a pattern between them. His hesitation lasted only an instant, but the anticipation was delicious, and when Izzy finally felt his lips against hers, she wanted to devour him.

Her lack of experience didn't matter, as instinct kicked in. Jake snaked one hand into her hair, holding her head in place as their bodies crashed together. She looped her arm around his neck, heaving herself up so her body could be closer to his, pressed against him, no room for daylight. His lips were on her chin, her cheeks, her eyelids, arms encircling her, but it wasn't enough. She wanted more of him. Needed more. The storm was gone, the cold spray from the waves, the damp sand, even the bracelet, the reason they were out there in the first place—everything vanished. All Izzy could see and hear and feel was Jake. And she wanted all of him.

Izzy wrapped her legs around his torso while he supported her weight with his thick arms. He kissed her more deeply, his tongue desperate to be inside of her. Then he sank to his knees and pulled away, looking her in the eyes.

"We should . . . go slow," he panted.

Izzy shook her head. She'd been going slow for too long. "I want you."

"I don't want you to regret—"

"My entire life has been a regret," she said, feeling for the first time how like her mom she truly was. "Things not done, things not said. I'll regret not being with you right now."

He stroked her face again. "You're so beautiful."

"I love you."

That was all Jake needed to hear. He inhaled her as they kissed, then gently, gradually, he lowered her to the sand. His hands were tentative, seeking permission as they caressed her body, but Izzy didn't want tentative. She'd almost died twice in the last twenty-four hours. She wanted to live every moment like it might be the last one.

She closed her eyes and moaned as Jake eased his body on top of hers, pushing her shirt up to her collarbone. His lips moved tantalizingly slow, kissing her stomach every few inches as he eased upward, until suddenly he stopped.

His body went rigid.

But not in a good way.

In a scary way.

Izzy's eyes flew open. Jake was looking out over her head, down the far side of the dune away from the beach. His jaw was slack, his skin sickly yellow. "Jake, what's wrong?"

He didn't answer, just continued to stare. She arched her head back and was just able to catch a glimpse of what had struck dumb fear into him.

Sticking out from the sand at the bottom of the dune behind them was a boot.

Attached to a leg.

Attached to a body that looked very much like Hunter's.

THIRTY-TWO

IT WAS IZZY'S TURN TO COMFORT JAKE.

They'd pulled their clothes back into place and rushed down the dune. Hunter's face was buried in the sand, and before Jake even touched the body, Izzy knew he was dead. The pose was unnatural, one arm flung wide, no attempt to shield his mouth and nose from the suffocating granules, but it wasn't until Jake tried to move him that they discovered the bloody aftermath of a dozen stab wounds in Hunter's chest.

Jake had called 911 immediately, which was impressive. Izzy wasn't sure she'd have been that functional if it had been Peyton lying in the sand, and though Jake's hand shook in hers while he gave directions to the emergency dispatcher, Izzy admired his ability to think calmly and rationally in the face of a personal tragedy.

As soon as the call had ended, Jake's arm had slumped to his side and he'd just stood there, staring at the lifeless remains of his best friend. Hunter's pale skin was practically white, and the stitches he'd received at urgent care had blackened, making the scene even more macabre. Izzy knew if they stared at Hunter's corpse any longer, they'd never get the image out of their minds.

She'd taken charge then, gently guiding Jake back down to the beach, making sure they trod the same path they'd made on the way up the dune just in case there was any evidence to preserve. Her years of obsessively listening to murder podcasts was coming in handy.

Once the police arrived and they'd given a statement, Izzy and Jake headed back to the parking lot, where they sat hand in hand on the open tailgate of Jake's pickup truck, blankets draped over their shoulders by a kind but ultimately impotent EMT who'd turned his attention to them rather than Hunter while police officers and forensic scientists combed the area. Normally, Izzy would have been deeply interested in their tactics, but now she only had one thing on her mind: Jake. And making sure he was okay.

As they waited in silence for someone to tell them what to do, Izzy felt the darkness intensifying around them. One glance at the black clouds overhead told her that the Storm of the Century was almost upon them. The authorities must have sensed it as well because the frenzy of activity on the beach shifted into high gear as investigators tried to gather as much evidence as they could before the storm wiped the beach—and the crime scene—clean.

Izzy shivered beneath her blanket at the memory of Hunter's body left abandoned in the sand. If they hadn't stumbled upon him, would he ever have been found? Judging by the ferocity of the waves at low tide, there was a good chance that a storm surge would swamp the dunes entirely, washing Hunter out to sea. His disappearance would be one of those cold cases Izzy followed on *Murder Will Speak*, and Peyton and his family would have been left forever wondering what happened, a wound that would never heal.

Not that learning your son or boyfriend had been murdered was some awesome thing. But at least, eventually, there would be closure.

As long as the police found the killer.

"Elizabeth Bell and Jake Vargas, correct?" A sheriff's deputy rounded the back of the pickup truck, hands shoved deep in the pockets of his parka. He was about Izzy's dad's age, that indeterminate range of adulthood that put him somewhere between forty and elderly, with a few grays cropping up in his light brown beard and crinkles in his pale, freckled skin around his mouth and forehead. His brown eyes were red-rimmed and watery, which could have been the result of the biting winds on the beach or perpetual insomnia.

"Izzy," she said after Jake didn't respond. She squeezed his hand, as if to say, *I've got this.*

"Deputy Porter." He nodded. "You discovered the body?"

They'd already given their statement to another officer, but Izzy sensed Deputy Porter's authority. "Yes."

He arched an eyebrow. "While . . ."

Izzy didn't appreciate the leading edge to his tone, as if he was insinuating some wrongdoing on their part. Not that she wanted to admit that they were making out on the freezing cold beach as a massive storm rolled in. She nodded to the metal detector that lay in the bed of the truck behind them. "I lost a bracelet here. Jake was helping me look for it before the storm."

Deputy Porter's eyes flitted down to Izzy's pants and UGGs. "In your pajamas?"

Before she could respond, Jake raised his head. "She was in the hospital last night," he said, tone steely. "She almost died from carbon monoxide poisoning."

"And then felt the pressing urge to come out here and search for a bracelet?"

Jake squared his shoulders. "Yeah."

A wry half smile cracked the right corner of Deputy Porter's mouth. "All right, calm down, son." His eyes shifted back to Izzy. "You're Taylor Bell's sister."

She nodded briefly, not that Deputy Porter needed the confirmation. He certainly hadn't phrased it as a question.

"And you work for Mike Bixby?"

Unlike Izzy, Jake didn't bother to confirm the deputy's statement that he worked for Hunter's dad. "I was Hunter's best friend."

That was the cue Deputy Porter had been waiting for. The smile vanished, and he was all business. "When was the last time you saw him?"

"Last night."

"When exactly?"

"I left his house around eight. He was home with his parents."

"And he didn't mention that he was going to meet anyone? A girlfriend, maybe?"

Izzy was about to pipe up with *Peyton didn't kill him!* when she caught the deputy's eyes flash in her direction. She bit her tongue. He was baiting her.

"No," Jake said with a firm shake of his head. "He took some of the pain meds he got from urgent care after they stitched up his face and was going to bed early."

Deputy Porter nodded, and Izzy sensed that Jake's story confirmed what he'd already heard, perhaps from Hunter's parents. Izzy winced as she imagined what they must be going through. Their only child. Murdered and dumped like trash.

"And do you know who gave him those cuts?" Deputy Porter continued. "Who might hold a grudge against him?"

"Yes!" Izzy blurted out. She couldn't help herself. She knew no one but Jake believed her, but there was only one person who would have done this. "Alberto Bianchi."

Deputy Porter cocked his head to the side. "Is that the Italian kid who's staying with you?"

"I don't think he's actually Italian," Izzy said. She wasn't holding back anymore. Someone needed to stop this monster.

"Why not?"

"Because he's barely spoken a word of Italian since he got here," Izzy said. "And he was on the same flight the FBI thought the Casanova Killer took out of San Francisco, and I think they arrested the wrong guy."

Deputy Porter blinked. "How did you know about the flight?"

Agent Michaels's card was back in Izzy's bedroom. She would just have to convince Deputy Porter that she was telling the truth. "Agents Michaels and Stolberg came to my house yesterday, asking questions. They definitely thought Alberto was a suspect. I know you arrested Greg Loomis, but I'm telling you, Alberto is dangerous."

"What makes you think so?"

"We weren't searching for *my* bracelet," Izzy said. She watched Deputy Porter's eyebrow raise a fraction, just like Agent Michaels's had. Was that a move they taught in law enforcement training? "Alberto gave my best friend a bracelet at the bonfire Friday night. Hunter ripped it off her wrist and tossed it into the dunes. That's what we were looking for."

"Why?"

"Because Agent Michaels showed me a photo of an earring Daniela

Margolis was wearing when she was murdered. A matching bracelet was missing from her body. I'm pretty sure that's what Alberto gave Peyton."

Deputy Porter stared hard at her for what felt like five full minutes but was probably more like five seconds. He was assessing her, trying to gauge whether or not she was full of shit. Izzy knew the FBI agents' names and that they'd traced the Casanova Killer to Eureka from San Francisco, but that information could have been leaked, and she could only hope that the sincerity on her face and earnestness in her voice sold her story.

Finally, Deputy Porter turned away, pacing around the side of the truck as he opened up a channel on his walkie-talkie. "Dutch, can you send a patrol around to the Bell house? Yeah, I know we're stretched thin, but make this a priority. Uh-huh, that's the address. Pick up an Italian exchange student named Alberto Bianchi and bring him down to the station."

Holy shit. He believed her?

Deputy Porter paused, listening, but Izzy couldn't make out what the other voice was saying. He clicked his tongue in response. "I know, I'll take the heat. Just call it a hunch."

"I hope you're right about this," he said, flashing his eyes at Izzy as he made sure the zipper on his jacket was hiked all the way up to his neck. "Arresting a foreign national could be my ass."

"I am." Izzy was surprised by how confident she sounded. That was new.

He grimaced; then without another word, Deputy Porter strode toward the beach, where a forensics team member waited for him.

"You did it," Jake said. His smile was sad, his eyes tired. "He believed you."

"I'm as much in shock as you are."

"You don't have enough faith in yourself, Izzy."

She certainly wouldn't argue that point with him. Between the burden of her ever-present fear and lack of self-confidence, she'd never taken a firm stance on anything, always second-guessing herself and deferring to a stronger personality like her mom, her dad, or Peyton.

Oh shit.

"Has anyone told Peyton?" she asked with a start.

"I don't know."

"I should do it." Izzy didn't want to be the one to break such horrific news, but if you couldn't shoulder that burden for a best friend, what kind of friendship even was it?

Jake nodded in understanding. "I'll take you."

She eyed the ongoing investigation on the beach. It didn't look like things would be wrapping up anytime soon. "Do you think they still need us?"

"I can't imagine why." Jake slid off the tailgate of his truck, searching for someone to ask. "I'll find out, and then we can—"

"Hey, Miss Bell!" Deputy Porter appeared from nowhere, trotting across the wet sand.

"Yes?"

"Wanted to let you know that we sent a patrol over to your house. Spoke with your mom."

"Okay."

"She told us that Alberto Bianchi wasn't home."

THIRTY-THREE

JAKE EASED HIS PICKUP TO A STOP IN FRONT OF PEYTON'S house. "Are you sure you want to do this?"

No. "She needs to hear it from me."

"Izzy." He placed his hand over hers on the bench seat, grazing her skin with his thumb. "I want you to know that you're stronger than you think you are."

Strong. Izzy had never really thought about herself that way. She was the youngest sibling in a house full of boys. She'd never won a single bout of wrestling, earned an academic award, or single-handedly beaten the state champs in debate team like her brothers had all done. But she knew Jake was talking about something deeper. Izzy was emotionally strong. Possibly the only member of her family who was.

When she really thought about it, Jake wasn't wrong. She'd been try-ing to keep her family together for years, trying to keep her mom together for longer than that, and while Taylor was the righteous brother, Parker the smart one, and Riley the likable Bell, Izzy had been the linchpin. She made sure everyone felt important and valued and cared for.

But who was looking out for her?

Not Taylor, who was busy with Martina and his firefighter career. Not Parker, lost in his own breakup and hiding in academics. Not Riley, because, well, he was Riley. Not her dad, who was increasingly checked out, spending long hours at work sites rather than at home in a tense house that made him uncomfortable. Hell, he hadn't even shown up when she was in the hospital.

And in a way, not even her mom. It was clear from the last week that this whole Italian Scheme was more about Elizabeth Bell than about Izzy. But Izzy had gone along with it. Why? It was the first tangible opportu-nity she'd ever had to escape. To move away and start fresh. Decide who she wanted in her life and who she didn't. Alberto or not, it had in some ways been the perfect plan up until a few hours ago.

Because there *was* one person in Eureka who was looking out for Izzy, one person who cared about her unselfishly, who didn't want her to change, and who didn't want her to go.

"Thank you," she said. As she gazed into Jake's dark brown eyes, Italy vanished.

Rain fell steadily as they trudged up the walkway to Peyton's house. Her mom answered the door, and one look at Jeanine's red eyes and drawn face told Izzy that she was too late: her friend had already gotten the terrible news.

Peyton was on the sofa in the living room, knees hugged to her chest. A box of tissues sat beside her, and a small pile of used ones littered the carpet at her feet. She wore no makeup, a rarity for Peyton, or at least no traces of it were left after hours of crying. Her eyes were puffy, lids swollen and red, and she breathed through her mouth as if her sinuses were clogged from a heavy cold.

She teared up the moment she saw Izzy and Jake at the door. "You came."

"Of course." Izzy rushed to Peyton's side, hugging her around the shoulders. She felt her friend heave a sob, then force herself under control.

"I've been calling you for hours," she sniffled.

"My phone's at home." Izzy paused, wondering how much of this story she really wanted to burden Peyton with while she was grieving. "I was in the hospital last night."

"What?" She gripped Izzy's arm. "Are you okay? What happened?"

Izzy waved her hand, as if the details of her poisoning weren't important. "I'll explain later."

"But you're okay?"

"Yeah."

"Good." Peyton reached for another tissue, dabbing at her nose. "Is . . . is it true? You found him?"

Izzy nodded, trying to force the image of Hunter's stiff limbs, blanched skin, and blood-soaked clothes from her memory. She prayed that Peyton never had to see photos of his dead body.

"How? What were you doing out there?"

That was more complicated than the mystery of Izzy's unanswered phone. It seemed logical to explain everything to Deputy Porter: if they were really dealing with a vicious serial killer, then everyone was safer with law enforcement involved. But rehashing the bracelet incident was like rubbing salt in Peyton's wounds. The last forty-eight hours of her relationship with Hunter had been strained at best, and now he was dead.

If Izzy shared her theory about Alberto and the bracelet, would Peyton blame herself for her boyfriend's death?

Izzy was still trying to decide which was better—the truth or a lie—when Jake jumped in.

"I took her to the dunes."

"Why?"

Jake swallowed, stepping toward the sofa, just close enough to sweep his hand across Izzy's back. "Because I needed to tell her something."

It took Peyton a moment to understand what was happening. Her brows were drawn together in confusion as her eyes darted back and forth between Izzy and Jake, and then suddenly they grew wide and her jaw dropped.

"You hooked up? While Hunter was missing?"

"We *talked*," Izzy said firmly. Why was she getting blamed for this? She hadn't even known Hunter was missing.

Peyton pushed herself to the other end of the sofa. "Are you here to gloat? Flaunt your new boyfriend?"

The mood whiplash was a blindside, like dealing with Izzy's mom when she was all worked up. "I'm here to make sure my best friend is okay."

"Took you long enough," Peyton muttered.

"We had to give a statement to the police," Jake said calmly. It was amazing how he was holding his temper in the face of Peyton's tantrum, especially considering she might have taken an active, though unwitting, role in Hunter's death.

"Alberto came over right away. As soon as he heard."

Izzy blinked. Alberto had been there? He'd been alone with Peyton and her mom? Izzy gagged, thinking of all the Casanova Killer's victims.

Jennifer Wei, 25, 5'4", black hair, brown eyes
Chantal Harris, 24, 5'6", red hair, blue eyes
Daniela Margolis, 24, 5'3", blond hair, brown eyes
Peyton Nowak, 17, 5'5" brown hair, blue eyes

"Don't let him inside your house," Izzy said, slowly rising to her feet. "Never be alone with him. Peyton, he's dangerous."

Peyton shook her head, lips wrinkled in disgust. "Seriously? You already bagged Jake, and you're still jealous?"

"I didn't *bag* anyone," Izzy said, fighting against the blush rising up from her chest. "And I'm not jealous."

"Oh, really?" Peyton stood up and faced Izzy, all traces of grief wiped clean from her face. "So you didn't throw yourself at Alberto? Show up in his room just begging him to be with you?"

"That's not why I was there," Izzy said, her eyes flashing in Jake's direction. She hadn't told Peyton about her encounter in Alberto's room, which meant *he'd* filled her in. Alberto was trying to drive a wedge between Izzy and her best friend.

Peyton rolled her head toward Jake, a nasty curl creasing her upper lip. "Believe what you want to believe, Jakey."

The irony of Peyton accusing Izzy of infidelity was mind-boggling. She'd come to Peyton's house to break the devastating news of Hunter's death, and instead, it had turned into a referendum on their friendship. Peyton stood with arms folded across her chest, lips pursed, just daring Izzy to contradict her. She wanted a fight, but Izzy wasn't going to give it to her.

"I need to use the bathroom," she said, heading toward the powder room off the kitchen. *To splash some water on my face before I say something I'll regret.*

The cold water was reviving, snapping Izzy out of the rage state Peyton had ignited. She had no idea why her friend was suddenly so petty, except that for the first time since they'd known each other, Izzy had a boy in her life. She was no longer a step down on Peyton's scale of life priorities, a social weirdo happy to cling to Peyton's coattails.

How sad that their years of friendship came down to this? Izzy stepped out of her lane and reached for something she wanted, and Peyton felt threatened.

She dabbed water from her face with a hand towel and paused as she inhaled. The towel smelled familiar. A woodsy scent that she'd experienced recently. Intimately. But it wasn't Jake. He smelled like bodywash, but this was more like aftershave. Or cologne.

Amberwood, Riley had called it. Izzy's dad's cologne.

Izzy felt the small bathroom spin around her, mirror and shower and toilet whizzing clockwise as several elements of her dad's behavior all fell into place at once. His increasingly frequent absences from home. A whole dude's shaving prep kit in his workshop bathroom. The sudden appearance of cologne. The fact that he was home early for dinner on the same night that Peyton's mom was out with her girlfriends.

She fumbled with the handle and staggered out of the bathroom, hardly noticing the sound of a car engine outside and a door flying open. And though the image horrified her, it wasn't entirely a shock when she found her dad in the living room of Peyton's house, sweeping Jeanine Nowak into an intimate embrace.

"I came as soon as I—"

Izzy's dad never finished the sentence. He froze the instant he spotted Izzy as she emerged from the bathroom. The color drained from his face.

She wasn't even surprised. Not really. More disgusted. "How long?"

He stepped toward her, arms raised in supplication. "It's not what you think."

"How. Long."

In the face of her simmering rage, Izzy's dad unconsciously stumbled back toward Jeanine. His hand searched for hers. He never could stand on his own. "I didn't want you to find out like this."

Was he joking? "You didn't want me to find out at all!"

"Izzy, it's complicated."

She wasn't going to let her dad control the narrative. He'd been cheating on his wife for who even knew how long, but still having a romantic night at home that Izzy was so unfortunate as to overhear. There was no world in which that was okay.

But Harry Bell wasn't the only one in the room who deserved Izzy's anger. She whirled on Peyton, who had curled back up in the corner of the sofa.

"You knew," she said. "And you didn't say anything."

Her dad cleared his throat. "I asked her not to, Izzy."

Izzy held her hand up in front of her dad, demanding silence. Their conversation could wait. This one couldn't. "I'm your best friend. I shared all my worries about my mom, my parents, their marriage. And you didn't say a fucking word."

"I . . ." Peyton looked as if she was about to apologize, then swallowed, pushing back that reaction. "This isn't my fault."

"Fault. Shit." As if who was to blame was the most important issue. Peyton's priorities were so messed up.

"Izzy, language," her dad said, trying to sound firm. It was ludicrous that he chose this moment to attempt parenting.

"Save the four-letter-word bullshit for Mom," she said. The gloves were off. "You bailed on your parental duties a long time ago."

"I am still your father."

"Technically." How had she not seen what was going on?

It was then Izzy noted that Jake hadn't moved. Hadn't said a word. To his credit, he wasn't avoiding her face like Peyton or her dad. Jake was looking right at her, his eyes full of sadness. Izzy felt ill.

"You knew too."

He nodded, silent.

"How could—" A choking sob cut the words off in her throat.

"I'm so sorry," Jake said. He was the first person in the room who had actually apologized. "I should have. I just didn't know how."

He stepped toward her, hand outstretched, but Izzy backed away. She didn't need him or any of them. She'd been an idiot to think she could rely on people.

"Izzy," her dad said in a stern fatherly voice that he had no right to use with her. "Let's talk about this."

"Just leave me alone!" she cried, realizing she sounded like a toddler having a tantrum. Not that she cared. She stripped out of Jake's shirt, tossing it onto the floor, then, without another word, dashed out into the storm.

THIRTY-FOUR

RAGE PROPELLED IZZY MORE FORCIBLY THAN THE GALE FORCE winds bombarding the coast, and she was oblivious to the rain and the cold and her utterly inadequate clothing as she sprinted down the sidewalk. She didn't know who she was the angriest with: her dad for cheating, or Peyton and Jake for hiding it from her.

Jake's betrayal hurt the most. His words still rang in her ears: *You're stronger than you think you are.*

Strong, but not strong enough to handle the truth about her dad? She zigzagged through the grid of streets, not even sure where she was going. Tears mixed with the raindrops on her face. Had Jake been giving her lip service just to get in her pants? Could she believe anything he said?

Half an hour ago, Izzy had been ready to abandon her plans to leave home and start her life over, but now she truly felt as if she had no one. Everyone had lied to her. Her parents, her best friend, the guy she thought she loved. And Italy wasn't even a viable option. Never had been. Her Italian was atrocious, her interest in Italian art lukewarm at best. The only thing in life that actually excited her was listening to true crime podcasts about people who murdered other people and occasionally got away with it. If college was about following your strengths, she needed to find a school with a major in suburban serial killers. Which might have been funny if it weren't so painfully real.

What was she going to do?

Izzy stopped on the sidewalk in front of a familiar wooden fence, the metal gate rusted almost to the point of uselessness. Without realizing it, she'd walked home.

The rain was heavier, driving at her as coastal winds propelled the storm onshore. Izzy shivered, her sleepwear soaked through, but she didn't open the gate. Alberto probably wasn't even there, according to Deputy Porter, and yet she felt a reluctance to go inside. The aging Queen Anne Victorian didn't feel like home anymore. Nothing did.

She spun around, turning her back on the house she'd lived in all of her life. Where could she go? Mr. and Mrs. Liang were probably home next door at Miss O'Sullivan's Victorian Bed-and-Breakfast. She could say she'd gotten locked out and spend the evening drying off in their cozy parlor room. That would buy her time, but not solve her problem. She wished she had her own car so she could just drive off. Head north to Portland, or south to LA. Disappear into a city and never look back.

As the rain intensified, Izzy caught movement out of the corner of her eyes. A dark figure at her shoulder. She was a nanosecond too slow to react. While one arm held her firmly around the waist, a hand clamped over her nose and mouth, forcing a cloth to her face. Izzy flailed, trying to loosen the viselike grip as she struggled to inhale against the cloth. It smelled sweet, almost like a floral perfume, and just as she wondered what it might be, she felt her eyelids droop.

* * *

Izzy was tired of waking up with a pounding headache. First at the bottom of the stairs, then in the hospital, and now wherever the hell she was, the disorientating pulse of blood through constricted capillaries was a sensation she could do without.

She struggled to remember what had happened. She was out in the storm. Someone came up behind her. Eyes still closed, she realized not only that she was lying on the ground, but that the rain was no longer pelting her. She must be indoors, but where?

A familiar thunk of wood against wood clued her in. It was the sound of the broken door in her dad's workshop, blowing open and crashing into the wall of the garage.

She tried to move and quickly discovered that her hands were bound tightly behind her back. She also felt pressure on her throat, as if something had been wound around her neck.

Izzy's eyes opened in a flash of panic. She was on the floor in the workshop, cheek pressed against the cold concrete, and somewhere, just out of her vision, a person was moving.

She scrambled to her feet, struggling for balance with both arms immobilized. Her dad's workshop looked the same as it always did, neat and tidy after a day of work, though a pile of broken wooden planks beside the door was new. Izzy was still getting her bearings when she realized what it was: the remains of the grandfather clock from her room that had literally saved her life.

A reminder that she needed to get the hell out of this garage.

Izzy made a dash for the door; even outdoors in the Storm of the Century was safer than in that workshop and whoever was there with her. But she only made it two or three steps before something tugged at her throat from above, cutting off her airway. She fell backward, struggling to stay on her feet, and noticed the rope around her neck extended up and over the garage door rails attached to the ceiling.

"You're awake. Good." The voice was familiar, and yet not. The intonation was all wrong. Izzy turned toward the voice and saw a tall blond figure leaning against the wonky door. Alberto.

"What's going on?" Izzy managed. Even though it was the first question that came to mind, the lopsided smile that spread across Alberto's face signaled that she probably didn't want to hear the answer.

"Just a little theater," he said, fanning his hands wide as if displaying a magic trick. Izzy understood why she didn't recognize his voice right away: the Italian accent was gone, as was the cheerfulness.

"You're the Casanova Killer."

He stepped toward her, menace emanating from every pore in his body. How did Izzy ever find that attractive? "Does it feel good to know you're taking that knowledge to the grave?"

Icy panic swept through her body, colder and deeper than the rain that had penetrated her clothes. Her arms bound, some kind of rope around her neck. She was essentially helpless. "What are you going to—"

Before she could finish the question, she felt her body lift off the ground, pulled upward by the rope around her neck. She gasped for air as the noose tightened, constricting her windpipe, and she kicked and writhed as she dangled, desperately trying to find a foothold to offset her body weight.

Suddenly, she felt something solid beneath the tips of her boots.

Standing on her toes, she was able to release the pressure on her neck and breathe again. Her eyes flew open as she heaved in a lungful of air.

Alberto had scurried back to the door of the garage, where he was busy fiddling with the doorknob. The joke was on him if she thought he was going to sabotage it the same way he'd messed with the door to her bedroom—that latch was already broken, and not even her dad had been able to fix it so it stayed shut.

"There," Alberto said, stepping back to admire his handiwork. "That should do nicely." As he moved to the side, Izzy saw that he'd attached a line of wire from the doorknob. It stretched toward Izzy, disappearing beneath her.

"It's attached to the stool you're standing on," he explained. Which seemed like a silly idea. If he was going to strangle her, why not just do it? Why rig up this whole Rube Goldberg machine just to yank the stool out from under her? Even as Izzy stood on the brink of becoming the Casanova Killer's next victim, her mind was thinking like a detective. The door with the broken latch. If Alberto opened the window on the other side of the garage, the wind from the storm would eventually blow the door wide open, ripping the stool from beneath Izzy's feet. But Alberto wouldn't be there. He was creating an alibi or a diversion, depending on his need.

"The police will see through it," she said. "They'll find the wire."

Alberto shrugged, leaning his right shoulder against the door, keeping it closed. For now. "It doesn't matter. It'll slow them down. Confuse them. I'll be long gone."

"Not in this storm," Izzy said, feeling smug. "All roads out of town are closed."

Again, a simple shrug, and Izzy read between the lines. He already knew about the road closures from Taylor at dinner last night, but he didn't care. He had another means of escape.

But there was only one other way out of Eureka.

"That's why you killed Hunter," Izzy said, sick at the idea that his death was all her fault. Cluing Alberto in on her suspicions must have accelerated his escape plans. "For the keys to *Bodega's Bane*."

"I didn't anticipate his body being found," he said with a lift of his left eyebrow. "But again, it won't matter."

"You *want* to take the boat out in this storm." Alberto's plan was bold. Dangerous, but bold. "No one will be able to track you, and if the boat's never found, you'll be presumed lost at sea."

Alberto paused, tilting his head to the side in contemplation. "You're smarter than she is."

She?

"In another life, we could have been . . . close, I think."

Izzy shuddered at the idea of being intimate with Alberto, horrified that the hands that had throttled the life out of more than a dozen women had caressed her own neck. "In your dreams."

"Your loss." He strode toward her, and Izzy tensed, wondering if he'd decided to do the job himself after all, but instead of kicking the stool out from beneath her, Alberto slid a folded piece of paper from his pocket and tucked it into her boot. "I'll be so sad to learn of your murder-suicide with Hunter. Who knew that you'd been secretly in love with him all this time?"

"No one will believe that."

"You mean your swarthy fisherman won't believe it," Alberto said with a curl of his upper lip. "But again, it's just a diversion, so I don't care."

He turned toward the window, and Izzy knew her time was running out. She needed to keep him talking. One thing she'd learned from *Murder Will Speak* was that serial killers had massive egos. Once caught and convicted, they loved to brag about how they'd gotten away with it for so long. Maybe she could exploit that weakness.

"Framing me for Hunter's death. That's hardly your MO."

Alberto glanced over his shoulder. "I have my reasons."

He wasn't taking the bait. "Do you even know anything about boats?"

"I'll have help."

She. Help. Shit, he must mean Peyton. How could she get wrapped up with him so soon after Hunter's death?

"A partner? Also not your MO."

"A temporary alliance." Alberto slid the window open, and Izzy felt the stool tremble beneath her toes as the door flapped a millimeter or two. "An angry sea is a great place to hide a body."

"Fuck you!" Izzy shouted. Now she wasn't just trying to save her own life, but her best friend's as well.

Alberto tsked, his face sagging with disappointment. "Such language! You need to listen to your mother about those four-letter words."

"Dick," she said defiantly. "Anus. Mofo. Twat."

"Izzy . . ."

She wasn't done. "And my favorites: shit and head."

"Such ugliness from a pretty girl."

"Ugliness? *You're* the murderer."

He sighed, weary of the conversation. "I only kill little sluts who deserve it."

"You killed Hunter!"

A blast of wind rocked the side of the garage and the stool shuddered, but before the door flew open, Alberto crossed the garage to the door, stopping it with his foot. The stool stilled. "Look, I don't enjoy killing men. There's no thrill in it for me." He licked his lips. "I can't *taste* it."

Izzy wanted to vomit.

"I can't be inside them while it happens."

"That's disgusting."

Alberto ignored her. "Kylie was exquisite. The salt of her tears. . . ." He sighed again, lost in the memory. He was rhapsodic now, the ego taking over. At least she'd bought herself a little time, even if it meant enduring this stomach-churning display. He stepped toward her, and Izzy thought maybe if she could lure him close enough, she could get her legs around his neck and strangle him. "I was never getting out of here without a utilitarian murder. Either Hunter or your brother. Couldn't be helped."

Her brother? Alberto's interest in Riley's travel plans. The pompadour hairdo he sported for the bonfire. "You were going to kill Riley and take his place on the flight. Just like you killed the real Alberto."

"If a plan ain't broke, don't fix it," he said, quoting Izzy's dad.

"But Riley is traveling with a friend, so—"

"Plan B." He smiled again. "See? We'd have made a great partnership."

"Temporary." *Come closer.*

Alberto laughed. "True."

A sharp ding pierced the howling wind, and Alberto's hand crept to his pocket. His phone. Peyton had just texted him.

"I'm sorry to say that our time together has come to an end," he said, backing toward the door.

Dammit. She was out of options, but she wouldn't give him the satisfaction of seeing her fear. "I'm not."

"Defiant even at the end. See, I like that. I wish I could stay. You must taste . . ." He exhaled. "Amazing."

"Maybe you should find out?" She forced a smile, hoping she looked as if she didn't have ulterior motives, but again, Alberto was having none of it.

"No time. A lady awaits." He opened the door just enough to slip his lithe body outside. The stool inched away, almost out of reach of her toes. "*Ciao*, Izz-ee."

THIRTY-FIVE

THE MOMENT ALBERTO'S SMARMY FACE DISAPPEARED, IZZY screamed.

"Help! Somebody help me!"

A howling wind was her only response.

She cried out again, as loudly as she could with the thick rope pressing against her larynx, but this time she couldn't hear herself, the roar of the storm swallowing her words whole.

Another gust blasted the side of the garage, and the door flapped. Izzy leaned back, her face tilted toward the roof so her body was elongated an extra millimeter or two. She was able to get the toe of her left foot in front of the stool. It skittered an inch across the concrete floor, and

Izzy pressed down with all of her strength. By some miracle, the swirling winds changed direction and snapped the door shut again. She'd avoided death for the moment, but with the storm intensifying, it was only a matter of time before the busted old latch gave and the door flew open with enough force that she'd be unable to prevent the stool from being ripped away.

She frantically wrung her hands, trying to break free of her bonds. If she could just loosen the knot, maybe she could slip her hands out and remove the noose. But Alberto, or whatever the hell his real name was, had tied it viciously. Rough fibers dug into her flesh, rubbing the skin raw as she twisted her wrists. Sweat coated her body as she contorted her fingers, trying to make her hands as slender as possible to slip one free. But it was no use. Her hands were swollen from the lack of circulation, and freeing them would be like shoehorning a basketball into a golf hole.

What were the odds she'd survive once the stool disappeared? Alberto had fitted the rope tightly around her neck so that even when she tilted her head back, she could feel the noose pressing against her windpipe. With the full weight of her body pulling her down, there was no way to prevent the noose from cutting off her airway completely. She was pretty sure death would be inevitable.

Fear, anger, and shame mingled in her heart. As shitty as her life felt, she certainly didn't want to die. Not only that, but unless someone stopped Alberto, Peyton would be his next victim. Once she'd helped him navigate out of the marina, there was nothing stopping him from strangling her, probably during some disgusting sex act, then shoving her overboard in the midst of the storm.

She hated Alberto. Hated that he'd won. Hated that he was going to live to kill again. How many women would die because Izzy hadn't trusted her instincts, hadn't gone to the authorities sooner? Those deaths were on her head, even though she wouldn't be around to feel the guilt.

Or to feel love. She shrieked in frustration, a heart-wrenching wail of impotence and regret. Her last words to both her dad and to Jake had been said in anger. They'd never know how much she—

"Izzy? Izzy?"

"Help!" she cried, practically choking on the word. She took a deep breath, and with the last of her strength, she screamed.

Izzy probably should have anticipated what would happen next, but even as the door swung open, she only felt an instant flood of gratitude and relief. Until the stool was ripped out from beneath her feet.

She dangled from the overhead beam, writhing as the noose instantly closed off her windpipe. The panic returned tenfold as she tried and failed to gasp for breath. Her eyes rolled back and she felt a tremendous pressure, like her entire head was about to pop off. She didn't even know who had come into the garage, and as the seconds stretched on, she wondered if it was Alberto, come back to enjoy his favorite moment: watching a woman die.

Suddenly, the pressure on her throat lessened. She felt herself being lifted into the air, and she gulped greedily for oxygen. Her lungs burned as if they'd forgotten how to breathe in those seconds she had dangled from the noose, but then they seemed to remember their primary function. Izzy's breaths were quick and deep, almost as if she was hyperventilating; she never even felt the noose being removed from around her neck.

Then she was back on terra firma, feet squarely on the ground, legs wobbly as she tried to steady herself. Two strong arms held her upright, and it took her a heartbeat to realize that the body attached to those arms was talking to her.

"Izzy? Are you okay? Holy shit, what happened?"

She looked up, vision still blurry, and Jake's face came into focus.

"How?" Izzy croaked. The sound of her raspy, muted voice startled her, a tangible reminder of just how close she'd come to death. "How did you—"

Jake stroked her damp hair. "Your dad and I both followed you outside, but you'd disappeared."

Like a pouty child. Her tantrum had almost been her undoing.

"He went to your brother's place, and I headed here," Jake continued.

"Thank you. For coming after me."

Jake took her face in his hands. "What happened?"

"Alberto. Or whatever his name is. He killed Hunter."

The muscles in Jake's jaw rippled. "Where is he?"

"Heading for the marina. He's got the keys to *Bodega's Bane*."

"He'll never make it out of the bay alone," Jake said.

Now it was Izzy's turn to clench her teeth. "He isn't alone."

"What?"

"Peyton's waiting for him."

"But . . . " He turned away, thinking. It was a lot to process, Izzy knew full well. "She won't be able to guide them out in this weather," Jake said, shaking his head in disbelief. "They'll capsize on one of the coastal bars."

She had only a passing idea of what he meant. "That's bad, right?"

"Deadly."

Which would take care of Alberto but wouldn't save Peyton. "Can we call someone?"

"Coast Guard, but they'll have their hands full."

"Deputy Porter?"

"If we can track him down."

Then Izzy thought of someone who might be able to help, someone with more pull than the local sheriff's department or even the US Coast

Guard. She grabbed Jake's hand and pulled him toward the door. "How about the FBI?"

* * *

In the dash from the garage to the house, Izzy and Jake were drenched to the bone, and as they ducked onto the porch and through the front door, Izzy was thankful her family never locked up.

The house was quiet again, only this time the silence felt menacing. Izzy knew that her dad was either still out looking for her or back at Peyton's house, but that still left her mom and her brothers unaccounted for.

"Mom?" she called up the stairs. It was dark on the second floor, so Izzy dashed through the dining room into the kitchen, her mom's usual stomping ground. "Parker? Ri?" The kitchen was empty. Izzy even poked her head into the laundry room and pantry to make sure, and when she backtracked to the living room, she saw that Jake had opened the foyer closets and even the cabinet of the grandfather clock.

"They must be upstairs," Izzy said. She flipped on the lights, more aspirational than hopeful that she'd hear a familiar voice drift down.

Jake placed a hand on her arm. "Maybe I should go first."

"You've never even been in my house, how could you . . ." Her voice trailed off as she realized the implication of Jake's offer, and the reason he'd opened the closets and grandfather clock. The Casanova Killer would cram his victims into small spaces in their own homes. Jake was afraid that her family had become Alberto's latest victims.

Without waiting for Jake to take the lead, Izzy raced upstairs, throwing open the door to her parents' bedroom. "Mom! Are you okay?" The room looked empty, but Izzy wasn't going to take that at face value. She checked under the bed, then in the bathroom and closets. Thankfully, she found nothing.

Jake was coming out of Parker's room as Izzy emerged into the hall. He looked as relieved as Izzy felt. "No one's here."

Relief replaced the menace, though the eerie emptiness remained. Izzy nodded to the door behind Jake. "That's his room."

Not that he'd be foolish enough to hide out in the Bell house after staging Izzy's death to look like a suicide. The whole point was that he'd be halfway to the marina by the time she died. Still, they needed to be sure, and a quick search of the room proved that Izzy was right. Alberto had left the room exactly as he'd found it—virtually untouched. Even the duffel bag was still on the chair. Izzy wondered if the security hair he'd placed over the zipper was intact as well.

"He'll be at the marina by now," Jake said. "But they'll have to gas up before they can leave, and that'll take some time."

"Okay." Izzy backed out of Alberto's room as if, even without him there, she was afraid to turn her back on the space. "Agent Michaels's card is upstairs."

She led Jake down the hall to the attic door. The frame was splintered, the door hanging off its hinges at a precarious angle. The last time she'd been there, she'd busted that door open with the giant grandfather clock, avoiding death by moments. She climbed up to her room slowly, expecting someone to jump out at her from the darkness, just like in a horror movie, but the room, like the rest of the house, was empty.

Izzy paused at the top of the stairs, her eyes falling on the window, now pelted by the onslaught of rain. She ran her fingers along the sill. This time, she didn't feel the cool metal nailheads, only small holes in the wood. The nails had been removed.

Jake stepped beside her, his hand on her back. "Is this where you—"

"Yep." She didn't want to hear him say the words "almost died" because now that phrase applied not only to her bedroom, and the main staircase, but to her dad's workshop as well. How was she going to live in a house that reminded her of death?

There were going to be more if they didn't get moving. Izzy pulled her eyes away from the window. Her phone was still on the nightstand, charging. Exactly as she'd left it. And tucked into the case was Agent Michaels's card.

The phone rang four times before an answering machine picked up. Generic outgoing message, and Izzy hoped that Agent Michaels was good about checking her voicemail.

"This is Izzy Bell in Eureka," she said, speaking quickly in case the messaging service had a time limit. "You have the wrong suspect. Alberto Bianchi is the Casanova Killer. He admitted to killing Kylie Fernández and Hunter Bixby, and he's tried to kill me three times in the last twenty-four hours. He's attempting to escape Humboldt Bay in a fishing vessel called *Bodega's Bane* moored at the marina on Woodley Island. I told Deputy Porter everything I know."

She glanced up at Jake, wondering if she'd forgotten anything. He smiled, nodding his head as if impressed, and flashed a thumbs-up. Izzy was about to beg Agent Michaels to alert the Coast Guard, when a bright flash of blue light illuminated her room, followed by a heavy popping sound.

Then the lights in her room, and the house, and all of Eureka below her bedroom window, went dark.

THIRTY-SIX

JAKE DROVE TO THE MARINA AS QUICKLY AS THE WEATHER and the complete darkness would allow. Izzy wasn't sure she'd ever experienced such an utter blackout. Electricity to the entire town was out, making streetlamps and porch lights useless, and thick storm clouds blotted out the moon. Torrential rain pummeled the windshield so fiercely the wipers could barely keep up, adding another layer of disorientation to the drive. Everything looked different, as if all natural landmarks had been wiped clean, and Izzy only recognized where they were when Jake turned onto the bridge.

Izzy glanced down at her phone, which she held in a death grip. The words "No Signal" mocked her. "I just hope Agent Michaels got that message." She left the rest unsaid, but she and Jake both knew the reality of the situation. Without backup from the Coast Guard, the FBI, the sheriff's department, or some other law enforcement agency, they had little chance of stopping Peyton and Alberto. Even if they could get onto the boat. Alberto had killed over a dozen people and was planning to add one more to that list in the immediate future. Why not make it three?

The power outage had come at the worst possible time. Not that it should have affected their plan, since her phone was fully charged and the grid of cell phone towers across the greater Eureka area should have provided them with some kind of signal, but when Izzy had dialed 911 at the house, she'd heard a long beep and then noticed the "No Signal" message on the phone's tool bar. Jake's phone said exactly the same thing. Along with the power, the cell phone towers in Eureka must have been completely knocked out.

She couldn't even text Peyton to warn her about Alberto. She'd typed and sent a half-dozen messages pleading with her friend not to trust him, but they all sat in her messaging app with ominous little red exclamation points signifying a failure to send.

Izzy had checked her phone every few minutes as they crawled down to the marina, hoping they'd eventually come into range of a functioning tower, but so far, she'd had no luck.

Water sloshed over the asphalt as Jake eased the car off the bridge, and the aged spruce and oak trees flailed around in the wind, their spiny limbs occasionally caught in Jake's high beams. The parking lot for the National Weather Service was, ironically, empty. Even seasoned professionals were riding out the storm in a safer location.

"I'm cutting the headlights," he said as a ferocious gust blasted the side of the pickup. "So they don't see us coming." Izzy could feel the cab rock back and forth on its suspension, and Jake had to muscle the steering wheel to keep them moving in a straight line.

"I guess driving without lights in this storm can't be that much more dangerous than driving at all," she said.

"Or trying to power a boat out of the channel with that surge."

The lot for the marina was also completely empty, and submerged in an inch or two of water. Luckily, Jake's truck was high enough off the ground to plow through. He pulled into a row two docks away from where *Bodega's Bane* was moored, cut the engine, and dropped the keys into the cup holder.

"Just in case you get back here before I do," he said, zipping up the rain jacket he'd borrowed from Parker's closet. Izzy understood the implication: *If I don't come back at all.*

"Do you think you can disable the boat?"

Jake nodded. "I just need to get into the engine hatch and I can take care of the twin Cats. They won't be able to leave the dock."

"Good."

"Yeah, no engine at sea in a storm like this would be a death sentence."

"I've already almost died three times this week," Izzy said with a wry smile. "I might be invincible." She was trying to lighten the mood in the face of an impossibly dark situation, but instead of playing along, Jake gripped her hand so tightly her knuckles cracked.

"Don't underestimate the sea," he said, his eyes hard-set. "She's merciless."

Izzy recalled the glee on Alberto's face when he left her to die in her dad's workshop. "So is he."

"As soon as Alberto is secured, I'll manually activate the EPIRB on the cabin roof. That will alert the Coast Guard."

Izzy knew as much about boats as she did Italian, but growing up in a fishing town, she'd absorbed at least some knowledge, and she was pretty sure the EPIRB was an emergency beacon. Which didn't seem like it would do them any good in this storm. "Will it work if the whole town is off the grid?"

Jake smiled, the first time since he found her strung up in the garage. "It's got a GPS beacon and works on a satellite system, just like the Marine VHF. The Coast Guard station on the peninsula has their own power generator. They'll literally be here in minutes."

"Okay." With communications down, this seemed like the only option. Stopping at the police station or Coast Guard would have wasted precious time, and once *Bodega's Bane* was out of the bay, the chances of anyone finding them were basically zero. The best shot was to disable the boat's engines so they could never even leave the dock, but Izzy knew it was a long shot, and a dangerous one at that.

"We'll have strength in numbers," Jake said, reading her mind.

"Right." Izzy took a deep, steadying breath and pulled the hood of her rain jacket up over her head. Without help from the authorities, their plan was to climb onto the boat under cover of the storm, disable the engine, and then restrain Alberto until they could get him to the police. It wasn't a great plan, but it was the best they could do on their own. And the only way they could think of to save Peyton.

"Mike's gun is in a storage cabinet beside the bilge pump. Enter the cabin through the aft door and it'll be at the base of the stairs up to the wheelhouse."

She didn't like the idea of bringing a firearm into the equation, but it might give them an advantage. "Got it."

Jake raised his eyebrows. "Ready?"

She wanted to tell him a million things while they were still in the relative safety of his pickup—about her mom and dad, her childhood, the way she'd become a caretaker, and how she didn't want any of that to affect her relationship with him. She wanted to tell him that she loved him in a way she'd never thought herself capable of loving another person, and how if they survived this night, he'd better be prepared to have Izzy in his life forever.

But they didn't have time, and so Izzy could only smile and nod, then push open the door of the truck and catapult herself into the raging storm.

Wind whipped at her face, fluttering the hood of her jacket, and she had to pull the drawstring even tighter to keep it from flying off. The storm roiled around her, pelting her from several directions at once as she sloshed through the partially flooded parking lot. She was instantly disoriented, and if it hadn't been for the truck behind her, she wouldn't have been able to tell which direction to go.

Thankfully, Jake knew this area like he'd been born in the marina. One hand on her elbow, he guided her through the pitch black toward the docks.

Even though she couldn't see the small, handwritten sign, the words "Caution: Slippery" were in her mind as they reached the gangway. She could hear the usually placid water of the inner reach slamming into the rocky barrier that surrounded Woodley Island, and as she half ran, half slid down to the dock, she felt a rolling wave push up from underneath them, submerging the gangway in an inch of water. Maybe she should have opted for her rain boots instead of running shoes?

Izzy had no time to contemplate her choice of footwear. Near the end of the dock, a light flared to life, piercing the blackness. It pitched and bobbed against the black background of the night, buffeted by the waves, and even through a sheet of near-horizontal rain, Izzy recognized *Bodega's Bane.*

The exterior boat lights hit the dock, dancing over other slips, many of which were empty. And as her eyes were adjusting to the light, she noticed that the boat was moving. *Bodega's Bane* was backing out of its slip.

Izzy had no time to think, no time to consult with Jake. She could only think of saving Peyton. She broke into a sprint, hitting the floating dock so fast she hydroplaned past two slips before she was able to regain traction. She could see a crouched figure moving on deck, and judging by its slight build, it had to be Peyton. Which meant Alberto was piloting the boat. It had cleared the dock, engine roaring against the onslaught of waves in the narrow channel, and was starting forward.

They were too late.

"No!" Izzy cried in frustration as she watched the boat begin to churn its way out of the marina. What were they going to do? She couldn't just leave Peyton to her fate. She pulled out her phone, already damp from her jeans pocket, and practically wept in frustration as she saw that she still didn't have a signal.

"I'm sorry," Jake shouted at her side. "It's too late."

Suddenly, a wave blossomed up in the middle of the channel, pushing the boat back toward Izzy and Jake. Its stern thudded against the dock, tantalizingly close. She could see Peyton rushing to port, checking for damage over the gunwale, and in that moment, Izzy made a decision. Without thinking, she launched herself forward at full tilt, pushing off the edge of the dock and propelling herself into the air. For a split second she was airborne, blasted by a gust from the north. She felt like fall leaves at the mercy of the breeze. She saw the boat beneath her, moving forward under the full force of its engines, and then as she fell, her foot caught the railing and she tumbled forward.

Just as she was preparing herself for a cold splashdown and a lungful of seawater, she crashed onto the slick deck of *Bodega's Bane.*

Izzy's hip took the brunt of the impact before her shoulder collided with the fiberglass bait station in the middle of the aft deck. She lay crumpled in a ball, catching her breath, expecting to be discovered at any moment. But Peyton had disappeared.

Izzy popped her head up, just far enough to see over the side of the vessel as it lumbered away from the dock. The stern running lights barely permeated the sheets of rain surrounding them, and Izzy couldn't even see the marina. She hoped that Jake hadn't tried to leap onto the boat behind her and was still on the dock, not fighting for his life in the angry waters.

Regardless, as Izzy knelt on the deck pelted by relentless rain, two facts were very clear: the boat was already moving, so disabling the engine was no longer an option, and she was very much alone.

She had to get to Mike's gun.

Creeping forward on her hands and knees, Izzy peeked around the side of the bait station. The deck was empty, the door to the cabin closed. She scurried toward it, crouching low against the wind, and was able to wrench the door open and dash inside.

It was dark in the cabin, the exterior running lights filtered by tinted windows, but a shaft of light from the bridge illuminated the stairs at the front end of the cabin. Clearly visible at the base of the steps was a cabinet with a shiny white-and-black label: "Bilge pump." Just as Jake described.

The engines roared below, rumbling the floor beneath her feet, and the boat pitched upward as it took a wave head-on. Izzy braced herself against a nearby table, then, as soon as they crested the wave and started down the other side, dashed forward to the cabinet, ripping it open in one deft motion. Her eyes swept over the contents: paperwork, flashlights, thickly coiled rope that made her think of the noose Alberto had used to string her up less than an hour ago. She quietly lifted a few items, searching for anything that looked like a firearm or a holster or a box that might hold either.

Then she heard a low female voice behind her. "Is this what you're looking for?"

"Peyton!" Izzy whispered. She spun around, ready with a list of explanations and supplications to convince her best friend that Alberto was dangerous, but the words died on her tongue.

Standing in the doorway to the crew quarters, aiming the barrel of a gun directly at Izzy, was her mom.

THIRTY-SEVEN

"MOM?"

The pitching of the boat paled in comparison to the dizzying emotions that overwhelmed Izzy as she stared at her mom in the cabin of *Bodega's Bane*. She and Alberto . . . How? When?

"Izzy," her mom gasped. Whoever she was expecting to find perving through the boat, it certainly wasn't her daughter. "What are you doing here?"

I could ask you the same thing was the first response that came into Izzy's head, but the sad reality was that she knew exactly what her mom was doing there. She must have known her husband was having an affair. Alone, depressed, looking for an escape, her misery had collided with

Alberto—handsome, attentive, *Italian* Alberto. Izzy had no idea what lies he'd told her mom in order to win her cooperation, but she was going to set the record straight.

"He's not who you think he is," Izzy said. "He's not even Italian."

Instead of protest or a look of confusion, Izzy's mom took the news in stride. "I know."

"You know?"

"I speak fluent Italian, Izzy. You think I'd be taken in by that accent?" Her mom lowered the gun and guided Izzy toward the door. "We need to get you out of here."

Not that getting off a moving boat in the middle of a storm was some simple feat, but even if it were, Izzy certainly wasn't leaving without her mom. "You're coming with me."

Izzy's mom shook her head. "I can't."

"But he's the Casanova Killer!"

"He's been *accused*, Izzy. Evan is completely innocent."

Evan. Was that even his real name? Doubtful.

"Mom, he tried to kill me."

Her mom's eyes grew wide, a mix of shock and disbelief. "What?"

"Three times."

"No."

"The stairs were tampered with. The dryer vent too." Izzy backed toward the aft door. "Mom, he's—"

"He sees me." Tears welled up in her mom's brown doe eyes. She looked young, innocent. "My body and my soul. He touches me."

Izzy shuddered. That whispered sexy time she'd overheard through the vents. It hadn't been her parents, but her mom and Alberto. He'd probably just come back from killing Kylie. There were so many disturbing layers to this onion, it was difficult to know which one to peel back first.

Her mom sucked in a ragged breath. "We're . . . we *were* going to start over together."

"He's killed at least thirteen women."

"He didn't."

"And Hunter."

"I can't . . . "

Izzy slowly raised her hands to her neck and unzipped her rain jacket, pulling the collar wide to expose the raw abrasions on her neck. "He strung me up by a noose in Dad's workshop. Tried to make it look like suicide."

Her mom's eyes flitted down to Izzy's neck, and then her body seemed to deflate, a balloon untied. She sank forward into Izzy, who wrapped her arms around her mom's sobbing body. *Bodega's Bane* pitched heavily to port and Izzy staggered back against the galley table to keep from toppling over, and just as she was trying to figure out how to get her and her mom off that vessel before it capsized—or worse—she heard a voice that chilled her blood.

"My love?" Alberto's voice floated down from the bridge. "Who are you talking to?"

Her mom stiffened in Izzy's arms.

"My love?" An edge in Alberto's voice now. The strain of his perilous escape attempt was fraying his confidence. Good.

"The crew quarters," her mom whispered, just loud enough for Izzy to hear. She slid her hand with the gun up to her chest, shielding it from the view of anyone who came up behind her. "Hide."

Maybe together they could overpower Alberto. Jake had said their strength was in numbers. Izzy and her mom might not equal one Jake

Vargas in terms of size, but in terms of fierceness, Alberto was about to have his hands full.

With a quick nod, Izzy took a step toward the crew cabin, tucked down into the bow, but as she moved, she saw a pair of legs descending from the bridge. They were too late.

"Izzy!" Alberto's voice was gleeful, his face smiling as he ducked down from the wheelhouse. "A family reunion. Lovely of you to join us." She was impressed by how cool he sounded, as if she'd just popped in for dinner. No hint of surprise at finding her alive.

"Your father never understood," Izzy's mom said, holding her daughter's gaze. Her eyes flicked down to the gun in her hand, and Izzy understood the message: *play along.* "He has always taken me for granted."

"'He's the sort who can't know anyone intimately,'" Alberto said, "'least of all a woman.'"

Izzy cringed. She knew that line. And Alberto hadn't written it.

"'He doesn't know what a woman is,'" Alberto continued. "He wants you for a possession, something to look at, like a painting or an ivory box."

"For fuck's sake!" Izzy said out loud. Four-letter words be damned. "You're quoting *A Room with a View!*"

Alberto looped an arm around Izzy's mom's waist and pressed their bodies together so fiercely Izzy was afraid her mom's diminutive frame would be crushed by the force. Her mom winced and tucked the gun into her armpit.

The boat lurched, pivoting to starboard. There was no one at the wheel.

"'He doesn't want you to be real,'" Alberto quoted, oblivious to the actual danger they were in, "'and to think and to live.'"

"You're not George Emerson," Izzy said, rolling her eyes. "Just a bad actor."

Alberto lowered his face to Izzy's mom, kissing her hair. "'He doesn't love you. But I love you!'" He spun her toward him and kissed her, passionately, one hand caressing the line of her chin while the other moved slowly, imperceptibly, toward the hand that was trapped between their two bodies.

"Mom, the gun!"

The kiss had been a misdirect. In the few seconds Izzy's mom had been distracted, Alberto ripped the weapon from her grasp.

Izzy knew she wasn't close enough to try to wrestle the pistol away from Alberto. She'd have a bullet in her chest before she made it halfway. Instead, Izzy dove for the aft door, throwing her body weight against it as she wrenched the handle. The wind whipped it open wide, taking her with it, while the boat careened dangerously on the chaotic waves, no hand at that wheel to guide it through the channel. Izzy tumbled out onto the deck, the howling wind immediately silencing all other noises around her. Though she was pretty sure she heard a loud pop. Like a gun being fired.

Mom! She was trapped inside with a serial killer, and if that had been a gunshot, then her mom might be gravely injured. Or worse. Either way, she had to get them off that boat, but how?

Water sloshed over the side as they tipped dangerously close to the churning surface. Rain and wind pelted her, and Izzy had to grip the railing to keep from hydroplaning. She had no idea what to do. Jake was the one with a plan, even if the first half of it was made moot once the boat left the dock. And the second half . . . activate the EPIRB? She didn't even know what it looked like. Jake had said it was some kind of

GPS beacon on the roof of the cabin, but that could have been anything. There had to be another way to call for help.

What had Jake said about the EPIRB? *It's got a GPS beacon and works on a satellite system, just like the Marine VHF.*

The Marine VHF radio. No phone line or cell tower required. She knew from Hunter's tour of the boat it was in the wheelhouse, figured it couldn't be that difficult to operate, and people who owned their own ham radios might run them on batteries. Or a generator. Or, like, maybe even the Coast Guard would hear? That was her best bet. It was worth a chance.

If she could avoid getting shot first.

Izzy crouched low as she inched her way around the port-side deck toward the wheelhouse. The wind pummeled the vessel, and Izzy had to plant a foot against the wall of the wheelhouse in order to get the door open against the onslaught. No flying bullets as she dashed inside, so that was a win, but she didn't have much time. There was no lock on the door, and no door at all to the stairs that led down to the cabin, but Izzy spotted a clipboard on the dash and jammed it between the handle and the wall, making it impossible to open the port door from the side deck. If Alberto had followed her out into the storm, he'd need to go all the way around the bow to starboard in order to reach her, and that should buy her a few seconds.

The radio was mounted on the ceiling, a little walkie-talkie handset thing attached beside it. She pulled the handset down, noting the "talk" button on one side of the microphone. The base had several dials but only one switch, which had to be the power. She flipped it, and the wheelhouse immediately filled with static. At least it was working.

The readout on the face of the mic showed the number sixteen, which could have been the volume setting, the battery life remaining, or the channel it was on, but Izzy didn't have time to figure it out. Not that it mattered. This was a Hail Mary pass at best. She pressed down the talk button, held the mic close to her mouth, and spoke as quickly and succinctly as she could.

"Mayday, Mayday." That seemed like the kind of thing that would get people's attention. "This is the fishing vessel *Bodega's Bane* somewhere in Humboldt Bay. The Casanova Killer is holding two victims at gunpoint." She swallowed. If anyone was listening, would they actually believe her? "He's trying to escape under cover of the storm. Mayday. Mayday. This is *Bodega's Bane* owned by Mike Bixby. My name is Izzy Bell, and I called Agent Loretta Michaels from the FBI to report this information—"

"NO!"

Izzy ducked instinctively at her mom's cry, just before she heard the gun explode again. The tinted window in the starboard door splintered, spindly cracks radiating outward from a single hole.

Izzy spun around and saw her mom hanging from Alberto's arm. He must have doubled back to the cabin and tried to shoot her from the stairs, but her mom had stopped him.

"Let go, my love," Alberto snarled, struggling to maintain his George Emerson persona.

"Leave her alone." Tears streamed down her mom's face as she wrestled with Alberto, who was nearly twice her size. "Leave my Izzy alone."

Alberto's arm waved back and forth as he struggled to maintain his aim, and Izzy ducked just as he pulled the trigger again. The bullet hit the windshield.

Before he could get a third shot off, Izzy's mom launched herself onto Alberto's back. He fell forward and tried to brace himself with the hand that held the gun. The instant the gun hit the floor, Izzy pounced, stomping on Alberto's wrist. He grunted, still trying to shake off Izzy's mom, and she stomped again and again, until his grip loosened and the gun slid across the wheelhouse floor.

As Izzy dove for the weapon, a thunderous roar emanated from outside. The ship shivered as if it had been struck by something very large, then the floor fell away, the boat pivoting like a toy caught in a bathtub eddy. Izzy reached for the captain's chair to brace herself, but the vessel pitched heavily to starboard, and she tumbled into the darkness.

THIRTY-EIGHT

IZZY SLAMMED INTO THE SPLINTERED WINDOW ON THE STAR-
board side of the wheelhouse and felt rather than heard the glass crinkle
and snap beneath her. *Bodega's Bane* listed heavily to starboard. Right was
now down, left was now up, and Izzy realized that they'd just hit one of
the sandbars Jake had been so worried about.

The cabin lights flickered, blinking erratically as the generator
struggled to keep running, and before Izzy could push herself off the
splintering window, a large object fell on top of her with a sickening crack
that sounded like an egg dropped onto the floor. Someone groaned, and
as Izzy rolled onto her side, she half expected to see Alberto's gun pointed
at her cheek. Instead, Izzy's mom lay limp beside her.

"Mom!" she cried, turning her over. A trickle of blood traced down past her mom's ear. "Mom, are you okay? We need to move."

Not so much as an eye flutter from her mom. She'd been knocked unconscious, either by the fall or by Alberto.

Alberto! Izzy peered up into the wheelhouse. In the flickering lights, she noted that the clipboard was still lodged into the port door, locking it shut, but Alberto was nowhere to be seen.

Icy cold water sloshed over Izzy's hand, pulling her thoughts away from the serial killer. Water seeped through bullet holes into the wheelhouse, and judging by the spiderweb of cracks in the tempered glass, it wouldn't be long before the entire pane exploded. The waterline was only partway up the side of the boat, waves crashing into the windshield like they were breaking over a reef, but the boat itself had stopped pitching, which meant they were stuck in the sand. For how much longer, she had no idea, but she had to get her mom out of there while she still had time.

Bracing her sneakers against the metal frame between the windows, she hauled her mom up. Thankfully, as her dad always joked, Elizabeth Bell was a "mite of a woman," and Izzy, who had four inches on her diminutive mom, was able to heave her over the back of the captain's chair before scrambling up the dashboard beside her. She had no idea what levers and buttons she activated on her way, but she seriously doubted she'd be lucky enough to somehow wake up the mysterious EPIRB. She had to hope that her Mayday had reached someone.

Getting her mom onto the captain's chair had been the easy part, but as Izzy half climbed, half clawed toward the port door, she realized that getting her mom out of the wheelhouse was going to be a bigger challenge. Other than the chair itself, there was nothing on the bridge she could use as leverage, just a fire extinguisher, mounted beside the door.

Were the straps that secured it to the wall strong enough to hold their combined weight? Impossible to know until she tried. Worst case scenario, the extinguisher would dislodge while Izzy tried to drag them up to the door, smash through the window below at the exact moment a wave moved *Bodega's Bane* off the sandbar, and sink the ship like a lead weight. Best case scenario, she'd be able to open the door and they'd make it out onto the deck of a partially capsized boat in the middle of the worst storm on record with a serial killer whose whereabouts were currently unknown.

Izzy wasn't sure which was the better option.

Though she supposed "waiting to die" wasn't it. At least outside the wheelhouse, they stood a chance. Even a slim one.

Izzy stood on her toes and was able to get the tip of her middle finger beneath the clipboard she'd wedged against the door earlier, sliding it out of place. It toppled onto the dashboard before sliding down across the buttons and dials. With the door free, she grabbed the waistband of her mom's jeans, and with more strength than she thought she possessed, Izzy lifted her mom's limp body off the chair and onto her shoulder. Panting from the effort already, Izzy slid her right hand around the back of the fire extinguisher. She gave it a little tug, testing its stability. The red canister didn't budge.

Now came the difficult part. With her mom still balanced precariously on one shoulder, Izzy pulled on the fire extinguisher and crunched her abs, curling her body upward. Her right shoulder screamed in pain, and she wondered if it was being dislocated by the weight hanging from it. Izzy's view of the port door, now effectively a ceiling hatch, was completely blocked by her mom's body, and as she blindly flailed for the handle, she wasn't sure how long she'd be able to dangle there before her muscles cried "uncle!"

She pawed at the door, her fingertips grazing nothing but smooth fiberglass. Once, then twice. The third time she didn't even make contact with the door. Her strength was draining away.

Izzy inhaled slowly, visualizing the position of the door handle, so tantalizingly close. On the exhale, she contracted every muscle above her waist and hoisted herself toward the door.

This time, she felt metal under her hand. She twisted the handle, releasing the latch.

Izzy only had to get the door open an inch before the wind did the rest of the work for her, whipping the metal and fiberglass from Izzy's grasp. Left with just one handhold again, Izzy dangled from the fire extinguisher for several seconds as she attempted to get one of her legs up though the open door. Second attempt was the winner this time. Izzy slid one leg onto the deck in the driving rain, and using that for leverage, she slung her mom's body out of the wheelhouse.

Holding her unconscious mom with one hand so she didn't slide into the bay, Izzy clawed her way through the now-hatchbacked door out into the storm. It was difficult to see in the driving rain, and the fiberglass exterior of the boat was slick as sheets of water poured across it. Izzy gripped the door frame with one hand, her mom's arm with the other, and tried to assess their situation. The stern of the ship was still mostly above water, leaving the engine room dry, but the bow was partially submerged. The exterior lights flickered erratically but were still fighting to remain on, and the relentless waves hadn't been able to dislodge the boat from the sandbar yet.

But the waves were brutal. Some came from the bow, others from behind, and Izzy fought to maintain her hold on both her mom and the door frame. She had no idea how long she'd be able to lie there on her stomach, keeping both of them from disappearing overboard, when a crash of frothy water dispelled that mystery.

Two converging waves must have smacked into one another on the opposite side of the boat because the angry surge that careened over the top of the wheelhouse was so violent it ripped her mom from Izzy's grasp. She watched in horror as her mom slid feet first toward the starboard side of the bow, which was slowly sinking beneath the waterline.

Without thinking, Izzy let go of the door frame and slid down after her mom. The railing on top of the gunwale broke both of their falls, and Izzy managed get an arm around her mom's chest, hauling her face out of the water.

Her mom's head lolled to the side. Izzy couldn't let go of the railing to even check if she was still breathing, let alone perform CPR if necessary. She braced herself and hugged her mom fiercely to her chest.

Izzy's arm ached, the metal railing digging into the crook of her elbow while she desperately tried to stay connected to the sinking vessel. She couldn't feel her fingers anymore, numbed by the icy water. Her mom's head flopped back and forth with every surge, a marionette whose strings had been cut, and Izzy's muscles burned trying to keep her mom's mouth and nose clear. Their clothes were so waterlogged she was sure she and her mom weighed an extra fifty pounds, and it felt as if needles were pricking every inch of her exposed skin. She wondered which would claim them first: drowning or hypothermia.

Suddenly, through the chaos of the storm, Izzy thought she heard something different. An even, mechanical whirr. Was that a boat's engine, or was her mind playing tricks on her?

A flashing red light appeared from the darkness, followed by the sharp bow of a speedboat, where Jake stood at the helm in an orange life vest.

THIRTY-NINE

A BILLION QUESTIONS FLOODED HER MIND, BUT THEY COULD wait. The only thing that mattered now was getting off *Bodega's Bane.*

"My mom!" Izzy shouted.

Jake flashed her a thumbs-up and attempted to bring the boat alongside, an almost impossible feat in the heavy surf. Every swell of water propelled Jake upward, while the fishing vessel remained stuck in the sandbar. The speedboat's engines roared as Jake tried to keep it steady, but he couldn't maneuver it alone. Finally, he picked up a coil of orange line.

"Tie it on!" he shouted.

Izzy nodded. The only way she could do that without sprouting a third arm was by letting go of the railing. And she'd probably only get one shot.

Jake held up three fingers, indicating that he'd throw on three, then bounced his body as a countdown. The exterior lights dimmed ominously, their intensity fluctuating at random intervals. Izzy tried to ignore the unreliable lighting and focused on Jake.

One. Two. *Three!*

His toss was perfect, and the rope flew directly over her head as it uncoiled. Izzy felt it hit the deck beside her and released her grip on the boat railing. She slapped at the undulating water where the rope had landed, desperate to feel the rough fibers in her palm, but she was sluggish from the cold, her fingers almost completely numb, and when she lifted her hand from the water, she expected to find it empty.

Instead, her fingers gripped the orange line, which was quickly being pulled through her palm.

She couldn't even feel it.

Izzy looped the rope around the railing and pulled it taut, tethering the speedboat to *Bodega's Bane*. Jake took advantage of a lull in the waves and accelerated toward the fishing vessel. The bow of the speedboat scraped along the hull of *Bodega's Bane*, it's shallow hull allowing it to maneuver around the dangerous sandbar, and Jake deftly grabbed the line. As if he'd been doing boat-to-boat water rescues all his life.

Hand over hand, Jake pulled the two boats together until they were close enough for him to get a hand on Izzy's mom. He tied off the line with a fisherman's efficiency.

"Are you okay?" he shouted, leaning over the side of the speedboat.

Izzy nodded, then looked down at her mom as if to say, *I don't know about her.*

Bracing himself, Jake reached out. A swell in the waves lifted the two boats, and Jake was able loop his hand through the waistband of Izzy's mom's pants, just as Izzy had done when evacuating her mom from the wheelhouse. She heard him grunt, and then, with one fluid motion, he landed her safely in the speedboat.

Jake's head disappeared for a moment, and when he popped up again, he was smiling. He flashed another thumbs-up, which could only mean one thing.

Her mom was still alive.

Izzy could have cried with relief. They were going to be okay. She pushed herself to her feet, ready to grab Jake's outstretched hand, when a massive wave bombarded them. The entire fishing vessel was lifted into the air, clearing it of its sandy anchor and propelling it into the speedboat. Izzy felt herself tipping forward toward the water as the wave righted the boat, and she was left dangling from the starboard railing.

Jake threw off the tether, then hit the throttle hard. The engines lurched the boat forward while he cranked the wheel, narrowly avoiding a collision. The lights of the speedboat disappeared back into the storm.

Izzy was alone.

She heaved a sigh of relief that Jake and her mom were okay, even as she swayed helplessly from the side of the boat. Her sneakers dragged through the swells beneath her, signaling how low the boat sat in the water. She had no idea if that meant it was sinking or had just taken on water from being capsized, but she wasn't going to hang around long enough to find out. She dragged herself back onto the narrow side deck and searched the sea for Jake and the speedboat.

That's when she saw a dark object racing toward her from the stern of the ship.

Though she shifted her body so her ribs took the brunt of a ferocious kick instead of her face, where it had been intended to hit, the impact sent her airborne, knocking the air from her lungs as she slid dangerously toward the bow.

"You bitch!" Alberto shrieked. He lumbered toward her, gripping the railing for support as the boat tipped steeply to starboard. Rather than fight the movement, Izzy let gravity pull her across the bow, putting some distance between herself and Alberto. She slid faster against the water-slick deck than she'd anticipated and hurtled into the side of the boat so viciously, her head whipped around and smacked the metal rail. Stars swamped her vision and mixed with the erratically blinking lights. Izzy was completely disoriented. She knew she had to move, but she couldn't quite tell in which direction. Water assaulted her from all sides, but the railing was firm beneath her numb, tingling hands, and she groped at it desperately, pulling herself down the length of the boat toward the stern.

Where was she going? There weren't many places to hide on a forty-three-foot boat that was half submerged in icy water. She could make a stand and fight back, but without a weapon, she doubted she'd be able to take Alberto down. Another swell of water threw Izzy against the shattered wheelhouse window. Gazing inside, she saw the contents of the bridge glide across the floor. The clipboard clattered to a stop against the leg of the captain's chair as another object raced by. Dark, matte metal.

The gun!

Izzy wrenched open the door and balanced herself against the frame. If she could get the gun, she had a chance to take down Alberto, but as she stepped into the wheelhouse, she saw a face in the window opposite her. Alberto's maniacal smile seemed even more terrifying with the strobe-light effect further contorting his features, but as she recoiled, Izzy noticed that he wasn't smiling at her. His eyes were downcast toward the floor of the wheelhouse.

He'd seen the gun too.

Before Alberto could open the door, the swells shifted, this time pitching the port side of the ship into the air. The clipboard broke free first, skittering past Izzy, followed by the gun.

Alberto's eyes grew wide as the weapon began to slip down the tilted floor. He threw the door open and launched his body toward the rapidly escaping Glock, but his fingertips missed the handle by an inch as it accelerated directly into Izzy's waiting hand.

Izzy didn't hesitate. Not even for a heartbeat. Alberto was on his knees when she aimed the gun and squeezed the trigger repeatedly at point-blank range until the chamber clicked, out of ammunition. She watched with grim satisfaction as his body recoiled from several direct hits to the chest and abdomen.

Alberto flopped onto his rear and attempted to crab-walk backward out of the wheelhouse. He made it as far as the doorway before his legs and arms gave out, his eyes wide in disbelief as he stared up at Izzy, unwilling to believe that she'd been his undoing.

A macabre smile crept across his face once more, spreading as slowly as the red patches of blood on his shirt.

"Izzy," he croaked. His voice gurgled like a drowning man's. "Isn't it delicious?"

Then he slid down all the way to the floor, eyes still open, head lying at an unnatural angle.

Izzy stood rooted to the floor of the wheelhouse, the sound of a powerful motor growing louder in the distance. She'd beaten him, avenged Hunter, saved her mother, but it wasn't enough. She needed to have the last word.

"You know what else is a four-letter word, Alberto?" Izzy said, not even caring if he was still alive to hear her. *"Ciao."*

FORTY

THE STORM BROKE JUST AFTER DAWN.

Izzy stood at the window of the Coast Guard station, huddled beneath a thermal blanket with a mug of sludgy coffee in her hand as a tentative orange glow pierced the thinning storm clouds, casting an eerie ray of sunshine on the ravaged coast. The feeble daylight revealed that Humboldt Bay had fared well, with most of the smaller boats riding out the storm in the marina. The blue-and-white fishing vessel half submerged in the shallows on the north side of the channel was a notable exception.

She stared at the listing hull of *Bodega's Bane*, glinting in the morning light, and wondered if Alberto's body would ever be recovered.

He'd still been in the wheelhouse when the Coast Guard had pulled her from the foundering boat, but when they'd gone back for him, the body had already been washed overboard. Which sucked. Not because Alberto was dead, but because Izzy didn't know for sure that he was. Wouldn't until they located his bullet-riddled, water-logged, fish-eaten corpse. And until that day, she'd never truly believe he was gone.

Her mom, thankfully, would be okay. Physically. Emotionally, it would be a longer road. For aiding and abetting a known criminal, Izzy's mom was facing jail time, but considering her state, Izzy hoped for an in-patient mental health option.

Jake was still in the conference room giving his statement to the police, his dad standing watch behind him. They'd hardly been able to talk since they arrived at the station, as she'd been whisked off immediately, to answer questions first about her mom from the medical personnel and then about Alberto from Deputy Porter. She'd waived her right to have an adult present for the interview: she didn't need her dad or one of her brothers to come to her aid. Never again.

She wasn't even sure where her dad was, though Peyton's house was a good bet. She assumed he was contacted soon after her arrival at the Coast Guard station, but hours later, he still hadn't appeared. Like at the hospital. Her mom might have been planning to run away with a serial killer, but at least she'd been there for Izzy. Her dad had completely abandoned her.

"Hey, kiddo."

Izzy turned her head sharply. Her dad stood behind her, hands shoved into the pockets of his work cargoes.

"Hey."

He paused, as if waiting for her to run sobbing into his protective arms or some shit, but that wasn't going to happen. She cocked an eyebrow, signaling that the ball was in his court when it came to opening the conversation. He swallowed, obviously uncomfortable with the shift in the power dynamic, and it was clear to Izzy that he had no idea what to say to her.

A buzz from his pocket saved him from further awkwardness, and he smiled as he pulled out his phone and handed it to Izzy. "Someone wants to talk to you."

Peyton's face filled the screen. Her eyes were still red rimmed and bloodshot, and large purple crescents extended down to her cheekbones. Izzy wondered if she'd been up all night as well.

"Hey," Peyton began. She sounded about as exhausted as Izzy felt. "I'm so sorry, Izz."

Izzy was about to ask what her friend was sorry for, but Peyton had already anticipated that question.

"About Alberto and Jake and your mom and . . . and not telling you."

"It's okay," Izzy heard herself say. She was still angry with her friend, a hurt that ran deep and would take time to heal, but an apology was a good start.

"It's not," Peyton said. "I should have told you, but . . ." She dropped her voice. "He and my mom made me swear not to. He promised he'd tell you himself."

Izzy glanced up at her dad. He'd walked a few paces away to give her some privacy, and suddenly Izzy understood Peyton's question from before Alberto's arrival: *Hey, have you talked to your dad recently?* It wasn't about Italy, it was about his affair. Not only was her dad cheating on his wife, but he'd made Peyton lie about it for who knows how long. The depths of his selfishness were truly astounding.

"It was not your responsibility, Pey," Izzy said, marveling at the strength she heard in her own voice. "And I don't blame you. I'm sorry my dad put you in this position."

Peyton's eyes were glassy as fresh tears welled up. "I've been a terrible friend," she sobbed. "And a terrible girlfriend."

The trauma of Hunter's murder would linger with Peyton for a long time, as would the trauma of what Alberto had done to both of their families. But at least they could help each other through it.

"You're not," Izzy said, smiling sadly. "You're still my Pey."

"I love you."

"I love you too."

Peyton wiped her cheeks. "Let me know when you're home safe, okay?"

"I will." Izzy's smile deepened. "And be gentle with yourself."

Peyton nodded silently, then ended the call.

Izzy's dad eyed her sheepishly as she walked the phone back to him. He was probably worried about what Peyton had told her. Good.

"I, uh, just want you to know this isn't your fault," he said.

Izzy froze. "What?"

"Your mom's problems." He placed an awkward hand on her shoulder, like he didn't know how to treat her anymore. "They're not your fault."

Izzy stared at her dad. Was he kidding? His watery blue eyes reflected concern and stress, but she wasn't entirely sure if either was related to her, since he'd never even asked how she was doing.

He flashed that boyish little half smile to signify in his cocky, white-man-privileged way that everything would work out. Izzy used to find that unfounded confidence reassuring, but not today. For the first time in her life, she saw her dad's affably forgetful, happy-go-lucky nature for what it actually was: childish and selfish.

She shook off his hand. "Of course it's not *my* fault, *Dad*," she said, laying emphasis on the last word to remind him who was the adult in this scenario.

He blinked, and his smile faltered. "Oh. Um, good." He stepped away, his fatherly duty finished. "I'm glad you—"

Only Izzy wasn't done. Not by a long shot. "Mom's mental illness is not my fault. Not anyone's fault. But leaving me to deal with her alone? That's on you."

"What?" He stiffened, instantly on the defensive. "I didn't leave you."

Izzy rolled her eyes. Just like Alberto, or Evan, or whatever the fuck his name actually was, Izzy's dad was a little boy who was unwilling or unable to take responsibility for his actions. "Yeah, you did. You all did. Taylor, Parker, Riley—they physically left. But you checked out years ago."

"Izzy," he said, squaring his shoulders and pulling himself up to his full five-foot-nine-inch height. "I have always been there for you."

"Really, Dad? Were you there when a serial killer tried to hang me in your workshop? Were you there when Mom almost ran off with him? Were you there when she came up with this whole stupid Italy plan in the first place?"

"I—"

"No, you weren't. You were fucking my best friend's mom."

"That's not fair."

"It's completely fair. You ran right over to their house when you heard about Hunter. But he was my friend too. Did you ever think that I needed comfort? Did you know that I discovered the body?"

"I . . ."

"You didn't even come to the hospital, *Dad*. I'm sure Mom texted you that I almost fucking died, but you couldn't be bothered."

His face reddened, and he sputtered out his next words. "I . . . I thought she was making it up."

"I wouldn't have blamed her if she was. You left. You left her alone in a town she hates, in a house she hates, surrounded by clocks she hates. And you don't care. You never even tried."

"I did!" He was whining now. Like Riley. "I tried for years."

"Then snuck off and started banging Jeanine Nowak."

"It wasn't like that."

Did men always try to justify their selfish bullshit? At least Jake had owned up to his ghosting, apologized without being prompted. At seventeen, he was already more mature than her own father.

"You know what, Dad? I don't care. I don't care why you cheated on Mom, and I don't care why you abandoned us." She shouldered past him, out of the room. She was utterly done. "Just understand, right here and now, that I will never forget this."

* * *

She waited for Jake outside the conference room where he was giving his statement to Deputy Porter. When he finally emerged, his dad lagged behind to speak to the deputy, which gave them a few moments alone.

He crossed the lobby in three strides and enfolded her in his arms, a gentle but strong embrace that felt like the closest thing to safe Izzy had experienced in a long time. Though she wasn't going to rely on other people for her happiness ever again, as she pressed her cheek against Jake's chest and inhaled his sea-salt scent, she thought it might be okay to have a partner by her side while she figured out her life.

"Are you okay?" he asked.

"I'm pretty sure I'll never be okay ever again," she said. Then she laughed. "But maybe years of therapy will help."

"It helps me," he said, passing a hand over her hair. "My relationship with my dad will never be normal, but at least it's better."

Izzy nodded. His empathy bolstered her confidence. "I'm down with better."

"And I'm here to help." He pulled away, lowering his head to her level. "Whatever you need or . . ." His eyes faltered. "Or don't need from me."

It was such a stark contrast: her father, who had spent his entire life making selfish decisions, doing what he wanted, when he wanted it, without giving much of a thought for the other people in his life. It had blown up his family, alienated his kids, and almost gotten his wife killed. And when faced with the truth of the situation, he'd gotten defensive, offered excuses, retreated. Never once had he taken responsibility for any of his actions.

Meanwhile Jake was standing by her side, despite his own grief after losing his best friend. He offered support in whatever form she needed, even if that meant stepping away from their romantic relationship, putting her needs before his own.

Izzy was pretty sure she'd hit the jackpot.

"I need . . ." She let her voice trail off, then slipped her hands into his, holding on to them for dear life. "I need you."

Jake's eyebrow shot up. "Yeah?"

"Yeah."

But instead of smiling, Jake's face clouded. "I know how you feel about this place. About this town. You probably hate it even more after all that's happened, and I'd be tethering you to that trauma."

Hate. Izzy had certainly shared how she felt about her hometown with literally anyone who would listen, and she'd spent the better part of the last year plotting an escape. Never running *to* anything, just from it. But while she still had no idea where her path was leading, Izzy had learned that it wasn't actually Eureka, California, that she was running from, but herself. And her family. And all of things that she knew weren't working, and that she felt utterly helpless to fix.

But that was going to change. *Izzy* was going to change. And maybe New Izzy didn't hate this town quite as much as Old Izzy thought she did.

"I don't hate it. Not this place, not my family, not my home. I just need to learn to live my own life despite them."

"I wouldn't want you to stay just for me."

"Oh, I won't."

He swallowed, stepping away. "I understand."

She tugged him back. "Jake . . . I mean, I can't leave this place. Not right now. Maybe not ever. Not as long as my mom's in treatment."

"Oh."

"I'm not staying for you. I'm staying for *me*."

"But you're staying?"

She nodded, pressing her body into his. "And I'd really like my life here to include you."

Izzy felt Jake's body relax. "I'd like that too."

She pulled his head down to meet hers. His lips felt so soft against her own, and when he broke away, she could actually feel the warmth radiating from his smile.

"I don't know what Eureka would do without you," he said, a hint of mischief in his eyes. "Who's going to catch all these serial killers?"

"No one, clearly." She laughed. Then a new thought grabbed her. "Do you think Humboldt State has a criminology program?"

"I wouldn't be surprised."

"Then maybe my mom wasn't wrong about everything."

"What do you mean?"

Izzy laced her fingers around the back of his neck. "Fate is also a four-letter word."

ACKNOWLEDGMENTS

Every time I write a set of acknowledgments, I am reminded of how lucky I am that I get to tell stories for a living, and of how little I could accomplish without the following people:

First, to Kelsey Sullivan, who helped me dig in and find the depth in Izzy's story. I appreciate her editorial insights every day.

To Ginger Clark, my publishing partner since 2008. Lucky novel number thirteen!

To the marvelous, supportive, ridiculously hardworking crew at Hyperion, who help make all of this look effortless: Marci Senders, who has knocked yet another cover design out of the park; Guy Cunningham, David Jaffe, and the entire copyediting team for putting up with so many commas; Holly Nagel and Danielle DiMartino in marketing; my publicist, Crystal McCoy, who gets it all done like a boss; Dina Sherman, who has been such a stalwart supporter through so many books; and my managing editor, Sara Liebling.

To Nicole Eisenbraun at Ginger Clark Literary, who works so tirelessly on my behalf.

To Mary Pender, who has always believed in me.

To Alessandro Polselli and international operatic soprano superstar Julianna Di Giacomo for fixing my terrible Italian.

To Emily O'Brien for invaluable insight into the foreign exchange student process.

To Cecilia Ortiz and Veronica Rodriguez, without whom I'd get nothing done.

To my mom: pinch babysitter, cheerleader, and a strong, working mom who led by example.

To John and John and Katie, who sacrifice a lot so Mommy can have some writing time.

And to working moms everywhere, because this shit is hard.